THE LEGACY QUEST TRILOGY
Book 1

STEVE LYONS was born and lives in Salford, near Manchester, in the north-west of England. He has contributed articles, short stories and comic strips to many British magazines, from *Starburst* to *Batman* to *Doctor Who*. He has also co-written a number of books about TV science-fiction shows, including the official *Red Dwarf Programme Guide*. He is the author of a dozen original Doctor Who novels and two full-cast Doctor Who audio adventures, and short stories for the Marvel-related anthologies *The Ultimate Super-Villains, Untold Tales of Spider-Man, The Ultimate Hulk,* and *X-Men Legends.*

AVAILABLE NOW

THE LEGACY QUEST TRILOGY
Book 1

By Steve Lyons

Interior Illustrations by
Jordan Raskin

MARVEL®

ibooks
new york
www.ibooks.net

DISTRIBUTED BY SIMON & SCHUSTER, INC

bp books inc
New York

Special thanks to David Bogart, Bob Greenberger, C. B. Cebulski,
and Bobbie Chase

X-MEN: THE LEGACY QUEST TRILOGY BOOK 1

A BP Books, Inc. Book

BP Books, Inc. trade paperback edition / June 2002

The BP Books World Wide Website is
http://www.ibooks.net

ISBN 0-7434-4468-X

PRINTED IN THE UNITED STATES OF AMERICA

10 9 8 7 6 5 4 3 2 1

For Peter Cooke

Author's Note: This trilogy takes place
shortly after the events recounted in *X-Men* #87.

CHAPTER 1

IT WAS the right kind of weather for a funeral.

The sun had not been seen all day. It had taken cover beneath a wispy blanket of clouds, as if sensing that it would not be welcome here on this gloomy November morning. The sky was gray, and its grayness seemed to leech all other colors from the cut flowers and the clapboard houses of this small, remote corner of New England. The air was cold enough to bite, and a weak but piercing wind howled as if in anguish through the trees.

The stranger took a deep breath, gathered his resolve and walked towards the wrought-iron gates of the town's small cemetery. He was a tall man, with a thin face, short red hair and freckled cheeks. At least, that was how he looked at the moment. As his feet crunched against the dead leaves on the ground, he felt an irrational fear that his disguise would not be good enough; that everybody would see through it, and see who—and what—he was. He buttoned up his black greatcoat, for the sake of appearances, as if trying to protect himself from a cold he didn't feel.

People had gathered at the gates. White vans sat among the black limousines, and the stranger recognized the logos of three different television networks on their sides. TV crews and newspaper journalists mingled with the crowd. Their presence seemed like

2

an intrusion. Bathed in artificial light, a young man made a live report to the nation. His words were emotive, his expression carefully earnest, as he spoke into his handheld microphone. The stranger felt a rush of anger towards him, but fought it. He had a job to do, after all.

The funeral party had arrived a few minutes earlier. The stranger could see them through the railings: a cluster of dark figures, almost swallowed up by a gray sea of headstones. He had watched, his heart going out to them, as they had struggled to clear a way through the gates, with the coffin of a lost friend or family member borne aloft on six shoulders.

Two grim-faced men had stationed themselves at either side of the entrance. They controlled the flow of people into the cemetery, and kept the paparazzi and the more obvious rubber-neckers out. They questioned anyone they didn't know, and searched them to ensure they had no cameras before allowing them to pass. The ceremony, they were determined, would be the one part of this tragic business that would not be broadcast to the world.

The stranger had to be there, but he hadn't reckoned on the guards. He quickened his pace slightly, turning his face from them even though they couldn't possibly have recognized him. He could probably have bluffed his way past them, but he couldn't have risked being searched. They would have found that his physical shape did not match his appearance.

And what would he have said to them anyway?

The stranger had traveled a long way to be here, and he wasn't sure why. He had never met the deceased. He had never even heard the name William Montgomery until a few days ago. And yet, the young man's death—and the media frenzy that had accompanied it—had had a more profound effect upon him than he could possibly have anticipated.

The stranger knew Montgomery's killer. He knew it very well indeed.

He rounded the corner of the cemetery, and kept on walking until the pack at the gates could no longer see him through the railings. He looked up at the metal spikes a foot above his head, and nodded confidently to himself. He cast one final, furtive glance up and down the street, to be sure that nobody was around to see what he did next. Then he crouched down, tensed his muscles and sprang forward, taking three bounding steps along the sidewalk before he launched himself into the air and twisted sideways. He somersaulted over the tops of the railings with an inch to spare, and made a perfect, almost soundless, landing on both feet on the far side.

For a long moment, then, the stranger squatted silently, almost expecting to hear shouts of outrage and fear. When he was sure his acrobatic feat had gone unnoticed, he pulled himself back up to his full height, adjusted his illusory tie and brushed dust from his coat.

Then, using the trees as cover, he picked his way stealthily towards the other mourners.

A weak, early afternoon sun was trying in vain to warm the frigid waters of the North Atlantic Ocean, where it met the North Sea off the coast of Scotland. Dark waves lapped against a lonely pillar of granite, which jutted obdurately out of the depths. Atop this pillar, light glinted off the towers and pylons of the Muir Island Genetic Research Center.

And, inside that center, one of the world's foremost geneticists was slumped over her lab bench, beginning to stir from a fitful sleep.

Doctor Moira MacTaggert didn't want to wake up, but an insistent pain in her neck and the stark electric light of her windowless laboratory dragged her from the comforting darkness. Perspiration had glued her face to the sleeve of her white coat. She tore it free, and sat up in her chair with a regretful sigh. Her throat was sore, but that was normal these days. She didn't know how long she had slept—this isolated, timeless environment gave her no clues—but she was still tired. Not just in body, but in mind and spirit too. The details of her dreams had already fled from her memory, but she knew they had been of a better world; a world that she was sorry to have left behind so soon.

The half-cup of coffee by her side was stone cold. A dry, brown ring stained the topmost paper in a haphazard pile of scribbled notes to herself. Notes that were all but useless now—but she still faced the dispiriting task of writing them up and filing them. There was always the smallest chance that some scrap of information might help in the future.

"I see no reason to continue," her lab partner had said yesterday morning. "Our initial hypothesis was hopelessly inaccurate. This entire endeavor has been an unmitigated disaster." Moira knew Doctor Henry McCoy well enough to know that the long words were an attempt to hide his feelings. But his strained tone had still betrayed his weariness and disappointment.

She had gritted her teeth and tried to ignore him, to focus on her work. On the slide beneath her microscope, a numbingly familiar chemical reaction had been playing itself out. "You can give up if you want, Hank," she had responded, "but I'm seeing this through to the end."

Was that optimism, she wondered now, or just blind stubbornness?

She dragged herself to her feet and stretched her arms and legs, pushing out the kinks in her muscles. She massaged her neck, and stifled a yawn as she opened the heavy doors that separated her from the rest of the world. She stepped out into the bare, clinical corridors of her research facility, and flinched from the cold sunlight that streamed through the small, high windows and made dust motes dance before her eyes.

Sleep must have overcome her, at last, just as everybody else was rising. She had been unconscious for over six hours, but it felt like six minutes.

She was not as strong as she used to be. A year ago, she had pulled regular all-nighters without a problem. Now, she was tired all the time, and she felt as if she had a permanent cold. She smiled to herself ironically. If only her ailment were something that simple.

At times like this, Moira could almost feel the virus eating away at her from the inside, sinking its tendrils into her DNA strands, rewriting her very genetic makeup. She wondered how much more time she had.

Yesterday's conversation flashed through her mind again. She remembered Hank's voice: "The virus has corrupted the DNA sequence in the cell samples. Even in the improbable event that our anti-vaccine could begin to slow the reaction now, it would be too late."

"It would be something!" she had insisted.

"A false hope, nothing more. We can't reverse that sort of damage, Moira. We'd have to learn to map the entire human genome just to begin to try."

Didn't he think she knew that?

It was unlike Hank to be so terse, so irritable, so insensitive to her feelings. But the strain of the past few months had begun to take their toll on him. She had watched it happening. She had watched him crumbling, piece by piece, with each new setback, each dashed hope. She knew what he was going through, but not how to help him. He would have to come to terms with it in his own way, his own time.

Yesterday morning, Hank McCoy had walked out of the laboratory, head bowed, fists clenched in frustration. Twenty minutes later, the security systems had informed Moira that he had left the center, left the island altogether. Good. He had needed to get away for a few hours, to find time to think. And equally, Moira had needed to be left alone, to bury herself in work, to pursue this latest futile experiment to its conclusion. That was how she coped.

"We've already reached the end, Moira." Hank's last bitter words to her, as he left. "You can hold out for a miracle if you wish, but you're only denying what we both already know. We've turned into another cul-de-sac. This line of research has reached a dead end."

He had been right, of course.

She wondered where he was now.

The center was silent, almost eerily so. This building housed some of the most advanced technology known to Mankind, but Moira strained her ears to hear even a distant hum, to hear anything above the regular sound of her own shallow breathing. An involuntary shiver caught her by surprise. She ought to have been used to this, after all these years living out here. She had always valued her privacy, and enjoyed the peace that came with solitude. But it seemed a long time now since she had truly been alone.

What if she died here? What if her time ran out today? When would they find her?

She walked to the kitchen alcove, her footsteps filling the emptiness with hollow echoes. She made herself a fresh cup of coffee using powdered creamer. She didn't like it, but she had become used to the taste. When you cut yourself off from civilization as she had, fresh milk was one of the many things that became a luxury. She leaned back against a worktop, removed her glasses so she could rub her weary eyes, and sipped at the hot liquid gratefully.

Hank had been gone for over twenty-four hours. Moira told herself not to worry. He had probably checked into a guesthouse on the Scottish mainland, or just roamed the Highlands overnight with no regard for the passage of time. But she couldn't rid herself of the nagging doubts. She had learned through experience that, where Hank McCoy and people like him were concerned, anything—almost literally, anything—could happen.

She wondered if she should call in the X-Men.

"So, what is the mood like in Newhill, Massachusetts today, Jon?"

"Very subdued, Peter. As you know, this is a small town, a very close-knit community, and the death of Mr. Montgomery from the Legacy Virus has affected everybody. The funeral is taking place behind me as we speak—just through these railings here—and many shops and businesses are closed in Newhill this morning, as a mark of respect."

"Have you spoken to Mr. Montgomery's family?"

"Not yet, Peter. They've asked that the funeral should be a private affair, that they be left alone to grieve. I'm hoping to get a few words with them as they come out. But I have spoken to some of the other local residents, and they all say the same thing. They just can't believe this has happened here, especially not to somebody so young. I think you said earlier that William Montgomery was only twenty-nine years of age."

"A community in shock, then."

"Absolutely. A state of shock. A feeling of 'how could this happen here?' I spoke to one woman earlier, and she told me there's never even been a mutant sighting in Newhill."

"But the Legacy Virus doesn't only target mutants any more, does it?"

"I'm afraid not, Peter. Mr. Montgomery's parents insist their son was not a mutant, and the results of the post-mortem seem to confirm their claim. I think, for many of the people here, that this is the most frightening aspect of this tragedy: that apparently, no one is safe from what, until recently, was seen as an exclusively mutant disease. On top of all this, of course, is the worry that we don't yet know how it might be transmitted: whether it's airborne, or if you can catch it from contaminated food and water. We just don't know."

"I'm sure a lot of our viewers, watching this, will be quite worried about this virus. What symptoms should we be looking out for, Jon?"

"Well, in the early stages, the symptoms are a sore throat and a runny nose—a mild cold, basically. But after that, it becomes more difficult to predict. The Legacy Virus attacks its victims' DNA, and there is still an awful lot we don't know about that. Very often, it causes outbreaks of boils and lesions on the skin. We also know that some of the earliest victims, some mutants—and of course their DNA is very different to our own—lost control of their actual mutant powers. What you have to remember, Peter, is that this is still a very new disease, and research into it is only just beginning."

8

"A lot of work still to be done, then."

"A lot of work—and a long way to go before we can hope for a cure. But I should remind our viewers at home that cases of the Legacy Virus are still quite rare. There have only been a few confirmed cases in human beings so far. It appears to be spreading quite slowly."

"But it *is* spreading, Jon."

"Yes, Peter. It is spreading."

Five time zones to the east of Newhill and its problems, a thin, almost gaunt, pale-skinned man sat in a small fishing boat with its engine turned off, and squinted at Muir Island through a pair of binoculars. Beside him, his partner—a stocky man with a full red beard, approaching middle age—struggled with the paddles to keep the boat as steady as he could.

The thin man's gaze lingered longest on the island's smallest building: a nineteenth-century crofter's cottage, incongruous against the bulk of the hi-tech facility that dwarfed it. When he had seen enough, he lowered the binoculars from his eyes, turned to the bearded man and gave him a curt nod of confirmation. No words were exchanged. No sounds were to be made at all, except when absolutely necessary. They pointed the boat towards a shaded nook at the foot of a low cliff. The bearded man set it on its way with an assured thrust of the paddles, then left it to drift towards its destination, with its two passengers, in silence.

The bearded man opened a black briefcase, rummaged through its contents and produced two black ski masks. He handed one to his partner, and pulled the other one down over his own head. Both men wore nondescript sweaters, faded blue jeans, gloves and boots that they would dump overboard once their mission was over. Reaching into the case again, the bearded man took out a rope and a grappling hook. He began to pay out a length of the rope, running his hands over it to check for knots, his eyes flicking towards the cliff top as he mentally gauged its height. The thin man occupied himself by taking another look at the schematics. He spread them out on his lap, nodding to himself as he matched the outlines of the buildings to the fresh evidence of his own eyes and ran through the details of the plan in his mind. Muir Island was protected by a sophisticated security system, and it worried the man a little that his blueprints were slightly out of date. But no system was impenetrable. Not if you had the right skills and tools for the job. And that cottage was the weak point.

He rolled up the schematics and slipped them back into their cardboard tube, which he tucked beneath his bench, out of the way. He reached for his laptop computer and booted it up, checking that all the programs he needed were still safe on its drive: programs that could root out and analyze data with phenomenal speed, cracking random combinations and even confounding enemy systems with false data. The men's instructions were that this mission had to be executed in total secrecy. If they set off an alarm, any alarm, then the deal was off.

As the fishing boat nudged against the rocks at last, the thin man took one final look at the target. Her image stared back at him defiantly from the small screen, her eyes alive with Celtic fire. Brown hair tumbled around a face that was still relatively young but careworn. In the picture, she was wearing a yellow and black bodysuit, as if she fancied herself some kind of super-hero. Her lab coat provided a bizarre contrast to the costume. But the thin man and his partner knew all about this woman. The bodysuit, they knew, was to give her freedom of movement, and an element of protection, in combat situations. She may have been an important scientist, but the nature of her work—and of the people with whom she mixed— had earned her some powerful enemies. She had to be prepared.

The thin man smiled a thin-lipped smile of satisfaction, as his bearded partner hurled the grappling hook towards the cliff top and it caught first time. All the preparation in the world wouldn't save Doctor Moira MacTaggert from them.

"No, we haven't heard from Hank in days. Is something wrong?" The speaker, whose image filled the screen of Moira MacTaggert's sophisticated communications console, was called Jean Grey. She was one of Moira's oldest, dearest friends.

"No more than usual," said Moira, with a sigh. "We've hit another brick wall, that's all."

"I'm sorry to hear that, Moira."

"Och, never mind that now," she said dismissively, trying not to show how much she was hurting. "We'll pick ourselves up and start again, like always. But Hank took it pretty hard this time. When he walked out of here, he was more down than I've ever seen him."

"How long has he been gone now?"

"The best part of thirty hours. I'm worried, Jean."

"I'm not surprised. This doesn't sound like the Henry McCoy I know." Jean pursed her lips and frowned thoughtfully.

She had long, curly, red hair and was quite strikingly beautiful—and Moira knew that she possessed the brains and the personality to complement her looks. But Jean Grey was also a mutant, born with a genetic abnormality that marked her as something different—and, in some people's minds, someone to be feared.

In many respects, she was lucky. Her genetic X-factor had manifested itself in the form of mental abilities—telepathy and telekinesis—and her outward appearance did not betray her nature, as it did the natures of many. She could have lived a normal life, at least some of the time—although there would always have been somebody out there, hating her for what she was and threatening to expose her secret. Instead, she had chosen a different path.

She had chosen to pursue a dream.

A long time ago, or so it seemed now, a man called Professor Charles Xavier gathered together a group of five young mutants, whom he christened the X-Men. Jean was one of those original five—as was Moira's current lab partner, the missing Henry McCoy—but many more came after them. Over time, the X-Men grew into an elite mutant cadre, who use their powers to protect a world that often seems to despise them. Their long-term goal is the peaceful integration of their kind into society. For now, however, they are forced to carry out their activities in secret, concealing their identities behind masks and code names.

Jean was wearing her costume at the moment: a body-hugging green bodysuit with a distinctive golden firebird motif to represent her chosen code name: Phoenix.

"Do you think he might be in trouble?" she asked.

"It crossed my mind," admitted Moira. "But I decided to do a wee bit of poking around with my computer here, just in case. I found Hank's name on an airline passenger list. He left Glasgow last night, changed planes at Newark and took an internal flight up to Boston."

"Boston!" repeated Jean, with the light of realization dawning in her green eyes.

"Aye, I thought that might set a few alarm bells ringing."

"He's heard about Newhill, then? About William Montgomery?"

"BBC News 24 has been running the story over here."

"It's the funeral this morning," recalled Jean. "You don't think—?"

"I think this death is the metaphorical straw that broke the camel's back, Jean. I think it's affected Hank more than he'll admit. And I don't think he should be left alone right now."

Jean nodded in agreement. "I get the message. I'll run a check with Cerebro, just to be sure. If Hank is in Newhill, then we'll get somebody up there right away."

"Thanks, Jean."

Moira broke the connection, and silence descended around her again. She gulped down the last of her coffee, and yawned. She ached all over, and her brain felt fuzzy. She was in no condition, let alone mood, to go back to work now—especially knowing that she would have to start from scratch and find a whole new angle from which to tackle the problem of the Legacy Virus. That was why she had come here, back to her cottage. She needed—and deserved—a few hours' proper sleep, in her own bed. Perhaps, by the time she woke again, there would be some good news about Hank.

She got to her feet, and headed for the stairs.

And, all of a sudden, there was somebody blocking her way.

"What—?" she began. But there seemed no point in completing the question. The man was wearing a black ski mask, and he was pointing a heavy gun in her direction. A footfall sounded behind her, and Moira whirled around to find another man—taller than the first and painfully thin, but also armed and masked—emerging from her kitchen. They were professionals, she knew that. Had they not been, they could not have got within a hundred meters of this building without her security systems telling her about it.

"All right," she said, in as stern a voice as she could muster, "what is this? What's going on here?" Her gaze darted from one gun to the other, her muscles tensing, ready to respond if it looked like one of the intruders was even thinking of firing. Outmatched she might be, but Moira MacTaggert would go down fighting or not at all.

"What's going on, Doctor MacTaggert," said the thin man, in a voice that was calm and measured, and slightly hoarse, "is that we represent some people who wish to speak to you."

"At gunpoint?"

"The guns are a precaution, nothing more. They fire a dart that will deliver a neural shock to your system, causing you to lose control of your bodily functions. It isn't a pleasant experience, but if you stay very still, keep your hands where I can see them and do precisely as you are instructed, then you won't need to find that out for yourself." The thin man produced a small, black device. It resembled a mobile phone, but it only appeared to have one button. He pressed it, and returned the device to his pocket without ever looking at it.

"Who are you working for?" asked Moira. Neither of the two men answered her. "What happens next?" she ventured.

"You will be collected," said the thin man. "But our employers have also asked us to ensure that you bring your files along with you."

"What files?"

"Please, Doctor MacTaggert, don't try to play dumb. It doesn't suit a woman of your obvious intelligence. You have been researching possible cures for the Legacy Virus. You keep hard copies of all your notes, and also back up the data onto rewritable DVDs. The disks will be quite adequate."

"Oh, will they indeed?"

"I believe you keep them in this house. However, our search has failed to uncover them. I suspect you currently have them about your person."

"And what makes you so interested in my work?"

"You'll find out," said the shorter man, gruffly, speaking for the first time.

The thin man gesticulated impatiently with his gun, and Moira knew the conversation was over. She would get no more out of her captors for now. Perhaps they knew nothing more. Throughout the exchange, she had been watching them, looking for a chance to seize an advantage, to overpower them or simply to run. There hadn't been one. Their eyes had remained upon her, unblinking. Their guns hadn't wavered. As she had already noted, they were professionals.

She had no choice. With a sigh of resignation, she reached into her inside coat pocket and produced three DVDs. The bearded man stepped forward, eagerly. Moira's stomach did a cartwheel as he snatched the precious disks from her. They were only the backup files, she told herself. But what if her unwanted visitors intended to destroy the originals too?

"And now," said the thin man, with satisfaction, "we wait."

Six thousand miles away, night had already fallen. In a sumptuously appointed office, the whirring of an overhead fan merged with the muted voices of revelers from the main ballroom at the front of the single-story building. A businessman sat in a plush chair, keeping his expression carefully neutral as he updated his latest ally on his progress.

"It is already done. The woman is on her way here."

"Are you insane?" The businessman bristled. His ally's voice was so heavily disguised by electronic filters that it sounded positively robotic. Even so, he managed to make his scorn quite audible. Likewise, his features had been digitally altered so that his image on the desktop computer—and to anyone who happened to intercept and unscramble his encrypted transmission—was unrecognizable. This being the case, the businessman wondered sourly why he had bothered to use a video link at all. He knew the answer well enough, though. The picture on the screen was an imposing one, despite—perhaps in part because of—its blacked-out features. His ally's eyes, in contrast to the rest of his face, burnt brightly with contempt. The businessman could see through the façade—he was not above manipulating images in such ways himself—and was determined not to be intimidated. It was no easy task, though. The businessman fancied himself one of the most powerful men on the planet, but he was talking to one of the few beings alive who actually worried him.

"The work was going too slowly," he defended himself. "I took a decision."

"Moira MacTaggert is a close associate of Charles Xavier's. They were lovers!"

"I know that."

"Then you should have appreciated the likely consequences of moving against her. Who do you intend to reveal our plans to next—perhaps Henry McCoy?"

"McCoy has returned to America. I waited until MacTaggert was alone before I acted."

"Do you think it makes a difference? Xavier's children won't rest until they find her."

"I believe it's a risk worth taking. Nobody alive knows as much about this disease as Doctor Moira MacTaggert. She has been working with it since it was first identified. She was the first baseline human being to contract it. We need her."

"The X-Men will bring this project down around your ears, you fool!"

"I daresay you're right." The businessman leaned back in his chair, affected a casual pose and returned his ally's steely glare. "But I'm gambling that, by the time they do, it will have served its purpose. The cure for the Legacy Virus will be in our hands."

CHAPTER 2

THE LAST good-byes had been said. The family and closest friends of the dead man were casting handfuls of earth upon his coffin. His mother was weeping. Doctor Henry McCoy was relieved to think it was almost all over. He wondered again what he was doing here.

There had been a good turnout. William Montgomery would have been gratified to imagine he had so many friends. But, from his inconspicuous position at the back of the crowd, Hank had overheard the buzz of a dozen muttered conversations. He knew that, despite the efforts of the guards on the gate, few of the onlookers were here for Montgomery's sake. They were here for the spectacle. They were here because they thought it would make them part of a story that had put their small town on the map. They were here because it gave them an opportunity to share their worries and suspicions with like-minded neighbors. Hank had tried not to listen to their ignorant theories about why Montgomery might have died. But he had heard the word 'mutant' mentioned several times, always with distaste.

It made them feel better, of course. To fool themselves into thinking that the young man had somehow brought on his own fate. To convince themselves that it couldn't happen to them.

It was only through the benefit of advanced technology that Hank himself could stand among them, without becoming a target for their unthinking prejudice. He dug his hands into his coat pocket and felt the stubby, metallic shape of the image inducer: the device that was casting a holographic field around him, to make him look like something he wasn't.

Once upon a time, he had been able to pass for human without such help. Well, almost. He had been marked out by his stooped posture, his overdeveloped leg muscles and his oversized feet—but his superhuman strength and acrobatic prowess had compensated somewhat for the stigma that nature had attached to him at random. He had joined the X-Men and christened himself the Beast, as an ironic gesture towards those who had mocked him, but also as a reflection of his own deep fears, that his animal nature might one day subsume him. And he had dedicated himself to the science of genetics. He had studied his own abilities, seeking to understand the genetic mutation that had made him an outcast.

In so doing, he had taken an unwise gamble. He had ingested a serum that hadn't been fully tested. He had unlocked the full potential of his remarkable genes—and, in so doing, he had turned himself into more of a physical freak than ever.

The voices of the crowd grew louder as they shuffled back to the cemetery gates, as if the end of the service had somehow drawn a line under the need for a respectful hush. Hank walked alone, tuning out their bigotry, looking for a way to escape. As soon as he was out on the sidewalk, he thought, he would turn left, walk back to the station and catch a train to the airport. He would leave this place and its troubles behind him.

He should never have come here.

He was halfway to the sidewalk when he realized that something was wrong. A knot of people was marching against the departing crowd, up the gravel path. Their faces were twisted by hatred, and they carried homemade placards daubed with misspelled slogans. Hank didn't need to read them to know what they said. He had lived through this scenario too many times.

The protestors were fighting their way through the onlookers, towards the family, who had stayed behind to share a quiet moment by the graveside. The guards at the gate had been over-powered; they ran after the protestors, shouting angrily, unable to stop them. They were followed by the journalists and the camera-men, seizing this chance to get closer to the action, eager for an incident to report. One presenter ran backwards, speaking breath-lessly into a pursuing camera, keeping the rest of the world updated. And the people who had already reached the gates were turning back, realizing that there was suddenly more to see.

The family saw the protestors coming, and read their placards. The younger members of the clan moved to confront the aggres-sors, their misery boiling over into anger. Montgomery's mother burst into tears again. A hungry crowd closed in around the bat-tleground, and Hank found himself pushed to its front. He felt exposed, but he couldn't get away.

"What are you doing here?" spat one of the family members. "We don't want you here!"

"And we don't want your kind in Newhill!" came the spiteful rejoinder.

"What 'kind'? What are you talking about?"

"Mutants!"

"There ain't no stinking muties in our family!"

"Oh yeah? Your brother just died of a mutant disease, didn't he?"

The young thug's friends supported him with a roar of agree-ment. A similar cry went up from some of the spectators. They had been thinking the same thing, and this altercation gave them the chance to vent their fears, to demand answers. A chill ran up Hank's spine. This was going to be ugly. And the presence of the cameras only made things worse. It incited the protestors to go further than they might otherwise have done, to put on a perform-ance.

"If he wasn't a mutie himself, he must've palled around with them!"

"Yeah, he must've been a mutie-lover!"

"Mutie-lover!"

"Your whole family are mutie-lovers!"

"How do we know Montgomery's not gonna come crawling out of his grave, eh? You see it all the time on the news. These muties, they're like super-villains. They never really die, do they? We ought to cut off his head and drive a stake through his heart or something!"

"Yeah, stop him coming back."

"Keep him from spreading his filthy mutant plague to our kids!"

The insults kept coming, and the denials grew ever more heated. Soon enough, words turned to pushes, and pushes became punches. One of William Montgomery's brothers grappled with one of the tormentors, and they toppled sideways into the crowd. The onlookers took sides. They aimed kicks and blows. Some tried to quell the violence by singling out the biggest agitators and bearing down upon them, but they only added to it. Others didn't have the nerve to join in, so they shouted encouragement to one side or the other, adding fuel to a fire that was already threatening to burn way out of control. A small number tried to escape, but they found this easier said than done. In the space of a few seconds, a minor skirmish had erupted into a riot.

Hank had seen it all happen a thousand times before.

This was nothing to do with him. He told himself that as he kept his head down, avoided the fists flying around him and looked for a way out. This wasn't his business.

But then, through the chaos, he caught sight of Mrs. Montgomery, sobbing onto the shoulder of the priest who had performed the funeral ceremony. And he wondered how things might have been different had he not wasted so many hours, made so many wrong guesses. If he could have cured the Legacy Virus in time to save this poor woman's son.

He wondered how much of this was his fault.

And, with a sigh, he reached for the image inducer. He hesitated for only a second before he thumbed the switch to deactivate it. And suddenly, the true form of the Beast was revealed.

The reaction was as instantaneous as it was predictable. A collective gasp of horror went up, somebody screamed, and the crowd contracted as the people nearest to Hank struggled to get away from him. One woman fell over, slipped between the cracks in the throng and couldn't get up again. Much as it hurt him, the Beast couldn't blame them for being frightened. A monster had just appeared among them. He remembered how he had felt upon first sight of his own newly mutated form, a lifetime ago. He remembered staring into a mirror, appalled at his own pointed ears and heavy brow and fangs. These features, combined with the blue fur—blue, of all colors!—which grew over his entire body, gave him the appearance of a malevolent werewolf from a dark fairytale.

His suit had disappeared, and he was clad only in a pair of stretchable trunks beneath his black overcoat, the only part of his disguise that had been real.

He would probably have caused a mass panic if he had stayed here. But that wasn't what he had in mind at all.

The Beast took a standing leap, further into the air than most people alive could have managed. He brought his hands down onto the heads of two startled men who hadn't been able to get away fast enough, using them to support himself as he swung the lower part of his body forward and somersaulted into the center of the fray. Some of the protestors, and some members of the Montgomery family, had been too caught up in fighting to see what was happening around them. They saw now. A blue-furred monster dropped into their midst, and, on a mad impulse, grabbed hold of the most vocal of the anti-mutant demonstrators and planted a big kiss on his lips. The youth tore himself away, spluttering and spitting, but the Beast's momentary good humor faded at the sight of an elderly lady, who had produced a handkerchief and was breathing through it, her eyes alight with fear for her life. He was distracted, frozen, for less than a second, but it was long enough. Somebody leapt onto his back, scratching at his face and kicking and screaming. The Beast twisted around beneath his assailant, loosened the man's grip and pitched him forward over his shoulders. Two more men rushed him, one from each side. He threw himself backwards, head over heels, and righted himself with a deft handspring as his would-be attackers collided with each other. But more and more people were becoming emboldened, wanting to take out their frustrations, and he couldn't avoid them all. Their voices merged into a cacophony of hatred as they trampled each other in their haste to reach him. Enemies of a moment before had become allies. "How gratifying," said the Beast, "to see that you all agree on one thing, at least."

Somebody had found a stout stick from somewhere. The Beast heard it whistling through the air, and sidestepped a fraction of a second too late. He winced, momentarily staggered, as it cracked against his ribs. The crowd took full advantage of his weakness, and suddenly he found himself beneath a pile of bodies.

This was not going the way he had planned.

He pushed one man away with the butt of his hand, another with his foot. He wriggled out of the way of a second blow from the stick. He pulled one thug down on top of him, using him as a shield and then pushing him into someone else, sending both to the ground. He reined in his anger, knowing he dared not use all his strength. These weren't evil mutants. They were normal human beings, and he didn't want to hurt them no matter how much they provoked him. So the Beast fought defensively, keeping them off-balance and guessing what he would do next, until he managed to open up a gap, and then he went for it.

The rest of the crowd had drawn in around the combatants, thinking themselves safe, baying for the blood of a monster they had thought defeated. They cried out in horror and shrank back as one, as said monster suddenly emerged from the melee and hurtled towards them. They tried to duck as he leapt into the sky, muttering apologies—"Pardon me...excuse me...oh, was that your face?"—as he bounded across their heads. And then, at last, he was clear, and the angry crowd streamed after him as he raced for the high railings at the edge of the cemetery. He knew that none of them would be able to follow him, as he cleared the barrier easily and landed on the sidewalk. But some of the mob had second-guessed him, and they were already spilling out of the gates just down the road and racing towards him.

The Beast ran—an easy, loping gait—until he was out of sight on a secluded street. He had achieved his objective. He had broken up the fight by giving its participants a common foe. Not that the trouble was over yet, of course. Some of them would not give in so easily. They would keep on looking for him, roaming the streets in gangs. There might be other skirmishes throughout the day—but they would be on a smaller scale, at least, and the police would be able to handle them. And, with luck, they would be far away from William Montgomery's grieving parents and his freshly dug grave.

All the Beast had to do now was remove their target.

He reached into his pocket and produced the image inducer. His face fell at the sight of the dent in its side, and he stared at the device in dismay as he operated it and nothing happened. He remembered the stick that had cracked into his side, and he realized with growing dread that he had nowhere to hide now. He could already hear footsteps and voices approaching.

"Excuse me, mister?"

The Beast whirled, ready for an attack, but the unexpected voice had come from a young girl, no more than about ten years old. She was standing in the small front garden of one of the neat, white, wooden houses, and there was no fear, no hatred, in her face.

"You used to be in the Avengers, didn't you? I saw you on the TV, fighting some scary man with a beard. My mom said you saved all our lives that day. You're a super-hero."

"Bless you," said the Beast, his features breaking into a toothy smile.

And then the angry mob rounded the corner behind him, and he was running again.

Hank! Hank, are you there?

The words bypassed his ears, popping into his head like thoughts, except that he hadn't thought them; it was not his own internal voice that had spoken them. He recognized and welcomed the telepathic presence of an old friend. *I'm here, Jean.* He formed the answer in his mind, knowing that she would hear it. *I'm in a small town called Newhill.*

I know. We're not too far away. Is everything OK down there?

Let's see—how can I put this? The Beast skidded around another corner, and came up short at the sight of a second group of people running towards him. He telesent an emphatic: *No!*

Hold on, Hank. I've got your position, and we're almost there.

Surrounded, the Beast sprang into the air again and landed on top of an orange, new-style Volkswagen Beetle. "Aren't you forgetting something?" he goaded the crowd, as they gathered around him, shouting out their hatred. "I believe it's customary for the lynch-mob to carry pitchforks and flaming torches!"

He performed a desperate dance on the car's roof, leaping over grasping hands and lashing out with his feet to repel anyone who tried to climb up beside him. This kept them at bay for a minute or more, before they started climbing up simultaneously from opposite sides of the vehicle. Then the Beast leapt past them before he could be overwhelmed. He bounced nimbly off the Beetle's curved bonnet, and onto the trunk and then the roof of the next car. One man tried gamely to follow him, but cried out as he fell short and hit the road hard. The Beast had gained another few seconds, as the crowd moved to surround his new perch. But this time, somebody had the bright idea of rocking the car beneath him, and he found it increasingly difficult to keep his balance and avoid his attackers' blows at the same time.

He was hugely relieved, then, to hear a familiar sound over the clamor: the *bamf* of a sudden displacement of air that could only have heralded the arrival by teleportation of one particular X-Man.

If the crowd had thought the Beast a character out of a dark fairytale, then they must have imagined Nightcrawler being birthed in that same evil place—if not somewhere worse. His skin, like the Beast's, was blue—a darker, indigo blue—his fangs and pointed ears were similarly pronounced and, in addition, he sported a long tail with a pointed end. His white-gloved hands and white-booted feet had only three digits each, and his yellow eyes glowed like headlamps. He resembled a shadowy goblin demon. Only the Beast, of those present, knew the gentle, chivalrous, Christian soul that was the real Kurt Wagner.

Nightcrawler seemed to hover in midair above the crowd for an instant, before disappearing in a puff of sulphurous smoke and materializing almost instantly, a few feet to the left. He teleported again and again and again, always before gravity could take hold of him, until it looked like he was almost surrounding the mob by himself. They panicked, as Nightcrawler had no doubt intended, running this way and that, forgetting their prey, confused and perhaps unsure just how many dark allies the Beast had called upon. And then Nightcrawler appeared on the car roof beside his teammate. "Komm mit, mein Freund!" he instructed, lapsing into his native German tongue—and they jumped down onto the road and fled side by side.

They gained a considerable lead before anyone thought to follow them—and even then, their pursuers were neither as numerous nor as enthusiastic as before. "You have my lifelong gratitude, my friend," the Beast panted. "I thought my branta canadensis was well and truly cooked." Nightcrawler grinned at his teammate's typically verbose turn of phrase. "I'm not sure we did much to further the cause of peaceful mutant-human relations, however."

"I've dealt with mobs like that before," said Nightcrawler. "You can't reason with them. If it's any consolation, half of them will be ashamed of themselves after the heat of the moment, when they realize what they've done."

"Which leaves us to worry about the other half."

"As ever, the story of our lives. It looks like our lift's arrived."

The Beast had already heard the drone of the X-Men's Lockheed SR-71 Blackbird stealth jet overhead. Nightcrawler *bamf*-ed away, taking the most direct route possible up to the airplane. He could have carried his colleague with him if he'd had to, but a tandem teleport would have placed a great deal of stress upon both of them. The Beast was not surprised when, having taken only a few more steps, he sensed somebody swooping down behind him; somebody who wrapped a pair of strong arms around his chest and lifted him bodily off the ground. He recognized the green-gloved hands of Rogue, another teammate, even before she told him to "Hold on, sugar!" in her familiar Southern drawl. The wind whipped through his fur, as his astonished pursuers—along with the town of Newhill, Massachusetts—dropped sharply away beneath him.

Five minutes later, the Beast sat inside the Blackbird with Rogue beside him, Nightcrawler in front and Phoenix at the plane's controls. "Not that I've any wish to look a gift horse in its oral cavity," he said, "but what exactly alerted the X-Men to my predicament?"

"We got a call from Moira," said Rogue. "She was worried about you, up and disappearing like you did." She had removed the hood of her green bodysuit, and shaken loose her shoulder-length brown hair with its distinctive white streak. Even in here, though, she didn't take off her gloves. Her costume covered every inch of her skin, from the neck down. The Beast was well aware of the reason for that. If he was ever tempted to pity himself for the problems that his mutation caused him, then he had only to think of Rogue. She was forever denied contact with other people, knowing as she did that she only had to brush her skin against theirs to absorb their physical abilities, their thoughts, their very lives.

"Ah, yes," said Hank contritely. "I'm afraid I owe the esteemed Doctor MacTaggert an apology. I haven't paid her much consideration of late."

"It was Moira who worked out where you'd be," explained Phoenix. Gently, she added: "She said you were pretty upset about what happened in Newhill."

The Beast sighed. As the adrenaline rush from his exertions subsided, depression settled back upon him like a heavy shroud. Not every problem in his life could be solved by a last-minute cavalry charge. "You didn't see William Montgomery's parents today, Jeannie. Two more innocent victims in the war between *homo sapiens* and *homo superior*."

"But what possessed you to go to the funeral in the first place?" asked Rogue. "You must have known the locals wouldn't exactly roll out the red carpet for a mutant right now."

"I hardly planned to reveal myself as a member of our beleaguered species." The Beast shrugged. "And, to answer your question as best I can, I don't entirely know why I came here. It was not my intention when I left Muir Island. I acted on instinct. I didn't know for sure that I'd be boarding a flight until I had reached the airport."

"Moira told me the work wasn't going too well," Jean prompted sympathetically.

"A polite euphemism, no doubt, for my latest abject failure."

"Don't you think you're being a bit hard on yourself?" said Nightcrawler.

"Am I? A man was buried today, Kurt."

"You can't blame yourself for the Legacy Virus!"

"I can blame myself for not stopping it in time. For how long have I been seeking the cure to this damnable disease? How many people have suffered and died for my mistakes? And how many distractions have I allowed myself in the meantime? I shouldn't even be here. I should be with Moira, working to ensure that nobody else has to lose a son or a daughter, and yet what am I doing? Indulging my own feelings. I didn't come here for William Montgomery's sake, nor for his family's. No, if I were to analyze my own behavior today, I would be forced to conclude that I was looking for a way to expunge my own deep feelings of culpability."

"What have you got to feel guilty about?" protested Rogue.

"The news reports didn't help," recalled Hank, in a distant

voice. "Every time I turned on a television set or listened to the radio, I was confronted by evidence of my own shortcomings; a reminder that the Legacy Virus is still spreading. I couldn't save its latest victim. I can't guarantee I'll be able to save the next one."

"You can't think like that," said Nightcrawler. "Legacy isn't the only disease out there, you know. It isn't even one of the most common. People die of cancer every day, but do you blame the doctors who are trying to find a cure?"

"Of course not." The Beast sighed again. "And I know you're right. This is something I'm going to have come to terms with." He leaned back in his seat and barked a short, bitter laugh. "Do you know what the most ironic thing is? While I was down there, sur-rounded by the rampaging mob, I felt more alive than I have in days. I felt like the bombastic Beast of old. I even found time to dispense a few quips—and not because the situation wasn't per-ilous, but because my enemy was tangible. I could act against it. I could leap past one of my tormentors, or knock one aside, and see how my actions improved my circumstances. I miss that feeling of accomplishment, that simple chain of cause and effect."

"You blew off some steam," said Rogue. "That's good!"

"Do you think so? Look at me: I pride myself on being a man of words, a man of science—and yet I appear to be most at peace with myself when I can attack a problem with my fists!"

"Sometimes we don't have a choice," said Rogue firmly. "Some people won't listen to reason—especially not those who'd cheer-fully see us all dead because of what we are."

"It's only natural to feel frustrated," said Phoenix. "You and Moira have set yourselves an almost impossible task. But I know you, Hank. I know both of you, and I know that, if anyone can cure the Legacy Virus, you can. It's not in either of your natures to give up."

"I'm gratified by the vote of confidence, Jeannie. And you needn't fret overmuch on my account. I believe I may have worked the surfeit of negative emotions out of my system for the present. In fact, if you wouldn't mind turning the Blackbird around, I would very much appreciate a ride back to the Muir Island research facility. I have work to do."

Jean half-turned towards him, and flashed him a radiant smile. "We're already on our way. Our ETA is in about one hour and forty-five minutes. I can think of a certain Scottish lady who will be very pleased to see you."

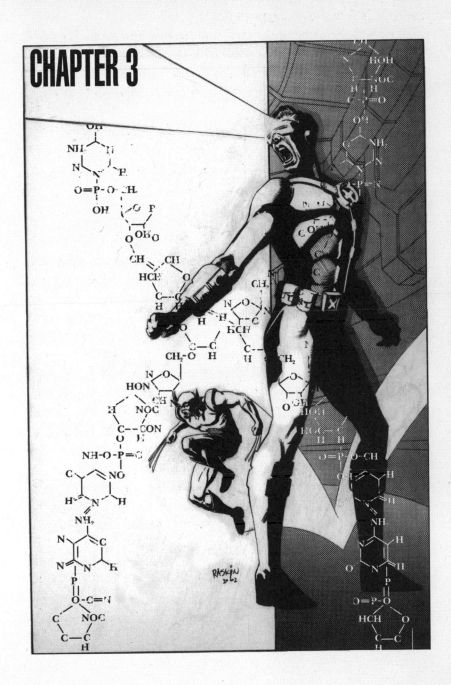

CHAPTER 3

SALEM CENTER was a small town in Westchester County, New York, just near enough to Manhattan to make commuting feasible, just distant enough to qualify as a peaceful suburb. Its peace, however, would have been shattered had its residents only been aware of what really went on in a certain building at the top end of Graymalkin Lane.

The Xavier Institute for Higher Learning was just far enough away from the town center—and set back far enough into its own grounds—for few people to notice the odd telltale sign of its true nature. And those who did see occasional flashes in the sky, or thought they heard the odd explosion, tended to assume that they were the results of some outlandish experiment being carried out within. They voiced concerns that, one day, Professor Charles Xavier's so-called gifted youngsters would go too far and wipe out the whole town, but they were only words. No one really believed them.

Inside Xavier's school right now, a young man was under attack.

The drones flew at Scott Summers from all sides, the nozzles of their tiny, in-built weapons flashing as their internal systems locked onto him. They were the size of dragonflies, but the shape of slightly flattened spheres, with silver metal plating. They were propelled not by wings but by antigravity systems, which allowed them to stop and turn on a hair.

He waited until they were about to fire, then dived. He passed beneath a cluster of drones, dropped into a crouch, and twisted around to face his attackers again. They had already reacted to his movement, and were swarming towards him in a great silver cloud. He rolled the fingers of his right hand into a fist, and activated the sensor in the palm of his glove. He opened his golden visor to its fullest extent, and a powerful beam of red energy ripped forth from his eyes and cut through the first rank of drones. They were halted in their tracks, each emitting an almost pathetic *bleep* as it clanged to the floor, a dead weight.

Explosions would have been more satisfying, but also more costly. Each damaged drone would have to be paid for.

Like all of Xavier's students, Scott Summers was far more than he seemed. His mutant power—his optic blasts—had earned him the code name Cyclops, and he was the original and current field leader of the X-Men. It was a role that often thrust him into fierce combat—which was why the Danger Room existed. This soundproofed, hi-tech training facility lay beneath Xavier's school, and offered the X-Men an environment in which they could hone their combat skills and learn to cope with their unique abilities.

"Hey!" protested Wolverine, Cyclops's Canadian teammate, from across the room. "I thought the object was to take these critters down one at a time. A test of reflexes, you said."

"Just narrowing the odds a little," grunted Cyclops, "that's all. Any objections?"

"Hell, no. 'Bout time you cut loose a bit, if you ask me. Can't be good for a fellow to be so uptight all the time."

"I didn't cut loose. It was a tactical maneuver. I'm perfectly in control."

"Whatever."

Cyclops had downed five drones, but the rest—another fifteen—

had split up again, to ensure that he couldn't hit more than one at a time. They learned fast.

He scowled, picked one of them at random and hit it with a narrow, focussed beam of exactly the right strength to trigger its cut-off circuit. But he had no time to bask in the satisfaction of having proved his point. As soon as he had turned his attention to one drone, three more had swooped in behind him. He tried to leap out of their way, but too late. A thin, yellow beam pierced his shoulder, delivering a stinging jolt of electricity. It did no more harm than that—Cyclops knew better than to operate the Danger Room on anything other than its lowest setting when there was no one in the control booth to monitor the session—but he was angry with himself for letting it happen. He had made a mistake, let his emotions influence his actions, and in combat that could have cost him his life.

Control was vital to Scott Summers. Without control, his optic blasts were a deadly danger to everyone around him. They could only be kept in check by a shielding of ruby quartz—the substance from which the lens of his visor was fashioned—or by his own eyelids. When he woke each morning, or during the night, he had to have the discipline to keep his eyes tightly closed until he had found and donned his special ruby quartz glasses.

To judge by his fighting style, however, Wolverine's temperament couldn't have been more different from Cyclops's. The man who was known to his friends only as Logan preferred to cut loose, relying upon his instincts. In battle, he almost resembled the wild animal from which he had taken his own code name. His mutant gene had endowed him with enhanced senses, a remarkable healing factor and three extensible bone claws in the back of each hand. Scientists in his homeland of Canada had added their own double-edged gift: they had grafted adamantium, the hardest known metal, onto his skeleton. And decades of experience—Logan looked forty, but his healing factor had retarded the aging process so that nobody could tell how old he really was—had made him, as he often boasted, the best there was at what he did.

He leapt into action now. He launched himself into the air, a yellow-and-blue-clad ball of hissing fury, and lashed out with his adamantium-laced claws. He had started the exercise with twenty drones, as had Cyclops. Wolverine's drones were golden in color, and programmed to target only him. They were also proofed against his claws, being reinforced with adamantium themselves. Still, a palpable hit would knock them, bleeping, to the ground. He had already downed eleven, without—as far as Cyclops had seen— being tagged in return. By the time he hit the floor again, three more drones had been deactivated. He landed nimbly on his feet, and rolled out of the way of the inevitable counterattacks.

His approach was effective, Cyclops couldn't deny that. It had also been the cause of bitter clashes between the two men in the past, when Logan's feral nature had—in his leader's opinion—gotten the better of him. He was unpredictable, and Cyclops didn't like that.

Scott was responsible for the X-Men's welfare—and, when Professor Xavier was away as he was now, that responsibility weighed particularly heavily upon him. He had been placed in charge of his mentor's dream—and he had no intention of letting the Professor down.

The drones were coming at him again, all at once, in a circle around him, maintaining their distance from each other. He gritted his teeth and set his jaw determinedly. He struck out four times with pinpoint accuracy, not one iota of energy wasted. At the last possible second, he ducked again and rolled, gratified to see that some of the drones had fired upon the spot where he had just been, and that two had hit and incapacitated their fellows.

He brought himself up into a crouch, and found himself back to back with his teammate. "Come on, One-Eye," taunted Wolverine, "why not admit that you only scheduled this workout 'cos of what we saw on the TV news?"

"I told you –"

"Yeah, yeah—and each time you blast one of these critters, you ain't seeing the face of one of them Newhill jerks. Right! What I want to know is, what did McCoy think he was doing, stirring up the ant's nest like that?"

"It wasn't his fault. It looked to me like he only stepped in to help." That wasn't what the news reports had said. They had played to their viewers' paranoid obsessions: mutants hiding among them, waiting to strike. Only the Beast had been featured—the camera crews hadn't been quick enough to catch him after he had fled the cemetery and joined his teammates—but rumors of an army of super-powered reinforcements had been presented as fact.

"Two gangs of mutie-haters tearing lumps out of each other? I'd have gotten myself a corn dog, sat back and watched them go at it!"

"No you wouldn't, Logan." Cyclops snapped his head around and blasted another drone, which had ventured too close to him.

"Doesn't help none though, does it, getting into a scrap on live TV? As if people need any more convincing that mutants are the cause of all the world's problems."

"They're scared, that's all."

"Scared of what they don't understand."

"Perhaps, in Newhill, they have cause to be."

"I don't see how you can be so damn reasonable!" Wolverine had been making himself a target, drawing his drones towards him. Now, with a scowl and a flash of metal, he closed the trap, and took out another two. "What, they think the Legacy Virus is a picnic for us? It's designed to kill mutants, for Christ's sake. So, how come it's our fault if a few poor *homo sapiens* get caught in the crossfire?"

Cyclops didn't answer. Wolverine wasn't saying anything that he didn't already know. He had spent most of his life fighting against anti-mutant prejudice, but the situation never seemed to improve—and Legacy had only made things worse. Scott had been present when Stryfe, himself a mutant from the far future, had unleashed his engineered virus upon the past in retaliation for a lifetime of mistreatment. He had been unable to stop him.

Stryfe's intention had been that his mutant kin should be

feared and shunned even more than they already were; that they should be treated like lepers. He had been more successful than he could ever have imagined. Even Stryfe hadn't anticipated that the virus itself would mutate, and begin to attack baseline human beings: those who weren't mutants.

Stryfe was dead now, but his legacy lived on in places like Newhill, Massachusetts. It threatened to destroy Professor Xavier's dream. But, most of all, it had exacted a very personal cost from the X-Men themselves. It had struck closest to home when it had taken the life of Illyana Rasputin, the younger sister of their currently-absent teammate Colossus. Now, Moira MacTaggert was also threatened.

Cyclops shared Wolverine's frustration—and, if the truth were known, he did find some release in loosing his powers and knocking drones out of the sky.

The impromptu training session, however, was interrupted by an insistent electronic chirping. The communications console at the Danger Room's door. Cyclops felt a stab of dismay at being recalled to the real world and its problems so soon, but he controlled it. The silver drones were mounting another attack, but he focussed past them and fired a thin optic beam, which hit the emergency cutoff switch on the wall. Wolverine found himself swinging at empty air as his remaining drones clattered to the floor around him.

Cyclops hurried to the console and took the call, a knot of worry forming in his stomach at the knowledge that it would almost certainly be bad news. Still, a smile played on his lips as the monitor revealed a head-and-shoulders shot of Jean Grey Summers, Scott's wife and the love of his life. He could see from her expression that something was wrong, so he skipped the small talk and got straight to business. "What is it, Jean? Is Hank OK?"

"He's fine," said Phoenix. "We took him back to Muir Island in the Blackbird. It's Moira. There's no sign of her, Scott. She seems to have disappeared into thin air."

Cyclops's mind was already working, racing through a checklist of the X-Men's many enemies who might have a grudge against Moira or who might use her to get at them, and who could pull off a stunt like this.

"You'd better tell me everything," he said.

Phoenix had just recapped the situation for Cyclops, and broken the connection to New York, when she heard the door of Moira's cottage opening. She sensed the Beast's thought patterns before he had joined his three teammates in the living room, and she knew he had nothing good to report.

"I've been over every inch of the research center with a fine-tooth comb," he said. "I can find nothing damaged or missing, nothing out of place at all. No indication that anybody other than Moira and myself has entered the building in weeks."

Phoenix nodded. His detailed inspection had only confirmed what an earlier quick search had suggested. She had performed a telepathic sweep of Muir Island herself, and knew that its sole inhabitant was not present. At least she could stop fearing the worst now. She knew that Moira had contracted the Legacy Virus, that it was eating away at her on a cellular level—and a dead woman would have no thoughts for her to read. She hadn't voiced her worries, but she knew that Nightcrawler, Rogue and the Beast had shared them.

Moira's boat was still tied to its moorings. Her helicopter still rested on its pad. She hadn't left the island in either—which meant that somebody must have collected her. And the fact that her sophisticated security system had been deactivated suggested that she had left in a hurry. Or, as was beginning to seem likely, been taken against her will.

"It's the same here," said Nightcrawler. "It's like the *Marie Celeste*. I can find nothing to suggest that Moira hasn't just stepped out of the house for a few minutes." Kurt knew the cottage well, having lived here for a time as a member of Excalibur: Britain's own team of mutant heroes, now disbanded. "Except that, if she did, then where is she now?"

38

"I wonder," said the Beast thoughtfully. He padded across the room to a wooden cabinet, pulled open a drawer and began to rummage through its tidy contents.

"I checked the security logs," said Phoenix. "There were no incidents recorded in the hours before the system was shut down—but there are some blind spots in the data. I'm running a program to correlate them, but my guess is that somebody fooled the sensors and gained access to this cottage. They must have surprised Moira here."

"The disks!" Hank turned back to the others, and Jean could have sworn that his face had turned a paler shade of blue. "Moira and I always backed up our work onto rewritable DVDs, in case something happened at the research center. She kept them in this drawer."

"And they aren't there now?" asked Phoenix.

"But why would somebody want to take them?" asked Rogue.

"To sabotage your work?" suggested Nightcrawler.

The Beast shook his head and began to pace the room, pinching his lower lip. "No, no, I don't think so. I checked the files at the center. They were all present and correct. If this was sabotage, then our unknown foe would have destroyed them too, if not the center itself."

"It could be a coincidence," said Rogue. "What if Moira just happened to have the disks with her when she left?"

"It's possible," the Beast conceded, nodding thoughtfully to himself. "I suppose we can't form any solid conclusions at this juncture. If only I had been here..."

"It's my guess," said Nightcrawler, "that our perpetrators waited until you weren't."

"Exactly," said Phoenix. "And, instead of trying to deduce why Moira was kidnapped—if indeed she was—then I think we should ask ourselves how. She was taken by surprise in her own home. There are no signs of a struggle, and she didn't have time to alert us, even though she has a communications console in this room with a direct line to the X-Men."

"So either she knew her assailants and welcomed them into her home..." said Nightcrawler.

"Or they landed on Muir Island silently," concluded Phoenix.

"Which rules out an aircraft," said the Beast, "unless Moira was so engrossed in her work that she didn't hear its approach—and a would-be intruder would be unwise to gamble upon such a possibility."

"Could she have been taken in by a shape-shifter like Mystique?" asked Rogue.

"Maybe," said Phoenix, "although Moira has had enough experience with our mutant enemies to be cautious."

"I would suggest a teleporter," said Nightcrawler, "but the security sensors were calibrated to detect any sudden displacement of mass."

"Which they didn't," said Phoenix.

"Nevertheless," said the Beast, "it behooves us to investigate the possibility. With the equipment at the research center, I can conduct a thorough scan for residual energies."

Phoenix nodded. "OK, Hank, you do that. Kurt, you stay here and help him. Rogue and I will go for a quick flight, and see if we can locate any witnesses."

"You think somebody might have seen something?" asked Rogue.

"Yes," said Phoenix, "I do. Something like an unfamiliar boat on the sea this afternoon."

The TV news was still covering the morning's events in Newhill. Bobby Drake stared morosely into his glass at the warped reflection of his own young, open face and his mousy brown hair, and he tried to tune out the presenter's voice. He had come into Salem Center to avoid thinking about what had happened. He had spent hours wandering aimlessly around the town's shops, but had ended up in this bar because he was sick of seeing sensationalistic headlines on the afternoon and early evening editions of newspapers. He had already declined Wolverine's offer to vent his feelings by joining him and Cyclops in a Danger Room training session. This was one of those days on which he needed to forget that he was a mutant, and specifically the X-Man known to the world as Iceman.

But the television, mounted on a wall bracket above Bobby's head, wouldn't let him forget.

The blue-furred interloper at William Montgomery's funeral had been identified as Doctor Henry McCoy. This news program was more responsible than some: the presenter suggested that Hank had been trying to end the trouble, not cause it. He even reminded his audience of the Beast's one-time role as a member of the Avengers: a UN-sanctioned super hero team who enjoyed a degree of regard and even adulation that was denied to their mutant counterparts.

It was too late. Bobby knew that too many minds had been made up already.

To his left, further along the bar, a swarthy man in a lumber-jack's shirt and jeans made a less than polite comment about how 'muties' were appearing everywhere.

"Too right," agreed the bartender, operating the pumps. "It's frightening, that's what it is. If a freak like that Beast guy can pass himself off as human, then how're you supposed to tell? There could be half a dozen of them in this bar right now."

To Bobby's surprise, one of the bartender's colleagues—a young woman—came to mutantkind's defense. "Oh, Chuck," she said, rolling her eyes, "if you can't tell the difference, then what's the problem? They've got to drink somewhere!"

"Problem is," said the male bartender, "they're worming their way into decent society, that's what the problem is."

"We already know how they're planning to replace us," said the swarthy customer. "They should be rounded up and put into camps, where we can keep an eye on them."

"Or at least sent back to their own country. That...that Genosha, whatever it's called."

Bobby scowled, and told himself not to get involved. He gritted his teeth and tightened his grip on his glass, accidentally lowering the temperature of his beer by a couple of degrees.

It was like this all over the country, the television assured him. Longstanding fears had been inflamed. People were looking at their neighbors, talking behind their backs, wondering if they might conceal a dangerous secret. Wondering if they might be hiding and watching, and biding their time. There had already been four reported attacks against suspected mutants. One was dead, another injured. As yet, there was no evidence that any of the four possessed the mutant X-factor, although one had been found to be infected with the Legacy Virus.

The newsreader moved on to another story, and Bobby listened to it, because the conversation to his left hadn't finished and he didn't want to hear any more ignorant comments. The gist of the item was that a Mrs. Scott from upstate was making a fresh appeal to the public for sightings of her husband, a prominent biochemist who had been missing for three weeks. He had been carrying out research into the genetic modification of crops, and it was speculated that his disappearance might have something to do with anti-GM protestors.

"If they've got nothing to hide," asserted the swarthy customer, his voice rising as he swilled down his beer, "then why'd they kick up such a fuss about the Mutant Registration Act? Why object to letting our democratically elected government know who they are and what they can do?"

Bobby left his glass half-full, and walked out of the bar before he lost his temper and said something unwise. The evening was beginning to draw in, and he hadn't brought a coat, but the cold didn't affect him. He stuck his hands into his pockets and trudged back towards the school, his shoulders stooped.

He couldn't help wondering how the people of Salem Center would react if they knew that some of their suspicions were well-founded: that mutants really did live among them, and that they really did disguise their true natures in public and hold clandestine meetings at their top secret base, in which they formulated battle plans.

Sometimes, Bobby Drake just wanted to be normal.

Sure, his powers could come in handy. Iceman could do some pretty cool stuff: form ice and snow out of the very air, even skate from A to B on a self-created ice slide. And he was lucky: in battle, he surrounded himself with a tough shell of ice, but, when he was in civvies, there were no visible signs of his mutant powers. Unlike poor Hank or Kurt, he didn't need an image inducer to be able to hide in a crowd. His earliest days with the original X-Men—he had been their youngest member—had been some of the happiest in his life. But things hadn't seemed so bad in those days. The world hadn't seemed so hostile.

Being a mutant had never been easy—but there had been a time when Bobby had been able to get away from it all, at least for short spells. He had taken several leaves of absence from the X-Men, spent time with his family, dated girls and gone to college. He had even enjoyed a degree of public acclaim as a member of a Los Angeles-based super-group called the Champions. Perhaps he had just been naïve, he thought now. Perhaps he had been blind to the tensions that had been building up around him even then.

It was harder, nowadays, to forget that he was different. Harder to escape the reminders. Harder to ignore the fact that mutants had many enemies, some of whom had ways of finding them and attacking without warning.

Bobby had recently learned that, as Iceman, he had the potential to become one of the most powerful mutants yet born. He had been accused of squandering that potential. But he had no wish to devote his entire life to being the best mutant he could be. He wasn't Wolverine. He wasn't even Cyclops. He still wanted a normal life, outside of all this.

He wondered how long it would be before the choice was taken from him altogether.

It was with a heavy heart, then, that he entered the mansion home of the Xavier Institute, to be greeted by a worried-looking Cyclops and the fateful words: "We've got a situation." He listened with mounting despair as the X-Men's leader filled him in, and he wondered if his life would ever be his own again.

Scott, it transpired, had spent the last few hours with Wolverine and another teammate, Storm, compiling a list of likely suspects for the probable kidnapping of Moira MacTaggert. With nothing else to go on, they were working on the assumption that one of the X-Men's many enemies had chosen to get at them through their human friend. Bobby felt a pang of guilt when he realized that he was hardly listening to the details. It wasn't until they were halfway to the conference room that he suddenly stopped, and allowed a half-remembered fragment of a television news broadcast to resurface in his mind. "What if," he proposed tentatively, "this was nothing to do with us? What if somebody wanted Moira for her skills?"

Cyclops gave him an inquisitive look. "We've considered that possibility, of course. What makes you say that?"

"Because," said Bobby—and, to his own surprise, he grinned—"Doctor Moira MacTaggert isn't the only scientist specializing in genetic research to have disappeared recently."

The old fisherman in the homely dockside tavern was reluctant to talk to them at first.

Jean Grey smiled at him sweetly, and bought him another half-pint of mild—whatever that was. In return, he mumbled into his graying beard about the state of the fishing industry nowadays, what with EEC quotas and the Eastern European factory trawlers. Rogue felt quite sorry for him, as he talked about a way of life that was gone forever. But she became gradually less sympathetic as he continued to talk and talk, without answering the questions that her teammate gently put to him.

They had borrowed some of Moira's clothes, and donned them over their costumes, before flying under their own power to the nearest population center to Muir Island: Stornoway, on the Isle of Lewis in the Outer Hebrides. They had started at the harbor, asking questions of one person after another. It hadn't taken long for one woman to remember that, looking out to sea, she had seen a large aircraft coming in to land at about half past one. She didn't know where it had put down exactly, but she had seen it again, flying in the opposite direction, about fifteen minutes later.

"Looks like it was a plane after all, then," Rogue had said.

But Phoenix had disagreed. "Like Hank said, too noisy. Somebody might well have flown to Muir Island to collect Moira, but I'm betting she was already a prisoner by then."

It had taken another two hours after that—until Rogue was about ready to give up—before they had found another lead, which had brought them here.

At last, the fisherman confirmed what had already been suggested to the two women by a witness. But not before explaining that he lived off a meager state pension these days, taking out his old boat only when the pain of his gout and arthritis subsided enough to make such an undertaking feasible. There was no living to be made at his game any more. That was why (and he was getting to the point at last now), when he had been made a generous offer this afternoon, he had taken it. He had hired out the *Sea Tiger* to a pair of strangers. They had returned it a couple of hours later, and the old man had thought no more about it.

Finally, Rogue thought, they were getting somewhere.

Except that the fisherman refused to say anything more about his customers. They had sworn him to secrecy.

Jean didn't seem to mind. She smiled again, thanked the old man and bought him another drink, then ushered Rogue out of the tavern. With the coming of night, a bitter chill had descended upon this part of the island. Despite her near-invulnerable skin and two layers of clothing, Rogue shivered as a fierce sea wind whipped against her face.

"Tell me that wasn't a complete waste of our time," she said. "Tell me you read his mind!"

Jean smiled knowingly. "Our suspects had Scottish accents," she said.

"Locals, then."

"Let's hope so. They certainly didn't leave in the plane with Moira. But they were very careful not to let anything slip. I've been through every word they said to our man in there. They gave him names, but they didn't produce any forms of identification. They were almost certainly using pseudonyms—and they didn't say a thing that might help us find out who they really are or where they came from."

"If only *he'd* been so secretive," said Rogue, wryly. "Couldn't you have rooted out this information an hour ago, before we had to sit through the story of his life?"

"I don't like to invade people's privacy unless I have to," said Jean. "Anyway, I spent quite some time in our fisherman friend's mind during the course of our conversation."

"Oh?"

"He might not know the kidnappers' names, but he did see their faces. The images are still very clear in his memory. I was studying them, memorizing every detail. I think I can safely say that, if I were to see them now, I'd recognize them."

"So, what do we do next? Look at mug shots?"

"In a way," said Jean. "Tomorrow morning, we'll take a ferry to Ullapool on the mainland. It's the only way the kidnappers could have arrived on, and left, the island—and somebody at the terminal must have seen them. I can scan a few minds, and look for images that match the ones in here." She pointed to her own head.

"You're planning to follow them all the way across Scotland like that?" Rogue was incredulous. "Won't that be a bit like looking for a needle in a very big haystack?"

"Not necessarily. If they were in a private car, then a worker at the terminal will have spotted it, and might remember the registration number subconsciously, even if they think they don't. If the kidnappers used public transport, they'll have left an even clearer trail in the memories of ticket clerks, bus drivers and regular commuters."

"Are you gonna describe these fellows to me then?" asked Rogue. "Since it looks like we'll be catching up to them pretty soon, and all."

"I can do better than that," said Jean. "I can place a picture of them into your mind—and in Hank's and Kurt's too, when we get back to Muir."

Rogue grinned. "These guys sure didn't know what they were getting themselves into when they messed with a friend of the X-Men, did they?"

"OK, people, change of plan."

Cyclops was standing in the Xavier Institute's main conference room, stooped over the head of an oblong table, his gloved knuckles resting on its oaken top. Three other X-Men were present. Wolverine leaned back in his chair, champing on a foul-smelling cigar and glaring at his team leader as if ready to question his every utterance. Iceman had changed into his costume, which, at present, consisted simply of a pair of black trunks with a large red X sewn into the yellow waistband. Having most of his skin exposed helped him to use his powers more effectively, apparently—and he didn't feel the cold. If the X-Men went into action, then Bobby would shift into his armored ice form, anyway.

Rounding out the quartet was Ororo Munroe, better known as Storm. Before joining the X-Men, she had been worshipped as a goddess in the rainforests of her native Kenya—and, when she wielded her ability to control weather patterns, it was easy to see why. Storm was tall and elegant, with dark brown skin and long, white hair, which she kept off her forehead with a black headband. To see her hovering serenely in the midst of a gale of her own creation, her black cloak billowing around her as she brought down lightning bolts to smite her foes, was like looking at a raw force of nature.

"Thanks to Bobby," said Cyclops, "we now have a lead. We've been searching through archived news stories on the web, and we've learned that Moira is only one of at least four accomplished geneticists to have vanished in the last few months."

"The disappearances were each weeks apart," said Iceman, "and in different countries, which is probably why no one's thought to connect them before."

"And of course," said Cyclops, "no one else knows about Moira yet." He handed out color printouts of downloaded photographs. "A Doctor Takamoto from Tokyo was reported missing first. She's been gone for almost four months now, and the Japanese police have found no leads at all. They've begun to work on the assumption that she's dropped out of sight on purpose. The older gentleman is a Professor Travers from London. But the nearest victim is also the most recent. His name is Clyde Scott, and he lives right here in New York, up in Poughkeepsie."

"I saw his wife on the TV news this evening," said Iceman, as the others inspected a picture of a middle-aged, African-American man with cropped, graying hair.

"So," said Storm, "we are now working on the assumption that Moira was kidnapped, like these other people, because somebody needed her specialist knowledge."

"Precisely," said Cyclops, "which unfortunately widens the field of suspects somewhat."

"What's the plan then, boss?" Wolverine asked.

"I think we should pay a call on Mrs. Scott tomorrow."

WE KNOW *who you are.*

Allan Coleman started, jerking his head up from the puddle of stale beer on the bar top. He looked behind him, over first one shoulder and then the other, searching for the woman who had spoken. He saw nobody. Nobody who was interested in him, anyway. *Oh man,* he thought, *it's much too early in the night to be this smashed already!*

Come to think of it, he had no idea what time it was.

He contemplated his near-empty glass, then shrugged his shoulders, swigged down the last of his bitter to steady his nerves, and counted the loose change in his threadbare pockets, wondering if he could scrape together enough to order a chaser with the next pint. Business hadn't been good lately. With many of his associates enjoying extended holidays at Her Majesty's pleasure, the flow of merchandise had slowed to a trickle.

Allan looked around the seedy bar again, reminding himself of the surroundings in which he had settled into an alcoholic stupor, who knew how long ago. He frowned at the unexpected sight of a beautiful woman, sitting at the bar, three stools along. He rubbed his eyes and squinted, trying to focus. Was he seeing things, as well as hearing voices?

The gorgeous redhead certainly looked out of place among the White Lamb's usual Friday night collection of thugs and tramps. Allan rummaged through his change again, this time to see if he could afford to buy her a drink. It would be a hopeless gesture, he was sure, but Allan Coleman was nothing if not a hopeless, even mindless, optimist.

He levered himself up from his stool, wondering why he hadn't remembered that the floor was so far down and that it sloped at such a treacherous angle. He leaned against the bar to support himself, let out a controlled breath, and set his sights upon his prey.

We know who you are, Allan Coleman, and we know where you live.

This time, he let out a strangulated cry of fear. His head thrashed about wildly as he tried to find the source of the mysterious voice, but it was beginning to penetrate even his pickled brain that there *was* no source; that the voice was contained within his own mind.

"Who are you?" he cried, aloud, staring up at the nicotine-yellowed ceiling. "What do you want with me?" He attracted a few looks, but no one was really interested in, nor cared about, his unseemly outburst. They were used to such behavior in here. From Allan, more than most.

Oh, I think you know the answer to that.

"No...no, it can't be..."

What are you most afraid of, Allan? What keeps you awake at night?

"M-m-mutants! They've come for me! They've come for me!"

Remember the girl in the hardware store, Allan? Remember how she accidentally used her power in front of you: her harmless little ability, to create a small pyrotechnic display with her fingers? Remember what you did to her, Allan?

Allan Coleman tried to bury his head in his hands, to block out the terrible voice, but it didn't work. Tears streamed down his cheeks, and he was on his knees, and he realized he must have been shouting, begging for help. But people were no longer ignoring him; they were shaking their heads and moving slowly away from this gibbering madman.

The next thing Allan knew, he was being hoisted to his feet by Roger, the landlord, who was coming out with all the usual admonishments: he'd had enough to drink now, he was upsetting the other customers. Allan tried to resist, but he wasn't strong enough, and his terrified appeals went unheeded as he was propelled toward and through the doors.

He hit the pavement running, wanting to put as much distance between him and the public house as possible, knowing in his heart that it would make no difference. But the cold Edinburgh night acted like a slap to his face. As Allan came to an exhausted halt, bent double and wheezing in the shadow of the city's famous hilltop castle, he began to sober up. He began to realize that Roger had been right, that he had let the drink play games with his mind, that he had experienced nothing more than a half-waking dream. He felt foolish, but the feeling was nothing compared to the relief that washed over him. He laughed giddily, chiding himself for having believed such an unlikely fantasy, even for a moment.

Presently, Allan straightened up again, adjusted his twisted jacket and used his sleeve to wipe the sweat from his forehead. He swore never to touch an alcoholic drink again, as he did at least once every week.

And, just as he was about to set off for home—for his cramped, untidy and over-expensive third-floor flat—he felt a gentle tap on his shoulder.

Allan turned, and gasped to find himself face-to-face with a blue-skinned demon.

"*Guten tag*," said the nightmarish creature, its fangs bared, its luminous yellow eyes boring into his skull.

And then there was a ferocious *bamf!* of imploding air, and a sickly wrenching feeling in Allan Coleman's stomach, as Princess Street disappeared in a cloud of evil-smelling smoke.

* * *

Mrs. Pearl Scott had become used to receiving unannounced visitors over the past three weeks. Ever since she had reported her husband missing—ever since the fateful day when he had apparently left his Long Island laboratory as usual, but hadn't come home—she had answered the door to a steady stream of policemen, journalists and men in dark suits from various government agencies known only by their initials. At first, her heart had leapt at each new chime of the doorbell. She had raced through the hallway wondering if this was the one, the visitor who would tell her that they had finally found her husband. She had hoped for good news, but steeled herself for bad.

She didn't feel that anticipation any more. She had been disappointed too many times.

What Pearl hadn't got used to yet was the empty space in her bed, and the feeling of waking up in the morning alone, of going through the motions of life—sending her son off to school, reassuring him that Daddy was safe and well when she didn't believe it herself—even as fear gnawed its way through her stomach.

At least, if Clyde had died, she could have begun to accept her loss. This uncertainty was agony. She didn't know how to feel, what to prepare herself for.

There was something different about today's visitors.

It wasn't the couple's appearance that alerted her. Well, not really. The woman was of African descent, like herself, but younger, slimmer and taller, her hair a beautiful but unusual white. The man looked every inch the FBI agent he claimed to be, with his black suit and grim expression—but his red eyeglasses made for an odd fashion statement.

It wasn't anything they said, nor anything about the FBI passes they showed. Pearl had seen a lot of official cards and bits of paper recently, but how was she supposed to know if they were faked or not? How was she supposed to know what an FBI pass was supposed to look like, other than from brief glimpses on *The X-Files*?

No, it was nothing like that. Just a tingling sensation at the base of Pearl Scott's skull, as she let Agents Summers and Munroe into her house. An instinct, nothing more. A suspicion with no grounds in fact. But a powerful suspicion, nonetheless.

Could it be *them* at last?

The thought made her afraid, but hopeful at the same time. As the agents sat side by side on her sofa, she questioned them gently. She pointed out that she had already spoken to the FBI, and Summers smoothly explained that, in view of the lack of progress so far, the case had been handed to another department, but he didn't say which one.

"We'd just like to go through your statement again," he said.

"I've told you what happened a thousand times," said Pearl.

"Nevertheless," said Agent Munroe with an encouraging smile, "it might help to bring to mind a fresh detail, something you might have forgotten."

"Don't you think I've wracked my brains trying to think of something? I've got nothing new to tell you!" Archly, she added: "And you never take much notice of what I say, anyhow."

"I know it must be difficult for you, Mrs. Scott," said the young man, "but it really would be helpful to us if you could just go through it all one more time."

Pearl offered to make a cup of tea, then. In fact, she insisted, even when the agents indicated that they really weren't thirsty and would rather get down to business. She wanted to get away from them, to spend a few minutes in the safety of her kitchen, to think.

Almost mechanically, she lit a ring on the gas stove and filled the big old kettle, which, to Clyde's frustration, she had always refused to replace. And she wondered: what were *they* doing here? What had *they* done to her husband, and what did *they* want with her now?

She was drawn back down the hallway, to the door of the living room, and she pressed her ear up against the wood. She could hear her visitors talking, their voices unintelligible at first but a few words and phrases becoming recognizable as she strained to make them out.

"...pity Jean isn't here. She could just..."

"...gone through so much already...seems such a shame... lying to her..."

"...exactly tell the truth, can...both know how paranoid people can be..."

"...think she suspects, Scott?"

The hammering of Pearl Scott's heart, and the sound of her own heavy breathing in her ears, prevented her from hearing more. But she was sure now. She had always been sure, she realized. She had told the police, the special agents, the press, all about *them*, and no one had believed her. But she had always known she was right, and that *they* would come back.

Breathlessly, expecting to hear *them* behind her at any second, she tiptoed up the stairs and into the bedroom, the creaking floorboards seeming louder than they ever had before as she hurried to her husband's bedside cabinet, opened the bottom drawer and retrieved the gun from beneath his vests. She held it in her hand and looked at it numbly. It was heavier than she remembered. She had thought it would give her a sense of security, but it felt like a dead weight in her hand, and she was more frightened than ever because its solid presence made all this feel more real somehow. Her hands began to tremble, and she dropped the bullets three times as she tried to load them. By the time she reached the top of the stairs again, at last, the handle of the gun was threatening to slide out of her sweat-slickened hand, and the old kettle in the kitchen was whistling insistently.

She was glad for the noise at first, because it masked her footsteps, but she couldn't have been thinking straight because it hadn't occurred to her that *they* would hear it too.

The man emerged from the living room first. His face showed only concern but, with his eyes masked by red lenses, Pearl couldn't judge if it was genuine or not. He looked up to where she had frozen, halfway down the stairs, and he smiled when he saw her. "Mrs. Scott. I was worried that something was wrong. I think your kettle's boiling."

He saw the gun, then, before she could think of hiding it. He tried not to react, but he was taken by surprise and couldn't stop himself. He cocked his head, just a little, to one side—an inquisitive gesture—and Pearl could almost feel his hidden eyes boring into her. "Mrs. Scott," he said softly, gently, "what do you need the gun for?"

His words must have alerted his white-haired companion, because she appeared beside him in the doorway. Almost involuntarily, Pearl retreated a step. The gun felt heavier than ever, but she dragged it up to point at them, squinting along the sights but unable to keep them steady. A trickle of sweat dripped into her eye. "You—you won't take me like you did my Clyde," she stammered, her throat dry. "You won't! I'll kill you first!"

"Mrs. Scott," said the man, in the same level, conciliatory tone, "I assure you, we didn't take your husband. We only want to find him."

"You lied to me. *They* sent you, I know *they* sent you."

The man and the woman exchanged glances.

"You aren't from the FBI. Deny it! I dare you to deny it!"

"You're right, Mrs. Scott," said the woman. "We aren't from the FBI."

"But we don't mean you any harm," said the man. "We do want to help."

Pearl didn't know what to do, whether to believe him, and she was shaking so much that she couldn't have hit either one of the strangers with a bullet if she'd tried. She was no threat to *them*, she knew that—but in that case, why didn't *they* do something? Why didn't *they* attack her, disarm her, do whatever *they* had come here for? Could she have been wrong? She was so confused, and she only wanted to put down the gun and cry, give vent to the dreadful feelings that had built up inside her over these past long weeks, but she didn't dare, so she gave voice instead to the words that were burning in her breast: "I know what you are."

And all the woman said was: "What do you think we are, Mrs. Scott?"

"You're *mutants*," sobbed Pearl, and she burst into tears. "You're *mutants*! *Mutants*!"

Allan Coleman wanted to be sick.

He didn't know how the demon had brought him here, to this dark alley where nobody would be able to hear his cries, but he felt as if it had turned his guts inside-out in the process. He tried not to think about the churning in his stomach. He was facing a brick wall, with a rusted fire escape ladder, which led only to a boarded-up window. There was only one way out: he could hear the faint sounds of traffic behind him. The demon had vanished—not in a puff of smoke this time, but simply melting into the shadows—and Allan made to run.

But, as he turned around to face the distant road, he found another monster behind him.

This second creature was blue too, but this one had fur. It squatted on top of a dustbin, looking like a wild animal in humanoid form. And it smiled at him.

He gave a yelp of fear, and shrank away from it—then, realizing that his only hope was to do the opposite, to get past it, he galvanized his jelly legs into action and propelled himself forwards. The creature leapt from its perch, too late. For a blissful, hopeful moment, Allan thought he had outrun it—until something blue passed over his head, and the creature landed in front of him, still smiling.

"Not intending to leave our company already, I hope, Mr. Coleman?" it said, in a voice that was surprisingly cultured.

"What do you want with me?" Allan stammered.

"I'm sure it's not like you to make hasty judgements based on cosmetic appearances," the creature continued, as if he hadn't spoken. "I have to say, I would be extremely perturbed if I considered for a moment that you were a man capable of such unreasoning prejudice."

"I'm not prejudiced, I swear I'm not. I've got nothing against mutants, honest!"

"In which case, sugar," came a broad Southern American drawl from behind him, "you won't mind doing us a small favor, will you?" Allan whirled around, to find a woman behind him. He had no idea where she had come from. She had either teleported in like the blue demon, or dropped from the sky. She was wearing a green bodysuit with a hood, which cast her face into shadow. She looked normal enough at first glance, but she had to be one of them too.

Allan backed away across the cobblestones of the alleyway, looking wildly from the animal-thing to the witch-woman and back, scared to take his eyes off either of them, until he felt cold brick behind him. 'Boo!' said a voice in his ear—the voice of the blue demon, although he couldn't see it—and Allan actually screamed.

Don't worry, Allan Coleman. We aren't going to hurt you. Not if you help us.

It was the voice from before. The one in his head. A woman's voice, he now realized for the first time. And, this time, an image came with it. The redhead. The one who had been seated along the bar, not looking at him. She was looking now. He could see her face in his thoughts, and she was smiling at him. She looked kind and trustworthy. He wanted to believe her, but he was frightened. Frightened of the demon and the creature and the witch, but more frightened still of this woman who could disguise herself as a normal human being, who could infiltrate his local pub, his world, his mind, without him even knowing it.

"What do you want with me?" he asked again, pathetically.

And, this time, she told him.

As Allan Coleman's hurried footsteps receded into the distance, Phoenix stepped off the roof of the old warehouse building, onto which she had levitated herself after leaving the White Lamb pub. As she lowered herself into the alleyway, Nightcrawler emerged from the shadows beneath her to join the Beast and Rogue. He seemed to be in good health, which was a relief. Jean knew that teleporting with another person was a strain for him, although his endurance had improved with practice.

The Beast sighed heavily. "Chalk up one more example of *homo sapiens* who will never regard a mutant with anything less than mistrust again."

58

"According to Jeannie," said Rogue, "he never did anyway."

"Rogue's right, Hank," said Phoenix, as she landed beside her teammates. "I don't like using scare tactics, but Mr. Coleman's mind was well and truly closed already. And if you knew some of the things he'd done..." She shook her head, trying to clear it of the images she had seen in the unpleasant little man's memories. "Anyway, the point is, we didn't have time to be subtle. Moira could be in danger at this very moment, and our trail had gone cold."

It had been a long, exhausting day for the X-Men's resident telepath. It hadn't been too difficult to trace Moira's kidnappers back from the ferry terminal at Ullapool, via a bus ride and a train ride, to Edinburgh's Waverley Station. But, in the bustle of Scotland's capital city, she had had her work cut out for her detecting even the most fleeting memories of the two men's faces in the crowd. She had found a couple of people who had seen them on the street, and some more who had spotted one or other of them in shops. It was enough to confirm that the men almost certainly lived locally, but it didn't tell her where.

Then, at last, she had found somebody who frequented a particular rundown, back-street drinking establishment, and had seen her targets there on several occasions. Many of the White Lamb's patrons remembered them too, although Phoenix had been disappointed to learn that nobody knew much about them. They knew what the men did, but they didn't know their names. As she had noted back in Stornoway, they were good at keeping their secrets.

She had waited in the pub for a while, almost choking on the ever-present haze of cigarette smoke, hoping she might be fortunate enough for the men to show themselves there tonight. When they hadn't turned up, she had formulated an alternative plan.

"Well, let's just hope our Mr. Coleman can heat things up for us," Rogue muttered. "From the look on his face, I think he might just skip town and never come back."

"He won't," said Phoenix, confidently. "He's scared of our marks, but not nearly as scared as he is of us now. He doesn't doubt for a second that we could find him, wherever he hid."

"Besides," grinned Nightcrawler, "we got the telephone number off him."

"Nevertheless," said the Beast, "we stand a better chance of luring our friendly neighborhood guns-for-hire to a rendezvous if the initial contact is made by somebody whose voice they recognize, and whom they trust."

Phoenix "listened" with her mind for a moment. Allan Coleman was still nearby, and she was familiar enough with his thought patterns now to pick them out of a crowd. She smiled. "He's in a public call box," she reported. "He's dialing the number. With a little luck, we can look forward to meeting Moira's kidnappers within the next hour or two."

Scott Summers and Ororo Munroe sat in Pearl Scott's living room and sipped at hot tea from delicate china cups with saucers. It seemed odd, Scott reflected, as he reached for an oatmeal cookie, that the woman had gone from threatening them with a gun to offering them such hospitality in the space of only a few minutes. But then, Mrs. Scott had been confused and upset and, after making her announcement on the stairs, she had simply buried her head in her hands and sobbed. When Scott had approached her and carefully taken the gun from her, she had acquiesced without a struggle. And, upon realizing that he and his colleague really did mean her no harm—that, indeed, they meant to find her husband, along with their own missing friend—she had been relieved and almost pathetically grateful.

This still left the question of how she had guessed that her two visitors were mutants, but Scott thought it best not to pry too deeply. Perhaps it was just women's intuition. Perhaps it was paranoia: Pearl Scott had expected mutants to come and, by pure coincidence, had chosen today to believe it had happened. But it wasn't beyond the bounds of possibility that she might be a mutant herself, albeit not a strong one; that her power might simply be to sense when other mutants were in the vicinity. If so, it was probably best she didn't know about it. Scott knew of far too many people who would do anything to get their hands on somebody with such a power, and Pearl Scott deserved to live a normal life.

She was still a little flustered. She had apologized repeatedly for what she had done, and Scott and Ororo had repeatedly assured her that it didn't matter. "It's not that I'm against mutants or anything," she explained, "goodness, no. My husband, Clyde, was—*is*—a geneticist. He explained it all to me, and...and, well, hating somebody because they were born with a...a...twist in a DNA strand, it's about as sensible as hating somebody because they're...they're...well, because they were born with dark skin, isn't it?"

Ororo smiled encouragingly.

"But there are...I mean, you know, there are...evil mutants out there, aren't there?" Mrs. Scott spoke hesitantly, looking at her two visitors to see if she had offended them. When she saw that she hadn't, she continued, a little emboldened: "I mean, people like that Magneto one, and...and...what was he called? Onslaught." Scott resisted the urge to wince at that particular name. "I mean, it's not that...well, they're...*you're* the same as the rest of us, aren't you? Some good, some bad, some in between."

"And you believe your husband's disappearance may have had something to do with mutants?" asked Ororo.

"There's been no mention of it in the news reports," Scott pointed out.

Mrs. Scott's eyes flashed with a mutinous fire, which hadn't been there before. "No. No, well there wouldn't be, would there? It's a cover-up!"

In Scott's opinion, that wasn't very likely. Typically, the media were all too quick to jump at the merest suggestion of mutant involvement in something like this. However, he kept his own counsel for now, as Ororo questioned their witness further.

After some coaxing—and after making it clear, three times, that she didn't know anything for sure, she only had suspicions—Pearl told them her story. She told them about the day, just a week before her husband's disappearance, when two men in dark suits had come to the house and insisted upon talking to him, even though he had been busy. Mrs. Scott hadn't heard their conversation herself, as the three men had gone into the living room and closed the door behind them—but her Clyde had related the salient points to her later.

"They wanted to hire him, freelance like, to do some work for them. I didn't really understand the details, but it was something to do with mutants…with studying mutants' DNA and working on some…some…well, I don't know what it was. But Clyde said they were very insistent. And he couldn't help them; he was in the middle of a project for the government—but when he told them this, they started asking all kinds of questions. Was he prejudiced against mutants? Did he think they didn't deserve his help? That kind of thing. I mean, my Clyde, he didn't—*doesn't*—have a prejudiced bone in his body. He just couldn't help them, that's all, but they took it really badly, and they…well, they didn't get nasty exactly, but I remember Clyde saying…he said he didn't much care for their attitude. Like they didn't want to take 'no' for an answer, you know what I mean?"

Ororo nodded, understandingly. "Do you know who these two men were, Mrs. Scott?"

Scott chipped in: "Do you have any reason to believe they were mutants themselves?"

"Oh, no, no, no," Mrs. Scott assured them, "nothing like that. No, no, I think they were normal…well, I mean…they weren't mutants. Not that I'd know. They didn't *seem* like mutants. It's just that they talked about mutants, you know? And they did say their names, but I can't remember them. I wish I could. But I do know who sent them."

"You do?" Scott raised an eyebrow.

"Yes, well, that's the problem, isn't it? I've told the police, I've told the FBI, I even told a nice young gentleman from the TV news. But, as soon as I say the name, as soon as I mention that… that organization, they just look at me as if I'm stupid. They say

I'm being paranoid, that these are respectable people and they'd never do anything like kidnap my Clyde, and I keep thinking, perhaps they're right. But I just keep coming back to it in my mind, and...well, all I know is, I didn't trust those men. And nor did my husband."

"We don't think you're being paranoid, Mrs. Scott," said Ororo.

Pearl Scott looked hopeful, but she was still nervous, still fidgeting with her hands and talking quickly. "Sometimes I think it's a big conspiracy, you know. It feels like they've got friends everywhere, like you can't say anything against them because they're too powerful, and part of me knows that's stupid, like it's something off the TV, but it's how it feels."

She faltered again then, and Scott could guess what she was feeling. She didn't want to give them the name, because they might react like all the others. She was holding on to the hope of this moment, the hope that they might believe her as nobody else would. She didn't want to face the fear that they might not.

He reined in his impatience, and let Ororo do the talking. She assured Mrs. Scott that, as mutants, she and her friends had come up against conspiracies before, and that they would listen to any theories she had with open minds. The conversation became sidetracked, as Mrs. Scott sympathized with some of the X-Men's experiences, although Ororo resisted going into too much detail. Eventually, the woman could find no more excuses to stall.

She took a deep breath, and told her visitors the name of the organization; the people whom she believed responsible for the kidnapping of her husband. It was a familiar name, and Scott Summers couldn't help but smile and shake his head at the logic of it all.

He believed her without question.

The meeting had gone well.

The thin man and the bearded man had turned up at half past ten, right on time. They had recognized Jean from Allan Coleman's flattering—if somewhat sexist—description of her, and had sat with her at a small, circular table in the White Lamb's darkest corner.

The Beast, disguised by an image inducer, had pretended to bury himself in a newspaper nearby. Having originally picked up *The Independent*, he had had to be talked into swapping it for *The Sun*, the better to blend in. Nightcrawler had concealed himself on the roof, while Rogue had begun the long flight back to Muir Island, under her own power, to fetch the Blackbird.

Jean had given the two men a false name. They had declined to give her their names at all, but she had picked them out of their thoughts, along with their addresses and plenty of other information about them. She had put on a bashful act, as if she had never done anything like this before, as she related her cover story to them. By the time she was halfway through her sorry tale about the fictional no-good husband whom she wanted put out of his misery, she had already learned everything she wanted. She had continued to talk, though, to allay their suspicions. They had become impatient, and the thin man had begun to wonder why Coleman had thought this woman worthy of their attention. Picking up those thoughts, Jean had had to assure him that she could be very persuasive. No matter how she might feel about her reluctant informant, he didn't deserve to be hunted down and murdered.

Eventually, when she had thought it safe, she had made a show of deciding that she didn't want to go through with the contract after all. The bearded man had made some vague, disgruntled threat about what would happen if she wasted his time again, and Jean had mumbled insincere apologies. Then the two men had left, Jean had followed them out onto the street a few minutes later and made a quick phone call, and the X-Men had regrouped.

Phoenix, Nightcrawler and the Beast stood in the back alley in which they had frightened Allan Coleman half to death, and they waited for the sound of their plane overhead.

"I called the police," said Jean. "I gave them the names and addresses of our two friends, and a list of crimes they might be able to connect them with, including three murders. I was able to give them enough names and dates to make them take me seriously."

"It must have been one of the most extensive anonymous tip-offs they've ever received," mused the Beast.

"And one that can never be traced back to us, nor to Herr Coleman," said Nightcrawler.

"But what news did you garner of our compatriot?"

Phoenix took a deep breath. "It was pretty much as we expected. Our men were hired at extremely short notice, and given blueprints of Muir Island's security systems. Their job was to capture Moira, and they were specifically instructed that they were to take her by surprise."

"Presumably to obviate the possibility of her contacting us," said the Beast.

"Once they had her, they activated a signaling device that was sent to them anonymously via Federal Express. Within an hour, a Hercules transport plane had arrived on the island. They handcuffed Moira to a fence-post nearby and left her, along with the signal device and a key, just out of her reach, to be collected."

"So, they weren't aware of the identities of their employers?" asked the Beast.

"They were contacted by e-mail, and paid by money transfers. I memorized the details, but I'd be surprised if the payments were traceable."

"And they never set eyes upon the occupants of the Hercules?"

"Ah, now that's where we get lucky!" said Phoenix. "Our men, you see, don't like not knowing who their employers are. They accepted this contract because the money was good—very good—but they weren't happy about it."

"So, let me guess," said Nightcrawler, with a grin. "They disobeyed orders. One of them sneaked back to get a look at whoever was in that Hercules."

"They saw Moira being loaded into the back of the plane by two men."

"So, we have another pair of faces to trace?" surmised the Beast.

"Not faces, no. These men were wearing masks." Jean let those words sink in for a moment, before smiling and adding: "Familiar masks. Flesh-colored, with no features: just slits for the eyes, nose and mouth, and a seam down the center. Dark blue uniforms with red highlights."

Nightcrawler and the Beast made the connection simultaneously, and all three X-Men announced their conclusion in unison:

"The Hellfire Club!"

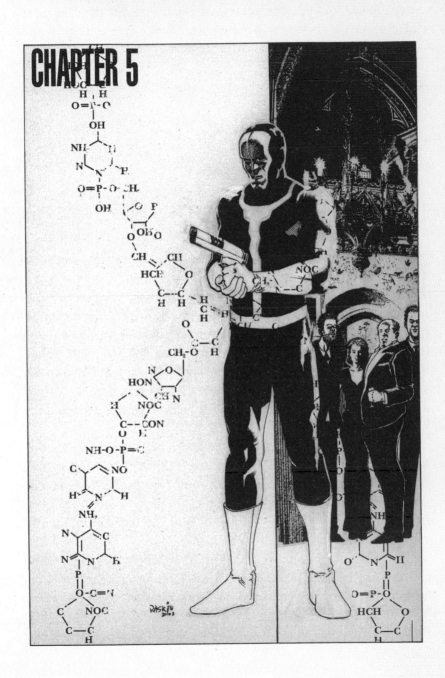

MOIRA MACTAGGERT slept again, but her dreams were less pleasant this time.

She dreamt of faceless men with guns. They were hunting her. She ran through Edinburgh's empty streets, heart pounding, breathing ragged, and all the time she was weighed down with the dreadful feeling that there was something she had to do. Something important. But she didn't know what it was. She had to get somewhere, but she didn't know where. And every time she turned a corner, one of the faceless men was in front of her, blocking her way.

The dread stayed with her as she surfaced from the nightmare. Moira tried to combat it by telling herself that everything was all right; that she was still at home on Muir Island and that she had simply dozed off over her lab bench again. But, as sleep fell away from her, her reactivated senses delivered the bad news that this simply wasn't true.

The first thing she noticed was the smell. The stink of engine oil assailed her nostrils. Secondly, she became aware of a throbbing lump on the back of her head. She didn't know where it had come from. Instinctively, she tried to raise her hands to it, but found that they were tied behind her back. Thick rope bit into her wrists, and her shoulders were aching. Moira's hearing kicked in, presenting her with fresh evidence: the distant beating of helicopter blades. She could feel the shape of an uncomfortable wooden chair beneath her. Her stomach was empty, and her chest was burning with the familiar cold-like symptoms of the Legacy Virus.

Finally, she tore open her leaden eyes to complete the picture. The chair to which she was bound stood in the center of a small, wooden-walled room. There was only one door, and the window beside it suggested that it led outside, even if the glass was too grimy to reveal more than a gray haze beyond. Another window, opposite the first, was covered by an old, stained, orange drape, which hung lopsidedly. There were only two other pieces of furniture—a desk and another chair—but, even so, the room seemed cluttered. The desk was stacked high with yellowing pieces of paper in torn manila folders, some of which had brimmed over onto the bare boards of the floor. Shelves lined the walls, filled with neglected tools, dirty cloths and old tins of paint and oil streaked by their own leaked contents. Dust lay on every surface, and cobwebs clung to the corners of the ceiling. Moira didn't recognize the room, but she did have a distant memory of running across tarmac towards a shed, with the faceless men chasing after her.

Or had that been part of the dream?

She shook her head in an attempt to clear it, and winced as a fresh stab of pain emanated from her wound. No, she thought, as her recent memories tumbled back into place, the faceless men had been real. Hellfire Club agents in their blue and red uniforms, with their all-concealing, featureless faceplates.

The costumes dehumanized them, taking away each agent's individuality. There was no way to tell them apart, no way to know who was under any one blank mask. Perhaps a close friend or a family member, or somebody who lived on the next block and watched you, furtively, as you went to work each morning. The shadowy group of businessmen who employed these mercenaries liked outsiders to imagine that they had eyes everywhere. To a certain extent, they had.

Moira had encountered the Hellfire Club before, and her experience of it had all been bad. Originally formed in London as an exclusive gentleman's club in the latter half of the eighteenth century, the organization now had branches across the world. Membership was considered not only a rare privilege but a status symbol, as was access to the club's famous—and often hedonistic—parties. As a result, those parties provided an environment in which the wealthy and the influential could meet on an informal basis. Many business deals had been struck and alliances formed over the punchbowl, beneath the cloak of secrecy that the Hellfire Club offered. Its influence extended into every corner of life—which made it the perfect cover for a handful of people who chose to use its resources for their own nefarious purposes.

Each branch of the Hellfire Club was ruled by a select Inner Circle, the self-proclaimed Lords Cardinal, who were accountable to nobody. An elite cabal within an elite cabal. They gave themselves ranks named after chess pieces, and dressed in Victorian clothing to symbolize their rejection of modern-day democratic values. Some Inner Circles did little more than arrange regular social events, but others took a more proactive stance. They were prepared to do whatever it took to perpetuate their own wealth and to ensure that political power remained where it belonged: in the hands of the rich.

Their agents were well trained. Moira's single attempt to escape from them, her act of defiance, had been brought to a swift, brutal end. Ah yes, she thought ruefully, that was where the lump on her head must have come from.

She had kept herself awake during the flight here. That had been a mistake. She had paced the floor of the Hercules' expansive cargo hold, hour after hour, until she had lost track of time. The door to the cockpit had been locked. She had listened at it, making out at least two voices but unable to hear their words over the engine noise. She had tested the door, finding it too sturdy. She might have been able to barge through it, but not at the first attempt—and, without the element of surprise, she would only have found herself staring down gun barrels again. She had bided her time, intending to stay alert, but the flight had gone on and on, and the hold had been so warm and dry. She had begun to feel airsick and so, so tired.

They had landed at last, and it had been easy for Moira to feign sleep as the agents had come for her. She had groaned realistically as a red-gloved hand had slapped her around the face to wake her. She had let two agents haul her to her feet, trying not to show surprise as she had recognized their outfits, and wondering which of the Hellfire Club's Lords Cardinal, from which Inner Circle, they had taken their orders from. She had leaned on them like a dead weight as they had manhandled her towards the back of the airplane, where a third uniformed man had waited.

She had pretended to stumble on the loading ramp, throwing one of her escorts off-balance but hopefully without making him too suspicious. She had forced herself into action, pivoting around to strike out unexpectedly. She had grabbed the second agent's lightweight machine-gun, but hadn't been able to wrench it from his determined grip. She had resorted to Plan B, leaping from the ramp and running for it, taking in her surroundings only in that split-second of adrenaline-fuelled excitement. She had been brought to a small airfield. The Hercules had been the only plane present, and Moira's heart sank as she had taken in the high wire fence around the compound, and the hills beyond it.

Her only hope, she had reasoned, was if the agents had been ordered not to shoot her. It seemed logical. Why bring her all the way here—wherever here was—if she wasn't wanted alive and, with any luck, undamaged? All the same, she had been too weak to outrun them. She had raced along a taxiway towards a small shed, intending to put it between her and her pursuers, to gain precious time to tackle the fence. It had been a desperate, hopeless, ploy. She hadn't taken more than a few steps before she had felt them behind her.

It had probably been a machine-gun butt that had clubbed her to the ground, bringing stars to her eyes and darkness to her mind.

She didn't know how long she had been unconscious, how long she had lost to dreams of men without faces and work left undone.

That helicopter was getting closer.

Moira tested the strength of her bonds. They had been tied well. She felt no give at all between her wrists. She tried to move her legs, but they were tied too, to the legs of the chair. The chair, however, was light enough. She could probably walk it across the room, after a fashion. She scanned the shelves, looking for something to make towards; something she could use to cut the ropes. It did occur to her that she wouldn't have been left with all these tools if her captors had been worried about the prospect of her escaping. More than likely, there was an armed guard or two—or all three of the men who had brought her here—outside. She decided not to think about that. She concentrated on the immediate problem.

She had been in situations like this before. Too many times before. Strange as it seemed, she had become used to having enemies, to having her home invaded and her person attacked, to having to fight against somebody or something almost every day of her life. Sometimes, she wondered how she had come to be here; how Moira Kinross, chieftain of an ancient Scottish clan and keen student of genetic science, had become a standard-bearer for a cause not her own, and a target for those whose own causes were different. Perhaps it had started with Charles Xavier, a fellow student at Oxford University; a man with a dream, and the passion to make her dream it too. Or with Joe MacTaggert, the abusive husband who had made her swear that she would never be a victim again. Or with Proteus, her son who had been born a monster, his mind deranged and his body consumed by his mutant X-factor.

There was one thing that the Hellfire Club might have overlooked. Moira MacTaggert had become used to fighting back. And she had the resourcefulness, the experience and the sheer bloody-minded determination to win.

There was a filthy glass jar on one of the lower shelves. If she could knock it off its perch, she would have some shards to work with. She hoisted the chair's back legs off the floor, and tried to hobble forwards. The effort was painful. After only a few steps, she needed to rest. But the sound of the helicopter outside drove her onwards. It was louder now, and there was no doubt in Moira's mind that it was coming here. She was running out of time.

Haste made her clumsy. The chair tripped her up, and she toppled to the floor, unable to put out a limb to save herself. She managed to twist so that she landed on her left arm, not on her face, but the landing still hurt. She lay there for a few seconds, breathing heavily, trying to work out how she was going to find the leverage to get herself upright again. She was just beginning to accept that it was impossible when she realized she had a leg free.

It took her a moment to work out what had happened: the chair had broken in the fall. A strut had snapped off, allowing the ropes to slip down over the end of its left leg. Moira smiled grimly to herself. Her captors had used good, strong rope, but they hadn't been so careful about what they tied her to.

The helicopter was landing, not too far away. She hoped it would mask the noise she made as she thrashed about and kicked at the chair with her free foot, trying to loosen more of its old joints. The right front leg broke off next, allowing Moira to lift herself to her knees and to crawl awkwardly towards the desk. She wedged the back legs of the chair beneath it and pushed up, as hard as her straining muscles could manage, until she heard the satisfying crack of the chair back splintering away from the seat.

In the sudden silence that followed, she realized that the helicopter engine had been stilled. She was acutely aware of the sound of her own exhausted panting. She made herself hold her breath for a second, and listened.

Footsteps approached the shed.

As heavy bolts were drawn back on the other side of the door, Moira leapt to her feet and grabbed blindly for a weapon off the nearest shelf. Her questing fingers found a large, rusted wrench, and its weight in her hand gave her some reassurance. The door opened inwards, and she concealed herself behind it, her heartbeat reverberating in her ears.

She brought the wrench down hard as soon as she had a target to aim for: a man's head, with black hair scraped back into a ponytail and secured with an elaborate red bow. It was a palpable strike, and Moira was dismayed to see that it had no effect.

As she had feared, she was facing one of the X-Men's mutant foes: the Hellfire Club was not a mutant organization per se, but mutants did dominate more than one of its Inner Circles.

And, slowly, she realized what this particular mutant's abilities were. Had he simply been invulnerable, then her hand ought to have been ringing now from the impact of the wrench. Instead, it felt as if the blow had cushioned somehow. She put two and two together, even as her enemy turned to face her. "Sebastian Shaw!" she hissed.

"Good morning, Doctor MacTaggert." His voice was silky-smooth, his eyes gleamed with confidence and his tight-lipped smile almost reached his ears. "I'm so glad you were able to meet me at such short notice. I trust you are as well as can be expected?"

"You smug git!" spat Moira. She put all her remaining strength into a shoulder-charge, even though she knew that physical force would be useless against him. Perhaps she could surprise him, make him step aside long enough for her to get through the door.

Hitting Shaw was like walking into a mattress. Moira wasn't brought up short, she just suddenly wasn't moving any more. Her legs almost buckled as her mind and body struggled to cope with this unexpected contravention of the laws of momentum. In contrast, Shaw didn't seem at all perturbed. The only part of him that moved was his left arm, and this shot out now with lightning speed. He seized Moira's right wrist and twisted it, sending a sharp knife of pain up her arm. She winced.

"Perhaps you are forgetting my unique ability, Doctor MacTaggert." Shaw's expression hadn't altered, but his eyes had hardened and his voice had developed a hard, almost sadistic edge. "I can absorb the kinetic energy of any attack you make against me. Absorb it—and convert it into raw power." He squeezed her wrist tighter, as if to prove his point. He was certainly strong. Moira gritted her teeth, determined not to cry out.

Then Shaw released his grip and his tone became light again, his words genial, as if nothing untoward had happened. "However, I didn't bring you here to demonstrate my strength. I must apologize, by the way, for the long flight. You must have been uncomfortable."

"As if you cared," muttered Moira.

"I would have had an associate of mine, Trevor Fitzroy, collect you by opening a subspace portal directly from here to your island. However, I'm afraid he would have left an energy signature that might have been identified. And a supersonic aircraft would have attracted the wrong kind of attention. I'm sure you understand."

"Oh, I understand. You don't want the X-Men jumping all over whatever sordid little scheme you've got going here."

Shaw tilted his head to one side, as if musing on that thought. "I was also concerned," he said, "that Fitzroy might get a little... shall we say, over-eager." His eyes glistened. "I'd hate him to suck your life force dry before I've finished with you."

Moira spat at him, and was gratified to see that, although the saliva hit him softly, it still hit him. The slightest shadow crossed his face, and he produced a silk handkerchief from inside his jacket and dabbed at his cheek. Then he clasped his hands behind his back, turned and crossed the room in a few strides. This simple act irritated Moira. He was showing his prisoner that he wasn't afraid to present his back to her; that he knew she couldn't harm him. The worst thing was, he was right. Her eyes flicked towards the door, which had closed by itself. He had left her a clear path to freedom.

"In case you are wondering," said Shaw without turning, "there are of course three highly-trained agents between you and my helicopter, and a fourth in the pilot's seat."

"Still paying those costumed goons to do your dirty work?"

"I still hold the title of Black King." He was facing her again, and Moira tried not to think about what an imposing figure he cut. It was something about his firm gaze and the way he stood, so sure of himself—as if nothing could touch him, let alone hurt him. He *was* the Black King: nominally the head of only one Inner Circle, but in reality probably the most powerful and respected of any of the Hellfire Club's Lords Cardinal. He wore a maroon velvet smoking jacket and waistcoat, a gray silk cravat, black breeches and thigh-length black boots. His long sideburns added to the image of a Victorian gentleman, although the façade was as misleading as that of the Hellfire Club itself.

His smile remained as fixed as ever, and Moira longed to wipe it from his self-satisfied face. "Oh?" she sneered. "Last I heard, your own son had deposed you and left you for dead."

"There were some... difficulties at our New York branch," said Shaw tartly, his smile turning into a half-snarl. She felt a thrill of achievement at having cracked his veneer, although it was only a small triumph. He took a deep breath and closed his eyes for a second, as if ridding himself of unwanted memories. When he looked at Moira again, his habitual smirk had returned. "However, I still control Hong Kong's Inner Circle."

"And that's where we are, is it? Hong Kong?"

"My private airfield." Shaw cast a glance at the untidy desk. "I acquired it rather suddenly from the previous owners," he said, by way of an explanation for the mess.

"So, are you going to tell me why you've dragged me halfway across the world?"

"With pleasure, dear lady." Shaw motioned Moira towards the remaining wooden chair. "Perhaps you'd like to take a seat? You appear to have left one intact."

"I'd rather stand," said Moira stiffly.

Shaw nodded. "As you wish." He pulled up the chair and sat down, crossing his legs and resting his hands upon his knee. "Now, as you are no doubt aware, we two have been pursuing a similar goal of late."

"If you mean we've both been trying to cure the Legacy Virus –"

"Precisely."

"Except that I doubt your motives are quite the same as mine."

"Please, Doctor MacTaggert," said Shaw with mock dismay, "I'm sure I don't know what you're trying to imply!"

"Is that what all this is about? You want to get your hands on my research?"

"Not at all. I had my operatives bring your notes because I thought they might be useful to you. As I'm sure you have guessed by now, Doctor MacTaggert, what I desire is your aid."

"You want me to join you?" Moira shook her head firmly. "You've asked before, Shaw."

"And you declined, as I recall. But how many people have died since then?"

"That's not fair!"

"Isn't it? I'm willing to admit that my research team hasn't had much success. Can you say any different? The American media has made much of this latest human death, haven't they? Your partner attended the funeral himself, I believe." Moira shouldn't have been surprised that Shaw knew so much. She was taken aback, however, when he leaned forward in his chair and fixed her with a compelling, earnest stare. "How many more funerals, Moira?"

She fought down a lump in her throat, and didn't answer.

Shaw leaned back again and steepled his fingers, thumbs resting on his chest. "I'm suggesting to you, once again, that we pool our resources. Come with me. Take a look at my research facility. I think you'll be surprised."

Moira's interest was piqued, despite herself. "How so?"

"Let's just say I have recently come into possession of some very interesting technology. I doubt if you can even imagine some of the new avenues that my scientists have begun to explore. In fact, Doctor MacTaggert, I will state here and now that, with the right team on this project, I fully believe that a cure can be found, in weeks rather than months."

"And you want me to be a part of this team?"

"I want you to lead it. You're the only person with the knowledge and the skills for the job. Naturally, you will have the best equipment at your disposal, not to mention the best people in the field. You've worked with Doctor Rory Campbell before, I think?"

"Oh, yes, I've worked with Rory."

"A very bright young man," said Shaw.

"Who just happens to know a thing or two about Muir Island's security systems," said Moira. Her tone was cold. Rory Campbell had been a friend. He had even lived with her on Muir Island for a time, acting as her assistant. After he had defected, she had changed her security codes, of course. She ought to have had the whole system replaced, but she had trusted him, at least that far. Campbell was not a bad man, or so she had thought: when he had left to work for the Hellfire Club, it had been for all the right reasons. He had believed he could make more progress against the Legacy Virus with the organization's resources behind him. Moira was still on speaking terms with him, just about—but she would have been lying if she had claimed not to resent his betrayal.

And now she had allowed him to betray her all over again.

Shaw's smile broadened. "I gave him my assurance that you wouldn't be harmed."

"Even if I refuse your kind offer?" Moira placed a sarcastic emphasis upon the word 'kind.'

Shaw pursed his lips as if giving the matter serious thought. "Harmed, no—although it may prove impossible to set you free with the knowledge you are about to acquire."

"That sounds like a threat, Shaw, however you dress it up."

He smiled again. "But then, why would you turn me down? I'm offering you a great opportunity: the best chance we have ever had to be rid of this virus. You could save millions of lives, your own included."

"And you're doing this solely out of compassion, of course."

"I'm a mutant, as are many of my associates. Is that not reason enough?"

"Where you're concerned, Shaw, no. I take it that, if this team of yours does find a cure, it'll be you who has control over how and when it's used; who gets to live and who doesn't?"

"Is it such a high price to pay?"

"You're damned right it is! When I beat this virus, it will be on my own terms—and you're the last person in the world whose hands I'd let control of a cure fall into."

Shaw laughed. "I can almost hear Xavier talking through you."

"I don't need Charles to tell me the difference between right and wrong!"

"No? You appear to have sacrificed the best part of your life to his cause."

"I don't expect you to understand."

"I understand," said Shaw, "that compromises must be made sometimes. You can't always live a dream."

"You can, if it's a dream worth living for."

"And dying for?"

"Yes!"

"I admire your principles, but I fear they are misguided." Shaw stood up slowly, straightened his jacket and brushed lint from his breeches. "We all share the same dream, in the end. We want to see a world in which *homo superior* are accepted as the natural evolution of *homo sapiens*. Xavier believes this can be brought about by reasoning with the primitives, by educating them. And yet, in the years since he formed his precious X-Men, anti-mutant sentiment has only grown. His methods have failed."

"And I suppose you'd rather fight it out," said Moira, sourly. "Survival of the fittest."

Shaw frowned. "Please, do not confuse me with the likes of Magneto and the so-called Brotherhood of Mutants. They believe they can take power by force, that they can *make* humanity accept them. But they'll start a war that can only end when the last human being is dead. No, Doctor MacTaggert, we live in a capitalist world. The only way to achieve true power, to affect real change, is to work within that system. Through the Hellfire Club, I have helped mutants to climb to society's highest echelons; to build economic and political influence."

"Fine words, Shaw," said Moira, "but I know your methods. Your battle plan might be sneakier than Magneto's, but you're no less ready to sacrifice anyone and everyone for the sake of your own twisted goals."

Shaw's face hardened, almost imperceptibly. "I'm sorry you feel that way. But I still believe that, once you have seen what I have to show you, you might change your mind. I sincerely hope, for your sake, that you do."

He swept past her, opened the door and strode outside. Immediately, a Hellfire Club agent stepped into the shed, gun at the ready. Moira marched after Shaw without waiting to be told. This must have been what he wanted, for the agent fell into step behind her.

"For my sake?" she shouted at Sebastian Shaw's back.

He was heading across the tarmac towards the large, black helicopter that must have brought him here. Its blue-and-red-uniformed pilot saw him coming, and started the engine. The rotors created a blast of air, which struck Moira in the face and blew her hair into disarray.

Shaw spoke softly, but she just made out his words above the din.

"For everybody's sake!" he said.

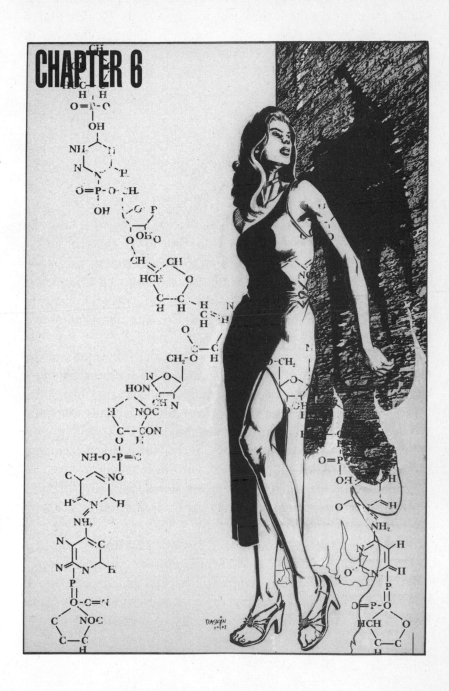

CHAPTER 6

THE X-MEN'S Blackbird had raced the night back to the United States. The village of Salem Center was wrapped in darkness now, but a light still burned at the top of Graymalkin Lane. In the conference room of the Xavier Institute, another meeting was taking place. A counsel of war.

"I think we're all agreed," said Cyclops, "all roads lead to the Hellfire Club. Clyde Scott was approached by its representatives shortly before his abduction, and Moira was delivered to Hellfire Club mercenaries." He cast an eye over his teammates: Phoenix, Wolverine, Storm, Nightcrawler, Iceman, the Beast and Rogue. Seven of the most powerful mutants in the world; eight, including himself. But they still had their work cut out for them.

"About time we shut those suckers down once and for all," muttered Wolverine, leaning back in his chair and resting his heels on the table.

"It's never that easy though, is it, sugar?" said Rogue.

"The Hellfire Club have thrived for centuries," warned Storm.

"Our next step," said Cyclops, "is to find out exactly which branch we're dealing with. Experience suggests that the various Inner Circles usually work independently of each other, and that the most likely candidates for a brazen move like this are New York, Hong Kong and London."

"As far as I know," Nightcrawler spoke up, "London's Inner Circle hasn't re-formed since the Black Air fiasco. I've spoken to Brian Braddock—Captain Britain—and asked him to snoop around a bit, but I think we can count them out for now."

"Which leaves us with Hong Kong and New York."

"Sebastian Shaw is still the Black King of the Hong Kong Inner Circle," said Phoenix, "and, the last we heard, Selene had taken control in New York."

"Didn't they used to be buddies?" asked Iceman.

"Selene was Shaw's Black Queen until recently," said Cyclops, "but I'd say they were uneasy allies at best. It's a good point, though. We can't just assume that Selene has defected. She might be working with Shaw to control both branches."

"Then I suggest we investigate both simultaneously," said Storm.

"I agree. That way, if they are still affiliated, they won't get the chance to send warnings to each other." Cyclops looked around the table, mentally dividing the eight X-Men into two teams of four. When he reached his wife, he hesitated. Then, looking away from her, he said: "Ororo, take the Blackbird and take Logan, Kurt and Rogue to the Hong Kong branch. Hank, Bobby, Jean and I will see what Selene's up to."

He felt Jean's smile in his mind, the telepathic equivalent of a loving squeeze of the hand. She was grateful to him for not sending her to China. They both knew why. No doubt some of the others did too. Phoenix would do her duty as an X-Man, of course—but if she could avoid meeting Sebastian Shaw in the process, she would be all the happier. More than that, there was one particular member of Shaw's Inner Circle whom neither she nor Scott ever wanted to encounter again.

"Hong Kong's twelve hours behind us," said Wolverine. "We can catch a few hour's shut-eye and still leave early enough on Saturday morning to be there by Friday midnight."

"At which time," said Nightcrawler, "there'll be a party in full swing, if I know the Hellfire Club. That should make it easier to infiltrate their headquarters."

"Agreed," said Cyclops, with a nod. "We'll wait until you're in position before we approach the New York branch."

"Good idea," said Iceman, with feeling. "If we have to confront that witch Selene in her lair, then I'll be a lot happier doing it in the full light of day."

To the mutant sorceress Selene, no sound was sweeter than that of human souls in torment. The screams that echoed around her catacombs, night and day, were her music, and she savored their harmonies now. As she walked, minor demons skittered out of her path and took refuge in the shadows. Fires burnt in wall-mounted braziers, and bathed the cracked stone walls in flickering light. The air was thick with the stench of brimstone. To most people, the heat would have been oppressive.

Selene had come from entertaining her more traditional guests upstairs. She still wore her low-cut, figure-hugging black evening dress. But it was the guests down here, in her true domain, who really interested her. Down in the lower levels of the building, nightmare chambers brought people face to face with their personal fears, in illusory form. But further below, in these stygian depths, mind scans and Virtual Reality devices were not needed. Here, Selene had constructed a nightmare that spoke to the shared terrors of all human beings—and it was real.

Externally, the grand old Hellfire Club building on Fifth Avenue, Manhattan, had hardly changed in three centuries. Like the organization that had owned it all that time, it retained its respectable façade. Inside, however, the new Black Queen had made changes.

The Hellfire Club lived up to its name now.

Attracted by the anguished timbre of one particular wail, Selene opened a cell door and peered inside. A man hung from his ankles, chains wrapped around his black tuxedo, over a pit of fire. Sweat beaded his balding pate. His jacket was torn where Selene's demons had attacked it with claws and whips. He looked at Selene with frightened but longing eyes, and tried to raise his head, but groaned with the effort.

Selene pursed her full, red lips into a smile, flicked her long, silken, jet black hair back over her shoulders and strode into the rough-hewn room. "Hush now, Mr. Pemberton," she cooed. "You wouldn't want to attract the further attention of my good friend Blackheart, now would you?" To underscore her point, she gestured with a hand and made the flames leap higher. They licked around Pemberton's forehead and threatened to burn what remained of his hair. He grimaced and breathed in deeply, but didn't make another sound. He was terrified of Selene's ally, the son of Mephisto himself. Almost as terrified as he was of Selene.

She nuzzled his chin with her long fingers, and wiped away a stream of blood, which oozed sluggishly down from beneath his collar. "Help me," he pleaded, in a dry, throaty voice. "I've had... enough..."

"Oh, dear," said Selene, with mock pity. "I think you're forgetting the terms of our agreement, Mr. Pemberton. *We* decide when you have had enough, not you." Her expression hardened, and she snatched her hand away and clicked her fingers twice.

In obedient response, a stooped demon appeared in the doorway. It was clad in the uniform of a Hellfire Club agent, and indeed it had been human once, before Selene had ripped its soul out of its body. It wore no mask. Its face—with its flaking parchment skin and blank, staring eyes—was exposed. At a cursory nod from its mistress, the demon's toothless mouth cracked into a malevolent grin. It scampered over to the fire and produced an iron poker, which it lay across the open pit to warm the metal. Mr. Pemberton whimpered, and tears trickled down from his eyes to evaporate in the heat of the flames.

To Selene's displeasure, her mystical senses chose that moment to alert her of something.

"Excuse me, Mr. Pemberton," she apologized, "but it seems I have more pressing business. My ears are burning, and I expect you know how uncomfortable that can feel." She smiled at her own little joke, and put a hand to her mouth, smearing his blood across her lips. "My servant will take care of you. I can promise you his undivided attention."

As she left the cell, Selene's expression darkened, and furrows appeared in the pale skin of her forehead. She muttered a short mantra in an ancient language, and activated a pre-prepared spell. She reached out her right hand, palm upwards, and her scrying device—what sideshow mystics would refer to as a crystal ball—materialized upon it.

Shadows chased each other across the globe's surface, resolving into the shapes of familiar faces. Cyclops. Phoenix. Iceman. "So," mused Selene, "I wonder what business the X-Men have with me?"

...the last we heard, said the voice of Phoenix, transmitted by the crystal into Selene's mind, *Selene had taken control in New York.*

Selene was Shaw's Black Queen until recently, said Cyclops. Then: *We can't just assume that Selene has defected. She might be working with Shaw to control both branches.* And: *Bobby, Jean and I will see what Selene's up to.*

Iceman was next. His words brought a smile to the eavesdropper's face. *If we have to confront that witch Selene in her lair, then I'll be a lot happier doing it in the full light of day.*

She sent the ball back to her inner sanctum, and lost herself in thought. In the cell behind her, Mr. Pemberton began to scream again. Idly, she licked his blood from her lips, and enjoyed its rich, salty taste.

It wasn't the same, though, she reflected wistfully. Torture was never quite as satisfying when the recipients were willing participants in the process. And indeed, some members of the Hellfire Club paid good fractions of their considerable fortunes for the privilege of enacting their masochistic fantasies. Selene had learned to content herself with the bittersweet mixture of pain and pleasure she could coax from them. She couldn't afford to draw too much attention, so it was rare that she allowed herself the treat of kidnapping a total innocent—usually a vagrant—and bringing him down here.

Sometimes, of course, she could go a little further than her customers wanted. It didn't stop most of them from coming back for more.

But now, the X-Men were paying her a visit. And, at the very least, this meant that the Black Queen could look forward to an entertaining diversion.

At best, perhaps she would be able to indulge herself after all.

The Hellfire Club's Pacific Rim headquarters was situated on the south side of Hong Kong Island. The building maintained a dignified distance from the overcrowded, noisy bars and evening markets of the north, while remaining as close as it needed to be to the bustling financial district and to the millionaire's paradise of Deepwater Bay. Its architects had sited it in the traditional manner, facing towards the sea, its back to the rolling hills. This had once been a peaceful, leafy area—but progress and the city center had encroached upon it, and concrete skyscrapers now grew between the trees.

The building itself was a wide, single-story construction in the classic Chinese style: all overhanging eaves and pillars. A two-story pagoda, housing a rooftop garden, rose from the sloping roof to a pointed spire. A broad flight of steps led up to a narrow plaza in front of the building. They were guarded by a pair of stone dragons on plinths, breathing real fire.

For some time now, Rogue and Nightcrawler had watched from the shadows between this building and the next, as a succession of well-dressed men and women, reeking of affluence, were drawn in by the lights that shone out from the veranda. The population of Hong Kong was 98% Asian—but, although the club had welcomed many Chinese guests tonight, it seemed to Rogue that it also attracted more than its fair share of expatriate white Americans and Britons.

A white limousine pulled up, and a woman poured herself out of the back. She was middle-aged and gray-haired, tall and slender, with a fur coat and a diamond necklace that had probably cost more money than Rogue had ever seen. This was obviously not her first port of call tonight. She could hardly stand. She rapped her knuckles on the car roof as a signal to her driver that he was no longer needed. In doing so, she leaned too heavily against the vehicle, and almost fell as it pulled away. She made circling motions with her arms to keep herself upright, then put a hand to her mouth and looked around with wide-eyed, sniggering embarrassment to see if anyone had seen.

"I think it's time," said Kurt.

They stepped into the light, Rogue leading the way. She had pinned up her hair, applied more makeup than usual and squeezed her muscular but shapely body into an elegant blue, long-sleeved frock. The result was a total transformation. Rogue didn't even *feel* like herself. She hardly dared move, in case her hair fell down or she burst out of her expensive clothing or was tripped by her treacherous high heels. Nevertheless, she managed a clumsy, teetering half-run along the sidewalk towards the drunken woman.

"*Dah*-ling!" she cried out, trying to soften her broad Southern accent. "Darling, it *is* you!" The woman, already halfway up the steps, turned and squinted at her myopically, without recognition. Rogue didn't give her the chance to put her sozzled brain into gear. She put a silk-gloved hand on the woman's shoulder and steered her back down onto the sidewalk, where her teammate was waiting.

It took more than a change of clothing to disguise the blue-skinned, demonic Nightcrawler. However, thanks to an image inducer, he currently wore a handsome face with a pencil-thin moustache, and a tailored suit. Rogue knew that the resemblance to Errol Flynn was deliberate. Between them, the two X-Men certainly looked like any one of the other young, wealthy couples who had passed through the doors of the Hellfire Club in the past hour or two. But there was one thing they still needed: an invitation.

"You've met my good friend Kurt, haven't you?" Rogue contin-ued, guiding the woman along the sidewalk. "Of course you have. So, how are you these days? It's been so long. You really must let me take you for a drink some time. We have so much to catch up on."

So far, the woman had allowed herself to be led. But now she resisted, shrugging off Rogue's hand and coming to a determined, if slightly unsteady, halt. Rogue glanced uneasily over her shoul-der. They hadn't come as far as she would have liked. But the woman, drunk though she was, had clearly begun to realize that she had never met these two strangers in her life. And, with another car already pulling up at the steps, Rogue couldn't afford to let her cause a scene.

She pulled off her glove, reached for the woman's face...

And hesitated.

As soon as Rogue's bare skin touched that of the woman, she would absorb her memories, her personality, her very self. It was her blessing and her curse. In her younger, wilder days, she had used her ability with abandon, exulting in the fact that she could steal the powers of other mutants and super-powered individuals. Now, though, she was more mature, and more aware of the conse-quences of her actions, both for her victims and for herself.

She had gone too far once. She had held onto a woman called Carol Danvers—the Avenger called Ms. Marvel—for too long. And something had gone wrong. Badly wrong.

Rogue owed her powers of flight, great strength and near-invulnerability to Carol. Unlike the other abilities she had absorbed over the years, they showed no signs of fading. But there was a part of Carol in her mind as well; a part that, at first, had railed against the injustice of Rogue's actions and had waged war upon her from within, almost tearing her psyche apart.

Rogue hated to use her innate ability now, but she couldn't turn it off. And it had grown even stronger. The only way she could control it now was by wrapping herself in heavy clothing, forever denying herself intimate contact with others. But she felt she had no choice. She knew what the real Carol Danvers had been through, and she wouldn't wish that kind of suffering upon anyone. And she was also fearful of allowing new voices into her head, of taking the risk that they would stay with her forever, chipping away at her old self until there was nothing left that was truly her at all.

Rogue looked at Kurt, and he must have seen the fear in her eyes because he responded with a reassuring nod. He would be here, if anything too bad happened.

She wished Phoenix could have been here too. Then she wouldn't have to do this.

There was a painful knot of anxiety in her stomach, and she had to will herself to reach out, slowly, with one finger, towards the inebriated woman's cheek until she just...*brushed*...against her skin... *and she was Mrs. Lavinia Smith, widowed but well provided for by her philandering husband Philip, who had been a director of an arms export business, and she had a taste for hard-centered chocolates but she couldn't stand dogs, nasty yipping little things, and she was sometimes lonely in that big old house in the hills and once, as a teenager in a West Hollywood school, she had lured Michael Craig from the football team into the stockroom and* she reeled with the onslaught of thoughts and memories pouring into her with the impact of a high-pressure hose, and she wanted to scream but she clenched her fists and redirected the sound into a low groan from her stomach, and the world shot out of focus and she hoped she had managed to separate herself from the woman *Lavinia, who didn't like the smell of after-shave and who always tried to put aside one hour in the afternoon to read* because she just couldn't tell.

Slowly, painfully, Rogue climbed back up to the surface of her own mind, relieved to find that she appeared to be intact and in control. Lavinia had collapsed and Kurt had caught her—but the woman still clung to consciousness, murmuring under her breath. Considering the state she had already been in, things had turned out remarkably well. Rogue put her glove back on, and answered Kurt's concerned look with a nod.

It was the work of only seconds, then, to search Lavinia's purse for her Hellfire Club membership card, which was exactly where she remembered leaving it. Her name was embossed into the golden square of plastic, below an upturned trident with a short handle. Simultaneously, Kurt scanned the woman's form into a spare image inducer.

By the time the next taxicab arrived, they were ready to bundle Lavinia Smith into the back, attracting only the briefest of gazes from the young Chinese couple who had arrived in the vehicle, and a world-weary sigh from the driver. "Our friend has had a little too much to drink, I'm afraid," said Rogue apologetically, before retrieving the woman's address from her borrowed memories, handing over some money and sending the cab on its way. The driver would probably have to help his customer through her front door, but she would be all right.

Then the two X-Men slipped surreptitiously back into the shadows. When they reemerged, a few minutes later, one of them looked very different.

The Fifth Avenue brownstone headquarters of the Hellfire Club's New York chapter stood only a few blocks from the home of the Avengers, opposite Central Park. As Scott Summers and Jean Grey climbed the steps that led to the entrance, people wandered past on the sidewalk behind them. It felt odd to be conducting X-Men business out of costume and in such a public place. But Scott was determined not to let the innocuous surroundings lull him into a false sense of security. Selene was a deadly, unpredictable foe. He was well aware that they could find themselves fighting for their lives at any moment.

The main doors were framed by a large, stone archway, into each side of which was set the club's familiar upturned trident symbol. They were locked, and the tall windows in the front wall were blank and dark. This building only came alive at night.

Jean pressed the bell, and Scott listened to its deep, sonorous tones echoing deep inside the mansion house. The couple exchanged a nervous glance as they awaited a response.

At last, footsteps shuffled down the front hallway, and the door was pulled open. Scott's eyes widened at the sight of a grotesque demon in the familiar costume of the Hellfire Club's mercenary agents. He tensed, and raised a hand to his ruby quartz glasses. They didn't give him the fine control of his visor, but he could lift them and unleash his optic beam if he had to. But the demon simply leered at its two visitors, and beckoned them inside with an expansive sweep of its arm.

Be careful, Jean telesent, not only to her husband but to Iceman and the Beast, who were waiting within telepathic range at the back of the building. *Selene might have been expecting us.* The sorceress was making a point by flaunting her club's true nature this way.

They followed the demon along a deep-carpeted passageway, past oak-paneled walls decorated with valuable old paintings, past the familiar ballroom with its grand staircase, and down a narrower, twisting flight of stairs to the first basement level. Selene was waiting beside an open door, leaning against the wall and studying her fingernails with a casualness that was belied by the steel-trap alertness in her deep, green eyes. She was provocatively dressed in a black leather teddy, which left her arms, the tops of her legs and a substantial section of her cleavage exposed. A cape, also black, was draped around her shoulders, and she wore knee-length black boots and long, finger-less gloves.

"Well, well, Mr. and Mrs. Summers," she greeted the couple, rolling the words on her tongue as if enjoying their taste. "And to what do I owe the pleasure of this visit? Perhaps you'd like to see how my Hellfire Club is faring under new management?" She pushed herself up from the wall and stalked through the door, beckoning Scott and Jean to follow her with a raised arm and a coiled finger, but not looking to see if they did.

Selene's office was furnished like a throne room, with gold trim and velvet drapes—and, yes, a large, central throne, upon which she now perched. But there was a dark quality to the décor, with light fittings and ornaments twisted into demonic shapes, framed paintings depicting vistas of various underworlds, and a raised stone dais upon which sat a crystal ball. Candles burnt in the corners of the room, but somehow didn't light them, and a thin veil of smoke hung over the air.

"I'm sure you are both aware," Selene told her guests, "that you don't qualify to become full members of the Hellfire Club in your own rights. Your, ah, financial situations do not permit it. Still—" She waved a hand, magnanimously. "——I am prepared to extend certain...facilities to you. You are, after all, close associates of at least two of our most valued members." She smiled, and showed her teeth. "And old friends of mine, of course."

"We aren't here to make small talk, Selene," said Scott, gruffly.

"No?" Selene gave him a look of disappointment, but shrugged it off. "I do apologize. If this is a formal visit, then you should have dressed the part." She made a gesture with both hands—and, before her visitors could react, their clothes came alive, rippling and transforming, changing shape and color, until Scott Summers and Jean Grey found themselves standing in the costumes of Cyclops and Phoenix.

"Nice party trick," said Phoenix, with false pleasantness. Cyclops was already worrying about how they would get out of here without causing mayhem. He would probably have to ask his wife to cloud the minds of any onlookers, to make them doubt what they saw.

"And you really should have invited your colleagues to join us," said Selene. She gestured again, and Iceman and the Beast materialized, looking thoroughly confused. "It is sheer bad manners to enter somebody's home uninvited—and by a rear window, at that."

"OK, Selene," said Cyclops, attempting to regain control of the situation, "you win that one. Now, let's get down to business."

"You mean your search for your lost friend." The four X-Men glanced at each other, and Selene took visible delight in having disconcerted them again.

"Then you *do* know where Moira is," said Cyclops, bluntly.

"The question is," she mused, "what kind of a mood am I in today? I might not feel predisposed towards assisting those who have tried to invade my privacy; who have, indeed, upset my plans in the past. Or perhaps I am feeling more...playful."

"You might be in the mood for playing games, Selene," said Cyclops, "but let me warn you now, I'm not!"

"Oh, Cyclops!" Selene was more amused than intimidated. She stood up and swept towards him, her cape trailing across the floor. "Always so earnest, so grim. Give me a few hours with you, and I could really loosen you up. And Iceman..." She caressed Bobby's chin with her hand. He recoiled from her touch. "Poor, scared little Iceman. You don't want to be here at all, do you? Unlike Phoenix here, who's hoping against hope that I'm the person you're looking for—because, if I'm not, she'll have to face her past all over again." Selene stopped in front of the Beast, who returned her gaze evenly. "Ah, but you, my little blue friend, your eyes tell the most interesting story of all. Your wishes conflict with Ms. Grey's, do they not? You, most of all, are looking for answers, but you'd prefer not to find them here. Your hopes are high, but your fears are still greater."

"Selene," growled Cyclops.

She turned her back on them, with a dismissive gesture. "I am bored with you all. But I suppose the easiest way to be rid of you is to reveal what I know about the MacTaggert woman's whereabouts." She retook her throne and leaned forwards, with a conspiratorial gleam in her eyes.

"Very well, then. I will tell you."

Kurt Wagner loitered by the French windows, flashing his Errol Flynn grin at anyone who looked his way, but avoiding too much eye contact, determined not to get drawn into conversation. The Hellfire Club was busy tonight, its ballroom packed with the cream of Hong Kong society. Well-dressed couples swayed on the dance floor to the strains of a classical orchestra, while fat men in business suits sat in plush, leather armchairs, smoked cigars and swapped bawdy jokes.

Kurt was relieved when Rogue finally reappeared from the direction of the restrooms. She had turned off her image inducer, and she looked slightly nervous to be braving the crowd with her own face. She needn't have worried. She blended in perfectly in her elegant clothes, and she was certainly drawing less attention than she had before. The inducer had been useful for getting the two X-Men past the doormen as Mrs. Lavinia Smith and guest, but the middle-aged widow had proved a little too popular with the club's clientele. Within minutes, Rogue had been intercepted by three different 'friends'. She had had to draw upon Lavinia's fading memories to put on a convincing act, until she could politely excuse herself.

Kurt took two glasses of champagne from a passing waiter, and handed one to his teammate. They drank and smiled, and gazed into each other's eyes, like lovers who didn't wish to be disturbed in their quiet corner. But, rather than whispering sweet nothings into Kurt's ear, Rogue was telling him about the security arrangements she had observed outside the ballroom. Presently, they linked arms, and she guided him casually across the room. There were three sets of interior doors, opposite the front windows, leading deeper into the building. Only one, however—on the far left—stood open.

Kurt stepped out into the corridor. Between him and the restrooms, a man and a woman were leaning against each other and giggling. He let their bodies cover him as he slipped behind a potted plant on an antique table and crouched down, pretending that his shoelaces needed tying. Peering between the leaves of the plant, he could see what Rogue had already described: two more corridors led off this one, directly away from the ballroom. In her Lavinia Smith persona, Rogue had affected drunkenness and stumbled towards the nearest, only to be turned around and sent back the way she had come by two muscular men in tuxedos who lurked just around the corner.

Kurt waited until the giggling couple had returned to the ballroom. Then, when he was alone, he turned off his inducer and crawled straight up the wall. And, clinging to the shadows where the wall met the ceiling, he advanced towards the first junction.

Nightcrawler's body tended to get lost in shadows. It wasn't just that his dark coloration made him blend in. It was one of the more bizarre effects of his mutant gene that, when there were no lights upon him, he became almost a part of the darkness himself, even down to the red and white highlights of his costume. Thus, as he rounded the corner and set eyes upon the two bruisers about whom Rogue had warned him, they didn't see him. They were deep in conversation below him, talking about a recent poker game, their postures relaxed, not expecting trouble. It was simple enough for Nightcrawler to slip past them.

He turned another corner, and was pleased to find himself in an empty corridor from which several doors led. One of these doors opened, and two Hellfire Club agents emerged, uniformed and armed. Nightcrawler caught his breath, but the mercenaries hadn't seen him. They marched away, in step with each other, and disappeared down a flight of stairs. He smiled grimly to himself. He was in the heart of the Hellfire Club building now. The real face of the organization was exposed to him; the one that the public weren't ever meant to see.

He checked the corridor for security cameras, but didn't see any. He relaxed his adhesive grip on the ceiling, and somersaulted to a soft landing.

Now, he wondered, which of these doors led to Sebastian Shaw's office?

He spent the next half-hour searching, peering through keyholes and listening at doors, staying in the shadows when he could, and scampering back up to the ceiling if he heard anything that sounded like an approaching footstep. He ventured inside a couple of likely-looking offices, but didn't find what he was looking for.

At last, through a keyhole, he spied a room that was conspicuously more opulent than the others, with expensive wallpaper and exquisite furnishings. *Fit for a Black King*, he thought. *And Shaw's never been one to be modest about his position, nor his wealth. If this isn't where he hangs his hat, then I'll program the image inducer to create a hat of my own—and eat it.*

His restricted view of the room hadn't revealed any occupants, but he decided to be careful. He climbed the wall again and, reaching down, knocked three times on the door. He waited long enough to be sure that nobody was going to answer, before dropping back to the floor and trying the handle. The door was locked.

After taking one final glance up and down the corridor, Nightcrawler concentrated, visualized the inside of the office, and disappeared in a cloud of brimstone.

The hairs on the back of Wolverine's neck stood up, an instant before the comm-set on his belt began to beep. "Sounds like Rogue and the elf are in trouble," he grunted.

The X-Men had found the office of a Hong Kong investments firm, deserted for the night, midway up a skyscraper overlooking the Hellfire Club building. Wolverine had spent the last two hours here, with Storm. They had made good use of the company's coffee-making facilities and had taken it in turns to keep watch at the window. Having seen nothing out of the ordinary so far, they had begun to hope that their teammates would return soon, their mission accomplished. This signal meant that, instead, they were in danger.

"Time to send in the cavalry!" said Wolverine. Storm had already thrown open a window and summoned a wind, to keep her aloft as she carried her Canadian teammate the short distance to their enemies. But suddenly, Wolverine detected a faint whiff of ozone in the air, and, with a cry of, "'Ro! Get down!" he flung himself to the floor behind a desk.

Wolverine's enhanced senses made it all but impossible to sneak up on him. But one of Sebastian Shaw's subordinates in his Inner Circle was a teleporter, like Nightcrawler. Except that, in his case, he used the stolen life energy of others to open temporary portals between places, times and dimensions. Wolverine knew this, and he had been prepared—at least, as prepared as he could be—to face an attack from nowhere.

Sure enough, the air shimmered and the room itself seemed to turn inside out as a hole was ripped through the fabric of reality. An upright circle of roiling energies opened to hang, impossibly, suspended in midair, and a dozen or so costumed mercenaries emerged, guns at the ready.

Standing in their center was a green-haired young mutant, almost swamped by his cumbersome battle armor. Wolverine knew his name. It was Trevor Fitzroy—but these days he was also known as the White Rook.

This was obviously part of a two-pronged attack. Whatever danger Nightcrawler and Rogue had found themselves in, they couldn't expect any help from their backup team now.

They were on their own.

CHAPTER 7

FIVE MINUTES earlier:

Sebastian Shaw had left his desktop computer on: its monitor displayed a screensaver on which an eternal flame licked at an upturned trident. If nothing else, it provided a useful light source, as did the glow from the streetlights outside, which filtered into the office through bamboo blinds. It may not have been much—but Nightcrawler had excellent night-vision, and he was able to search the room without turning on any telltale lights. He found nothing of note, however, until he turned his attention to the computer itself.

He took a quick look around its directories and noticed that there was something in one of the CD drives. A backup? Could he be that lucky? He clicked on the CD icon.

And, at that moment, he heard a sound outside the door. A key in the lock.

He leapt onto Shaw's desk and bounced up towards the motionless ceiling fan, via a backward flip that landed him squarely on the underside of its four rotors. He only just made it before the door opened, and two uniformed mercenaries burst into the office. They were followed by an albino woman, with angular features and long hair that was as white as her skin. She was clad in red leather, which matched the severe shade of her lipstick and nail polish, and left much of her skin exposed. Nightcrawler recognized her face, if not the costume. Her name was Scribe, and she had worked for the Hellfire Club's English branch before its downfall. He remembered hearing that she had been bailed out of prison—and that she, along with another of the club's associates, had dropped out of sight. But she had never been a member of London's Inner Circle, merely a paid lackey, and he hadn't expected to find her here.

She was looking right at him.

With a narrow-eyed smirk, she reached for two switches, which sat side by side on the wall. She flicked them both. A harsh light robbed Nightcrawler of his concealing shadows, and he leapt from the fan, startled, as it began to turn. He could have stayed out of Scribe's reach on the ceiling, but the agents were already bringing up their machine-guns to cover him and, now that he couldn't hide any more, he thought it best to take the fight to them.

Anyway, if this was the best the Hellfire Club had to throw at him, he shouldn't have to exert himself too much.

"Didn't anyone ever tell you it's polite to knock?" he quipped, as he planted a three-toed foot squarely in each of the mercenaries' blank-masked faces, throwing off their aims and staggering them. Before they could recover, he had 'ported across the room, putting Scribe between him and their weapons, and giving him a free attack at her back. It wasn't very chivalrous, he chided himself, but then the odds were three to one. He reached for Scribe's throat, but was dumbfounded when she evaded his grasp almost without seeming to move. He had never faced her in combat before, and he hadn't realized how fast she was. Indeed, she had already turned to face him, and she lashed out with savage precision. He threw himself backwards, but her fingernails still came within a hair's breadth of his face. While he was still reeling, she took an impossible standing leap backwards over the heads of the agents, giving them a clear target again. They strafed the front wall of the office with machine-gun fire, but their bullets passed through a cloud of brimstone.

Nightcrawler appeared in between them, took hold of their heads and knocked them together. They fell, but Scribe had already taken her opportunity to close in, and he felt a white-hot slash of pain as she raked her nails across his back. Instinctively, he teleported again, denying her the chance to press her advantage. But, almost as soon as he had appeared on the ceiling, Scribe reacted to his new position, swept up a heavy chair and hurled it at him. It hit the X-Man full on, dislodging him. He tumbled towards the floor, where Scribe was already waiting for him. "Come to Scribe, little goblin!" she cackled gleefully.

He teleported in mid-fall, materialized at her right hand side and immediately 'ported again to appear at her left. He had time to land just a single punch as she turned first one way and then the other, then he made three more 'ports in quick succession, and struck a second blow.

He kept up the hit-and-run tactics, trying to keep one step ahead of his opponent, but her speed was inhuman. She struck out at random, almost seeming to be able to attack in three directions at once. Her reflexes outperformed his; at last, her questing hands found the front of his red tunic and she drove him backwards into Shaw's desk, the impact winding him.

Nightcrawler gasped for breath as Scribe pinned him into place. He brought up his feet to kick against her—and his senses reeled as he thought he saw an insubstantial face, like that of a ghost, hovering in the air between them. He blinked, and suddenly remembered Scribe's erstwhile colleague: the second bail-jumping servant of the Hellfire Club in London.

That was when he realized how he had been tricked.

"Mountjoy!" he wheezed.

The spectral face was clearer now. Nightcrawler recognized its blank, staring eyes, and the lank brown hair that hung untidily down to its shoulders and formed a tuft on its pointed chin. The body-jumper must have been hitching a ride, inactive, inside Scribe, as he had done before, waiting for a chance to strike. His image was already becoming less distinct again as, instead of reforming his own physical body, he poured his essence into a second host. Nightcrawler could feel him, insinuating himself upon his every cell, taking control of his muscles. It was too late to teleport away. He could barely move his own arm, but he managed to reach inside his tunic for his comm-set, and to clumsily activate the emergency signal.

"He's summoned his teammates," Nightcrawler told Scribe, but the words didn't come from his mind even though he felt them emerging from his own throat, being modified by his own tongue and lips. "I couldn't take control quickly enough to stop him."

"Do you have full control now?" asked Scribe.

"I do."

She relaxed her grip, and Nightcrawler stood and flexed his arms and legs, testing out his muscles as if they were new to him. They *were* new, of course, to the intelligence that controlled him. Kurt Wagner didn't feel any different—he was still there, still conscious; he couldn't even feel Mountjoy's presence any more, not as such—but his body was acting independently of his commands. No matter how hard he concentrated on even such a simple act as lifting a finger, he couldn't make it happen. He could have screamed with frustration, except that he no longer had access to a mouth and lungs to scream with.

"Then we'd better make some more noise, hadn't we?" said Scribe, with a twisted grin on her face and a dark fire in her eyes. "I'd hate for the other X-Men to be unable to find us."

She seemed supremely confident, but Nightcrawler was sure that Rogue, Wolverine and Storm together could beat her, even if Mountjoy forced him to fight at Scribe's side.

He only hoped the Hellfire Club hadn't prepared any more unpleasant surprises.

Fitzroy was using the Hellfire Club's mercenaries as cannon fodder. They formed a living barrier, keeping Wolverine from reaching their White Rook, without any sign that they were worried about the likely cost to themselves. He ploughed into them hard. His adamantium claws popped through his skin with a *snikt,* and he sliced through the barrels of three machine-guns. The agents themselves he attacked with fists and feet. He didn't want to kill them, not if he didn't have to. Still, the first one who came too close—thinking he could grapple the X-Man to the ground—earned a shallow slash across his cheek that cut through his mask and drew blood. He would probably bear the scar for life.

Wolverine could have dealt with goons like this in his sleep. The frustrating thing was, it would take time, during which Trevor Fitzroy could be up to anything. Storm, meanwhile, had taken to the air, although the office had a low ceiling, which prevented her from climbing too high. More than Wolverine, she believed in using reasonable force; she had excellent control over her elemental powers and, where necessary, would soften her blows to avoid killing or maiming a foe. But she had faced Fitzroy before, and she knew the strength of his bio-armor. She brought down a lightning bolt, which smashed its way through the window, crackled over the heads of Wolverine and the mercenaries, and struck the villain squarely in the chest.

Fitzroy's armor, like the man himself, was a product of the future. His arms and legs were plated with a tough, golden metal, but his head and torso were protected by something more elaborate: a clear, crystalline substance, which looked like diamond and was probably as endurable. Something black and indistinct coalesced in its depths, around its wearer's chest and stomach: the unidentified energy that powered the armor. It flared white, and blue sparks coruscated around the outside of the crystal, as the armor absorbed Storm's blast and, Wolverine had no doubt, converted it into a useable form. He was gratified to see, however, that Fitzroy winced beneath his transparent helmet. Something had gotten through.

Two mercenaries reached up and seized Storm's ankles, dragging her down. She whipped up a wind to unbalance them, and to steady herself so she could land on her feet and face them squarely. But Fitzroy was free now, and—as if at a prearranged signal—six agents piled on top of Wolverine at once, and effectively blocked their leader from his view.

He shrugged them off within seconds, but by then Fitzroy was upon him. A golden gauntlet clamped onto his shoulder, and he found himself staring into the eyes of a lunatic. He could already feel himself weakening. Even through the armor, Fitzroy was draining his life force. He felt as if he had been fighting for hours, and his eyelids were beginning to droop. He had to break Fitzroy's hold now, while he still had some strength left.

He hacked at the armor with his claws, but they slid off without leaving a scratch. He aimed his next blow at Fitzroy's head—and, although this was repelled too, the young mutant recoiled instinctively. Wolverine shifted his weight and twisted, wrapped his hands around the giant metal fingers that held him and pried them apart, at the same time bringing up a foot and bracing it against Fitzroy's broad, crystalline chest-plate. He succeeded in levering himself out of his foe's deadly grip. He fell ungracefully, and his shoulder hurt like hell, but the drain had stopped. He was dizzy, and he wanted nothing more than to sleep, but Fitzroy was coming for him again, and the mercenaries were blocking his escape route.

Wolverine barged through them, as fast as he could, not caring where his claws landed in the process. He saw a desk and leapt onto it, scattering papers and, in one fluid motion, scooping up a chair and bringing it down onto an agent's head, rendering him unconscious. A hail of bullets came his way, but he leapt over them, and Storm quickly dispensed with his attacker, blowing him backwards into a wall.

The agents were all down now. Only Fitzroy remained. He stood with his back to the crackling disc of energy through which he had arrived, and his expression had lost none of its confidence. "I can deal with this jerk," said Wolverine, adjusting his stance on the desk and squaring up to his opponent. "Go answer that distress call; see what's up with the others."

Storm hesitated. "Are you sure?"

"Positive!"

"Yeah, right," scoffed Fitzroy. "I only have to lay one more finger on you, and you'll shrivel like a prune in the sun!"

"You're forgetting a little something, bub: my mutant healing factor. I'm all done and rested, and ready to kick your butt!" It wasn't quite true. Wolverine was beginning to feel better, but he was determined not to let Fitzroy know how weak he still was.

Storm glanced at both men, then made her decision and flew out through the pane of the window that her lightning bolt had shattered.

"Ready to dance this dance again then, are we, old bean?" Fitzroy taunted, in his cultured English accent. He circled Wolverine slowly, looking for an opportunity to pounce.

Wolverine showed him his claws, warning him off. He needed more time. "Think you can go the distance, Fitzroy? You ain't nothing but an upstart kid, cowering behind your toys."

"Do your worst. This bio-armor's constructed from omnium mesh. It's a hundred years ahead of your time; same as I am, old man!"

"If you were such a big shot in your own time," snarled Wolverine, "you wouldn't've come running to this one. You think your gizmos make you something special in the twenty-first century, kid? Think again! You're nothing but a snot-nosed punk, wherever you end up."

"I can still give you a lesson in manners, you psychotic midget!"

Fitzroy had fallen for the distraction, talking when he should have attacked. Wolverine was fully recovered now. Not only that, but his enemy's expression was priceless. He had the quick temper of immaturity, and he had let himself become riled. A cruel grin spread across Wolverine's face, and he added: "You ain't even learned how to grow facial hair yet. Time for your first razor, bub; get that green fluff off your chin!"

It might have been a childish insult, but it worked. With a yell of fury, Fitzroy powered his armor across the room, his hands outstretched to wrap around his tormentor's throat. Wolverine was ready for him.

Fitzroy probably expected his target to try to avoid him. Instead, Wolverine counter-attacked. The two deadly foes collided in midair, and hit the ground fighting.

Rogue's urgent, less than ladylike departure from the ballroom drew a few bemused looks and raised eyebrows from the other patrons. They were nothing, however, compared to the expressions of the two bouncers in the corridor outside, as the Southern X-Man literally flew at them. She downed them with simultaneous punches to the jaws, before they could raise the alarm. She touched down and paused for a second, listening. A loud crash resounded from a nearby side passage. Rogue kicked off her high heels, hitched up her impractical skirt and ran towards the source of the disturbance.

A second crash pinpointed the exact room. She shoulder-charged the door without hesitation, taking it not only off its latch but off its hinges too. It thudded to the ground, and Rogue felt foolish, in the sudden silence that followed, standing in the doorway in her fancy clothing, with her hair tumbling over her face.

The albino woman in the red outfit seemed amused. "An associate of yours, I take it?"

Nightcrawler grinned awkwardly. "Ah, yes. Scribe, allow me to introduce Rogue."

Rogue took a step into the room, confused and wary. "What's going on, Kurt?"

"I must apologize. I called for assistance a little prematurely. As you can see, everything is under control now." Nightcrawler indicated the two Hellfire Club agents who were sprawled, unconscious, on the floor. There had obviously been a fight here: chairs had been overturned, and books pulled from the shelves.

"And who's the lady? Call me a cynic, but I can't help noticing that clasp at her neck: you know, the one with the trident symbol that looks mighty familiar."

Scribe pursed her scarlet-painted lips into a smile, which was presumably meant to be friendly. However, her keen eyes continued to stare at the new arrival, and Rogue had the uncomfortable feeling of being sized up. "I don't blame you for being suspicious," said Scribe. "And indeed you are correct, I am a member of the Hellfire Club."

Rogue clicked her fingers, as well as she could through her gloves. "I remember the name now. Scribe. You were with the English branch. Their paper-pusher, weren't you?"

"I am the Red Rook of London's Inner Circle," said Scribe, with a hint of irritation.

Rogue ventured further into the room, making her way towards Nightcrawler but taking the long route. She kept her eyes firmly on Scribe as she circled her, alert for any hint of deception. She didn't know what it was exactly, but there was something about this woman that made Rogue distrust her. "I thought the English club went bust," she said. "Must be an awful bore for y'all, a Red Rook without a chessboard to play on. So, what's the skinny? You taking sides with the Black King now?"

"As a temporary measure, until I take my rightful place among the new red royalty."

Nightcrawler shot her a glance. "Although you could say that Scribe is playing for both sides already. She and I have come to an understanding."

"Uh-huh. That sounds like the Hellfire Club: so used to acting like snakes that they can't even trust each other. Not like the X-Men, eh, 'Nightcrawler'?"

It had taken her a while to work it out, but in the end she was just fast enough. Nightcrawler—if that's who he truly was—leapt at her, but Rogue took him by surprise. She plucked him out of the air and hurled him at Scribe. With dazzling speed, Scribe ducked beneath the human projectile and sprang towards Rogue, her fingers outstretched. Rogue put up an arm to protect her face. Scribe cut through her sleeve, but seemed to realize that she ought not to touch the exposed skin beneath. Rogue, in turn, tried to land punch after punch, but Scribe ducked and feinted and avoided each one, as if performing a speeded-up dance.

"Your instincts are good, I'll give you that," said Scribe. "What gave us away?"

"Whoever your friend is," Rogue grunted, "he does a lousy German accent."

Scribe was too fast for Rogue, and Rogue too tough for Scribe. They could have kept up this pointless battle all day, neither hurting the other. But Rogue realized that Scribe was just trying to keep her occupied, to distract her from the real danger. She forced herself to ignore the Red Rook, to look for whoever or whatever was in Nightcrawler's form. She had thrown him into a wall, stunning him, but he was already getting to his feet again.

She barreled towards him, not caring if Scribe was in her way or not, and caught him in the midriff. He hit the wall again, the breath knocked out of him. Rogue drew back a fist to send him down for the count, but hesitated at the thought of striking a friend. 'Nightcrawler' could have been a simulacrum, of course, or a shape-changer, but she was beginning to recall what little she had read about Scribe in the X-Men's files, and she knew she had previously worked with a man who could possess the bodies of others.

"You've realized the truth, haven't you?" her enemy taunted her, his English accent sounding strange in Kurt Wagner's voice. "Mountjoy's the name, and I'm in the driving seat of this body at the moment. You can't hurt me without hurting your teammate."

Rogue gritted her teeth. "If you're still in there, Kurt, I'm sorry about this. Truly, I am."

But then, before she could hit him, Scribe jumped onto her back and snatched the glove from her upraised fist.

It took Rogue a second to work out what to do next. She shifted her aim, intending to hit Nightcrawler's body in the stomach, where his costume would protect him—protect them both—from the danger that her skin posed. By that time, it was too late.

He teleported away, leaving Rogue facing a blank wall and

engulfed in a cloud of sulphurous smoke. Disoriented, she turned around...and recoiled, shocked to find Nightcrawler's face an inch from hers. He grinned at her, wrapped his hands around her head, pulled her closer and locked his lips to hers.

Rogue's eyes widened in horror. She tried to push him away, to break the deadly kiss, but she could already feel the change, weakening them both, and Kurt Wagner—the real Kurt Wagner—was inside her mind, screaming: *Don't worry about me, meine Freundin, just get him away from you!* He was trying not to fight her, to be as supportive as he could, but it didn't make the situation any easier to cope with. In that frenetic, dazed, upside-down moment, Rogue still couldn't tell which thoughts were his and which hers.

She screamed, and Nightcrawler was screaming too. As her vision blurred, she put everything she had into one powerful punch, hoping Kurt could forgive her, knowing they had already held onto each other for far too long. She was vaguely aware of the spectral form of a bearded man in a brown suit, fleeing from Nightcrawler's body as it crumpled to the floor. She prayed she hadn't harmed her friend too badly. She was on the floor herself, although she didn't remember falling. Her head was a mass of pain and, as she tried to focus on the carpet beneath her hands and knees, she saw that her skin had turned indigo blue.

"Very neat," said a man's voice: Mountjoy's, it had to be. "The X-Men defeat each other. So, what do we do with them now?"

"You heard Fitzroy's orders," said Scribe. "We kill them!"

And at that point, despite her best efforts, Rogue blacked out, her last coherent thought being to wonder why nobody else had answered Nightcrawler's emergency signal.

There weren't many lights on at the back of the Hellfire Club building, so Storm picked an illuminated window at random and struck it with a lightning bolt, blowing out the glass. A fierce gust of wind whipped the blinds up and inwards, out of her way, as she spread out her cloak behind her and glided smoothly through her makeshift entrance.

She had picked the wrong room. A middle-aged man in the seventeenth-century costume of the club's elite leapt out of his chair and cowered behind his desk, knocking over a bottle of malt whiskey in the process. Without so much as an apology for the intrusion, Storm hurried past him, pulled open the door and emerged into the corridor beyond.

A short way to her left, a rectangle of electric light spilled onto the carpet, and she could hear voices. She ran in that direction, and arrived in the doorway of a richly furnished office to find Nightcrawler and Rogue lying in the debris of a recent battle.

She took in the situation at a glance. Nightcrawler was unconscious, lying next to the wall at an awkward angle, blood trickling from a cut to his temple. Rogue's eyes were closed too, and she moaned fitfully to herself. Her skin was dark blue, and she sported a tail. Storm always made a point of keeping herself up to date with the X-Men's many foes, so she immediately recognized the man and the woman who had defeated her teammates. Scribe had a machine-gun: standard club issue, probably taken from one of the two agents who were also present and down. She was standing over Nightcrawler, pressing the muzzle of the weapon to his head. Mountjoy was watching, evidently enjoying the prospect of an execution.

"Get away from him, Scribe!" bellowed Storm. Even before she spoke, she had summoned a wind, which howled through the confines of the office and snatched the lightweight gun out of Scribe's hands. But Scribe reacted so quickly that she was upon Storm before she had even completed the command. She wrestled with her foe, obviously realizing that the wind-rider's powers were little use to her at such close range. Storm, however, had also realized this long ago, and had trained extensively in hand-to-hand combat. She broke Scribe's hold and seized her wrist, twisting it around behind her back and forcing the scarlet-clad villain down onto her knees. At the same time, she blew Mountjoy away—knowing that, if he touched her, the fight was over—and created a localized rain shower over Nightcrawler's head, hoping he wasn't so injured that a splash of cold water wouldn't revive him.

Scribe twisted out of Storm's grip, and coiled a foot around her leg, almost tripping her. While the X-Man was still off-balance, her foe punched her in the face, and dodged out of the way of her counterattack. "You bitch," she snarled, "you won't lay a hand on me again!" She slashed at Storm's cheek with her fingernails, leaving four shallow cuts.

Storm didn't respond to the threat. She gritted her teeth and concentrated on the air around her, sensing its currents and merging a part of her mind with them, coaxing them, guiding them and ultimately controlling them. Scribe broke off her attack, her white hair whipping around her face, as a veritable tornado sprang up inside Sebastian Shaw's office, with her at its epicenter. Papers, books, and—as the winds picked up—even furniture were scattered. Buffeted from all sides, Scribe did her best to remain standing, and even to press her attack. But, as good as her reflexes were, she couldn't possibly react to every sudden change in the wind's direction—unlike her opponent, who knew about each one in advance.

As Scribe lost her footing, Storm marched towards her. The Red Rook saw her coming and tried to back away, but she was blown instead into the X-Man's arms. Storm punched her—once, twice, three times—until her knees buckled and she fell. Then, the windrider allowed her miniature tornado to die down, and looked for Mountjoy.

She didn't see him. But Rogue—still exhibiting some of Nightcrawler's external characteristics—was on her feet now, facing her, and it only took a second for Ororo to realize that something was wrong. Something about her posture that was unfamiliar.

"Bright lady," she breathed in horror, "please, no!"

'Rogue' grinned, and slowly, deliberately, removed her remaining glove. "You know," said Mountjoy, in the voice of Storm's friend and teammate, "this body is just bursting with power. I've never felt anything quite like it. What a pity, then, that the mind of its real owner can't cope. While Rogue curls herself into a metaphorical ball and shuts herself off from the world, I can make full use of her abilities. I don't have to hold myself back for fear of what it might do to your poor friend's fragile psyche. I only have to touch you, Storm."

"I won't let you," said Storm, defiantly.

"Ah, but won't you indeed? This body is strong. Can you stop me without destroying it?"

"Rogue would want me to try!" Storm was already preparing to summon a lightning bolt, knowing that nothing less would penetrate Rogue's hide, fearing that what Mountjoy said could well be true.

"Might not be necessary, sugar," said Rogue—and Storm saw that a change had suddenly come over her. She seemed weaker. Her face was contorted with pain and she was clenching her fists and shaking as if engaged in some titanic inner struggle. Not only that, but her voice had regained its familiar Southern lilt. This could be a trick on Mountjoy's part, but Storm doubted it. Rogue was fighting him for control of her body.

For an instant, Rogue looked scared, and Mountjoy's English accent emerged from her mouth again. "What are you doing? This is impossible! You can't—!" Then, as if a switch had been thrown, Rogue was back. "Can't I? You made a mistake, Mountjoy. To take over my body, you had to touch me first. Even as you wormed your way in here, I absorbed a measure of your powers. You tried to take me over..."

Storm watched the bizarre battle, helpless to intervene. She gasped as her teammate's form altered again, her features lengthening, hair appearing on her chin, her very clothes darkening and changing shape until, in appearance at least, she was more Mountjoy than Rogue. But it was certainly Rogue who put the look of grim satisfaction on the combined entity's face and, using its mouth, completed her sentence: "Now, I'm taking *you* over!"

But the fight wasn't over yet. As Rogue's features began to reassert themselves, she turned to Storm and, rigid with effort, grunted: "Ororo, I can't hold him much longer. Take 'Crawler and get out of here. I'll follow you. Go!"

Nightcrawler was beginning to come round, but so was Scribe. Storm gathered up the injured X-Man and made for the window— but, groggy as he was, Kurt struggled in her arms. She let him go, and he practically fell on top of Shaw's computer, which had been blown off the desk and was lying on the floor, the screen of its monitor broken. He took a CD out of its drive, and grinned weakly. "Don't know what's on here, but it's something, right?" Then he fell against Storm, and lost consciousness again.

Wolverine was running rings around Fitzroy. He gave himself over to his animal instincts, letting them tell him when to attack and when to withdraw. He couldn't cut through the young mutant's armor, but he could use strength and leverage against him. He had brought Fitzroy crashing down to the floor four times already. Each time, he had swooped in and made an attempt to pry his omnium mesh helmet from his head. He hadn't been successful yet, but he figured he had at least loosened it.

Fitzroy, in turn, had punched him, head-butted him and tried with all his might to maintain a hold upon his slippery foe. He had probably drained enough energy from Wolverine to power a small town for a month. As long as he took it in small enough doses for the Canadian X-Man to recover between each one—and as long as he couldn't use the energy offensively—Wolverine didn't care too much. But he remained aware that, were Fitzroy to get a proper grip on him for any length of time, then that would be the end of him. It made for a long, grinding battle, but Wolverine took con- solation in the certainty that, even with his efforts magnified by his bio-armor, his opponent had to be feeling the strain more than he was.

Inevitably, Fitzroy made another mistake. He cursed as he was outmaneuvered and knocked off his feet, gravity and his heavy shell doing the rest. Wolverine was upon him again before he could stand, searching with his claws for a seam in his armor. He grunted with satisfaction as he found one. With the sound of wrenching metal, the helmet came off at last.

By that time, Fitzroy had reached up and seized both of Wolverine's wrists.

They glared into each other's eyes. Sweat was pouring down Fitzroy's face, but his expression was exultant. "You came too close, X-Man. You're dead, now!"

"Wanna bet, bub?"

Wolverine could feel his life force fading, and see it crackling inside Fitzroy's chest-plate. The powered grips of two armored hands would be difficult to break, perhaps impossible. But there was another way.

He retracted his claws and pushed down with all his strength. Fitzroy, who had expected him to try to pull away, was taken by surprise. Suddenly, Wolverine's fists were resting on his face—and the metal claw housings that were built into his gloves were pointing squarely at his eyes. "You just saw what adamantium can do to omnium mesh," he growled. "What do you think it can do to you?" Fitzroy set his jaw defiantly, so Wolverine spelled out his threat: "Give up now, or I'll dig my way into your brain, by the messy route! Better believe I can kill you before you can kill me."

"OK, OK, I give!" whined Fitzroy, sounding like a child.

"That's a good boy," said Wolverine. He could already feel his body repairing the damage, restoring him to health. "Now, since you're in such an obliging mood, I've got a few questions to ask you—about your boss, and a certain friend of mine."

"I don't know what you're talking about!"

"You'll have to do better than that, Trev."

Fitzroy spat in his interrogator's face. Wolverine snarled, and considered popping his claws after all.

But suddenly, all hell broke loose. A familiar *bamf* heralded an unexpected arrival. A blue-skinned Rogue teleported into the room, and crumpled to the floor with a cry of: "Logan, help me!" At the same time, a Hellfire Club goon leapt up from his prone position, picked up a chair and hurled it at Wolverine's head. Wolverine caught it, and sent the impromptu missile back the way it had come, but Fitzroy used the twin distraction. He pushed up hard, throwing the X-Man away from him and climbing back to his feet. He hesitated, as if wondering whether to attack again or just cut his losses. His decision was made easier as Storm swept into the office, carrying an unconscious Nightcrawler. Fitzroy dived through his dimensional portal and disappeared. Infuriated, and scenting blood, Wolverine made to follow—but his instincts told him better. He drew back, as the portal suddenly snapped shut: a deliberate attempt on the White Rook's part to cut any pursuers in half.

"Next time, Fitzroy," Wolverine muttered under his breath. "Next time!"

Now that the battle was over, a sudden silence descended upon the room. The sounds of laughter drifted up from the street below, and Wolverine's keen hearing picked out the muted strains of orchestral music from inside the Hellfire Club's ballroom. He could make out something else too: police sirens, approaching.

He hurried to Rogue's side. She was hunched into a ball, cradling her knees in her arms. He knew what had happened to her, just as he knew that there was nothing he could do to help. "You all right, darling?" he asked.

She looked up at him, and nodded bravely. "Too many stray thoughts whizzing about this old head of mine, that's all."

"And Mountjoy?" asked Storm.

"Gave up the ghost, so to speak. Soon as he got out of my body, I used Nightcrawler's power to 'port out of there. How is the elf? I'm afraid I hit him pretty hard."

"Concussed," said Storm. "He needs rest, but I don't think there's any serious damage. And he got what we came for." Wolverine could see that, even in his sleep, Nightcrawler was holding fiercely on to a compact disk.

"Time to beat a retreat then," he said. The sirens were louder now, and he could see from Storm's reaction that she could hear them too. "I think those cop cars are coming our way. We've attracted attention."

"And, since our raid on the Hellfire Club building wasn't exactly legal..."

"Took the words right out of my mouth, 'Ro. Let's get our butts out of here!"

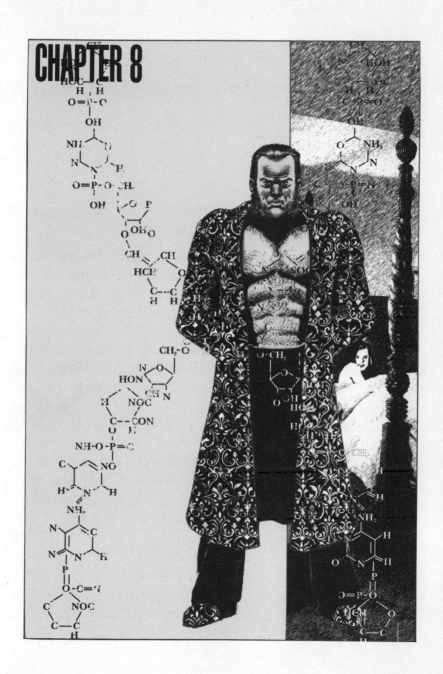

THE X-MEN'S Blackbird had always been fast—but, since it had been modified with alien technology, its speed was almost unbelievable. For Hank McCoy, however, the journey to China was still too slow. It gave him too much time to think.

"You, most of all, are looking for answers," Selene had said to him, "but you'd prefer not to find them here." His fellow X-Men had been discreet enough not to question him about what she had meant, later. But, much as he was loath to admit it to himself, she had been right.

Selene had been toying with them all, of course. She had promised to tell them what she knew of Moira's whereabouts. Then, with a cruel smile, she had announced: "Nothing. I know nothing." And she had broken into peals of laughter, which had soon subsided beneath Cyclops's glare. She had become thoughtful, then. "However, I am somewhat intrigued. Could it be that an old and trusted friend is keeping secrets from me?"

Hank's heart had leapt at that. He knew how deceitful the Black Queen could be—but, even so, he had believed her without question. And more: he had felt a tingle of excitement—of hope?—at the suggestion that this 'old and trusted friend' (and how many people could that be? Even the hint of sarcasm with which Selene had spoken the words pointed towards one associate in particular) could be the true culprit in all this.

Storm had contacted them, back at the X-Mansion, and her report had all but confirmed it. She had described how her team had battled the Hellfire Club in Hong Kong, and how Nightcrawler had escaped with half the contents of Sebastian Shaw's hard disk. Analysis of the data had revealed something interesting: that only a few days earlier, Shaw had deleted the schematics of Muir Island's security systems from his computer. It was enough to tie him in with Moira's abduction.

And so the X-Men had agreed to reunite in Hong Kong, to ponder their next move. In other circumstances, Hank might almost have welcomed the prospect of a forthcoming battle. It might have taken his mind off his problems. But why did Moira have to be involved?

It was sometimes easy to forget that Moira MacTaggert had the Legacy Virus herself. She faced her illness with a brave face and a determination to fight that was typical of her. Still, however bad Hank felt about his failure to find a cure, it had to be ten times worse for her. And he knew that, for each minute she was missing, each minute he spent searching for her, another minute passed during which no progress was made towards their goal. He felt sick to think of all that wasted time, of Moira's life—and how many others?—ticking away. And that made him feel guilty, because he knew he could have entrusted this rescue mission to the others. He could have returned to his work on Muir Island.

But there was a small part of Hank McCoy—a part he tried not to acknowledge, because it offered a hope that might be too cruelly dashed, and because he felt guilty about this too—which spoke to him of greater possibilities.

He had known for a long time that Shaw, like him, was trying to cure the Legacy Virus. If he had taken to acquiring geneticists, then there had to be a connection. But then, why attract the X-Men's attention by going after one of their associates? And why now?

"Your hopes are high," Selene had said, "but your fears are still greater."

What if the Hellfire Club had made a breakthrough?

Phoenix had taken the controls from Storm, to give her a rest. The African X-Man had already flown eight thousand miles to collect her teammates. She lay back in her reclined seat, her eyes closed— although she couldn't have been asleep, as the instruments showed that the Blackbird was still benefiting from an artificial tailwind.

Cyclops and the Beast were lost in their own maudlin thoughts, Cyclops staring out of the window in a futile attempt to prevent his wife from seeing how worried he was. Jean had to admit that she had spent most of the journey in subdued silence herself. The despondent air in the cabin had even rubbed off on Iceman: he sat and fidgeted restlessly, sensing the mood of the others and not wishing to disturb their reveries.

Jean didn't have to read Hank's mind to know that the Legacy Virus was at its forefront. As for Scott...well, his thoughts were an open book to her at the best of times. Right now, she could be sure beyond a doubt that they were thinking about the same thing.

Or rather, about the same person.

Once, back in the days when Jean Grey had been known as Marvel Girl, she had made a deal with a powerful cosmic entity. In return for her own survival when she ought to have died, she had allowed it to replace her temporarily on Earth. The Phoenix force had wanted to learn humanity, but instead—and with Sebastian Shaw's help—it had become a monster. It had saved the entire universe—but then it had destroyed a sun, and killed billions. It had learned something from its human host, though. In the end, it had taken its own life, to spare others. And, for a time, Jean Grey had been believed dead and buried.

That was when Scott Summers, still in mourning, had met Madelyne Pryor.

In some ways, it was flattering that, with Jean gone, Scott had fallen for a woman who looked almost exactly like her. But it was also somehow creepy, and neither Jean nor Scott liked to think about that chapter of his life. Madelyne was a pilot who had crashed her plane on the very day—at the exact moment—that the Phoenix, in Jean Grey's form, had died on the moon. She had walked out of the flames unharmed, with no memory of her life before the accident. To Scott, she must have seemed like his lost love reincarnated. In a way, she had been. He hadn't known it at the time, but she was a clone of Jean, created by the X-Men's old foe Mr. Sinister, as part of one of his typically Machiavellian plots.

After a whirlwind romance, Scott had married Madelyne. They had had a son, but he had been taken from them. They had been through a lot together.

And then Jean had returned.

Perhaps Madelyne had good reason to feel bitter towards the couple. Jean knew that Scott wasn't proud of the way he had treated his first wife during that difficult time. He had just found out that the only woman he had ever truly loved had apparently risen from the grave. He had seen at last that Madelyne Pryor had been nothing but a confused attempt on his part to replace her, to hold on to a part of Jean Grey forever.

But Madelyne wasn't Jean, and her hurt had festered and turned into hatred, and her hatred into madness. Jean and Scott still felt guilty about what they had put her through. But their guilt had been, in some small measure, assuaged by Madelyne's transformation into the Goblin Queen, which had proved her to be an imperfect reflection—a distortion rather than a copy, with a dark side that could never have been born of Jean herself.

Just like the Phoenix.

Madelyne was a member of the Hellfire Club now, a part of the Hong Kong Inner Circle—and, if the rumors were true, Sebastian Shaw's partner in more than one sense of the word. Storm's team hadn't reported meeting her in Hong Kong, but she would certainly be with the Black King somewhere, plotting and waiting for a chance to exact revenge upon the people who had wronged her. Her very presence would stir up feelings that both Jean and Scott had hoped to forget, and force them to confront a past they had thought long buried.

To a casual observer, it might have seemed like a ghost was operating the laptop computer.

The Hong Kong hotel room was in semi-darkness. A night breeze drifted through the open window, and made the blinds tap against the sill as if sending out a message in Morse code. The main source of light was the small screen, over which Nightcrawler hunched, parts of his body washed in color while other parts faded into the shadows.

Wolverine lay on his back, still wearing the lower half of his costume, on one of the two beds. From the regular rhythm of his breathing, Nightcrawler had assumed he was sleeping. He was surprised, then, to hear his voice.

"Shouldn't you be getting some rest?" asked Logan, disapprovingly.

"I had a few hours' sleep before we flew out here. I'm OK."

"Rogue hit you pretty hard—and it's likely we'll be facing off against the Hellfire Club again tomorrow. Think how she'll feel if you keel over as soon as the fists start flying."

"I told you, I'm OK. Anyway, Rogue did the right thing."

"Try telling her that."

"I already have. Mountjoy wasn't about to let either of us go. If she hadn't punched me, I don't know what would have happened. I could have ended up like..." Kurt didn't want to complete the sentence. Lamely, he finished: "You know."

"Like Carol Danvers," said Wolverine, never one to shy away from words.

Nightcrawler sighed, and turned away from the screen, his eyes adjusting quickly to the darkness of the rest of the room. His teammate, he saw, hadn't changed his position, hadn't even opened his eyes. "You're probably right, mein Freund," he conceded. A set of squared-off numbers shone from a digital clock radio between the beds. It was later than he had thought. "I thought I'd found something else in the data we salvaged from Shaw's computer."

"Like what?"

"Like a heavily encrypted communications link. I can't trace it, though. I can't even reconstruct any of the incoming messages. They've been very efficiently purged."

"Don't sweat it. A man like Shaw knows plenty of people. Doesn't mean to say they're all involved in whatever he's got his fingers into right now."

"I suppose not," said Nightcrawler. "At least we know now that he was interested in Moira. Chances are, he has her and the rest of the missing scientists. If only we knew where..."

"Get some rest," said Wolverine. "The rest of the team'll be here in a few hours, and then we can talk about rounding up Fitzroy and his pals and beating the information out of them."

"Come back to bed, Sebastian."

Shaw hadn't realized that Madelyne was awake. He had been pacing fretfully in his dressing gown, feeling confined in the small, basic quarters that were so much less than he was used to. There were no windows in this underground room, only a subdued artificial light. Not that the discomfort bothered him too much. He had bigger problems.

He looked at Madelyne, thin sheets clinging to the curves of her body, long red hair flattened by the pillow so that it seemed to form a halo around her beautiful face. She was a most enchanting diversion. But even she couldn't divert him from his worries tonight.

"You're brooding about Doctor MacTaggert, aren't you?"

He climbed back onto the bed beside her, and raised an inquisitive eyebrow. "The perils of living with a telepath, I suppose."

"Of living with a woman, Sebastian. I don't need to read your mind when I can simply read your face."

He smiled demurely, and wondered if she was lying to him. He had put the question to her deliberately, as a test. Fond as he had become of his Black Rook, he knew he couldn't trust her. He had learned through bitter experience never to trust anyone.

"I misjudged her," he confessed. "I knew she was stubborn, but..." He sighed. "Perhaps I should have heeded the advice I was given. Perhaps I should have been patient. I have some of the best people in the world working for me—but somebody like MacTaggert, somebody with her insights and skills, could have guaranteed our success."

"I can change her mind," said Madelyne.

"I doubt that very much," said Shaw. "She's already dying from the Legacy Virus. What more could any of us do to her?"

"Make sure it hurts!"

"She would still resist, spitfire. I was sure I could reach her. Our facility here offers the good doctor her best chance of survival. I believed that when she realized this, she would join us." Shaw clenched his fists in frustration. He had offered the Scots woman everything she could have desired: achievement, recognition, life itself. He couldn't understand the mentality of somebody who would turn down all that on a point of principle.

But then, he had always found it difficult to understand others. Because of this, and because of the circles within which he moved, he had found himself betrayed on many occasions. He surrounded himself with people who could further his cause, regardless of the fact that such people were likely to have their own agendas. *Keep your friends close,* said the old adage by which Shaw lived, *and your enemies closer.* That was why he didn't—couldn't—trust Madelyne. That was why he suspected Selene's motives for striking out on her own, without his sanction, and taking over the New York branch. She hadn't opened hostilities against him yet, but he would have been a fool if he hadn't prepared himself for that possibility. And were the Black King and the Black Queen to go to war again, then not all of the other pieces would choose his side. Trevor Fitzroy, in particular, was surely only biding his time until his mistress summoned him.

The game was falling apart around him.

"Everybody can be bought," said Madelyne, leaving Shaw to

wonder again if she had been eavesdropping on his thoughts. "I can look into her mind if you want, see what she truly desires. If she has a price, I can find it."

"Maybe," he said, thoughtfully.

"Where is she now?"

"In a bunkroom. I want her treated well, for now. I will talk to her again tomorrow. Perhaps she can still be persuaded." He didn't really believe it, though. He rolled onto his back and rested his head on the soft pillow. His dressing gown fell open, and Madelyne drew closer to him, and ran a hand over his exposed chest. Shaw didn't respond to her touch. "We're running out of time, Madelyne," he said quietly. "By moving against Doctor MacTaggert, we've attracted the attention of the X-Men."

"Fitzroy's letter?"

He nodded. He had prohibited all radio contact between this facility and his headquarters on the mainland. But, just a few hours ago, a tiny wormhole had popped into existence in his office here, above his desk, and a note from his White Rook had been pushed through. The X-Men had been sniffing around in Hong Kong. Fitzroy was sure they had learned nothing, but Shaw knew his old enemies better. They would be arriving on his doorstep before long.

"We can defeat the X-Men," said Madelyne, seeming to relish the prospect of a fight.

"And keep the project safe in the process?"

"It means a lot to you, doesn't it?"

"Far more than anything else."

He didn't want to talk about it any more, so he turned his back towards her. A second later, however, he felt Madelyne's breath upon his neck, and her hands massaging the tension-knotted muscles of his shoulders. He was irritated, at first, by her insistence upon invading his personal space. But the sensation was a pleasant one, and he found himself smiling as a weight lifted from him. She was a very enchanting diversion after all.

It took him a minute to realize that she had invaded his head too. She was massaging his mind as she massaged his body, relaxing him and pushing his worries away. But, by this time, he didn't care much any more.

He drifted towards sleep, idly wondering if Madelyne knew that he didn't love her.

"I don't think we have much choice," said Cyclops. "The Hellfire Club know we're in Hong Kong, and we can be fairly sure they have Moira, but we don't know where."

"So, we make them tell us," said Wolverine.

Cyclops nodded. "I think we have to take the offensive, yes."

Seven X-Men, dressed in civilian clothing, were eating breakfast in a quiet corner of a small cafeteria, a block away from the hotel in which three of their number had spent the night. Only the Beast was not present. Upon arrival in Hong Kong, he had professed himself to be dog-tired. The strains of the past week or so were beginning to tell, from working through nights on his ultimately abortive cure for the Legacy Virus, to lying awake and worrying about Moira. He had decided to skip the planning session, crashing down in Wolverine and Nightcrawler's room for a few hours, and asking Cyclops to fill him in later on what had been decided.

"We already know that Fitzroy, Scribe and Mountjoy are likely to be present," Scott continued. Storm had briefed the rest of the team on the previous night's events. "Rogue, I hate to ask you this, but I think you're our best chance against Mountjoy. After last time, he should think twice about using his power against you. You need to hit him hard and fast, get him out of the picture before he can get his hands on anyone else."

Rogue nodded. "I can do that, with pleasure."

"What if he's already hiding inside someone again?" asked Nightcrawler.

"I'll perform a telepathic sweep as soon as we're inside the building," said Phoenix. "By all accounts, Mountjoy doesn't control the mind of his host; I should be able to detect both his thoughts and theirs, as two separate patterns. I'll point him out to Rogue."

"Against Scribe," said Cyclops, "we need a good hand-to-hand fighter, someone who can match her reflexes. Wolverine..."

Wolverine shook his head. "Got me a score to settle with Fitzroy. He's mine!"

Cyclops scowled, and was about to remind Logan once again who was leading the X-Men when Nightcrawler jumped in to defuse the situation: "Scribe should be easy enough to deal with, if we double-team her. I can keep her busy while Bobby piles ice around her feet. That should slow her down."

"Suits me," said Iceman.

Cyclops decided not to make an issue of Wolverine's intransigence, this time. "Which leaves the rest of us to deal with however many mercenaries the Hellfire Club can throw at us," he said, "keep them off the others' backs while they handle the big guns."

"Gave yourself the easy job, I see, boss-man," remarked Wolverine. "Should be like shooting fish in a barrel." Cyclops ignored him. He was only trying to provoke a reaction.

"However," he continued, "we should be aware that Fitzroy has had plenty of time to call in reinforcements by now."

"Sebastian Shaw," said Phoenix, unhappily.

"Shaw likes to remain in the background," said Storm. "He doesn't usually involve himself in combat situations. If he does, however, then I believe I can handle him. He may have the ability to absorb kinetic force, but I can strike him with electrical energy."

"Makes sense," said Cyclops. "But if Shaw does turn up, he might have his personal assistant, Tessa, with him. She isn't one for brawling either, but we have to be prepared. She might decide to make an exception."

"Tessa's psi-powers are no match for my own," said Phoenix. "If it comes to a battle between us, I can take her. But I suspect I'll have other problems." She said the words with a hint of resignation, and Scott's heart ached to hear them. He looked at his wife, and she smiled back at him bravely. *It's all right, Scott,* she told him, mind to mind. *You can mention her name.* Aloud, for the benefit of the others, she said: "Madelyne Pryor's abilities are equal to my own, but I have the edge in experience. At the very least, I can keep her occupied until the rest of the Lords Cardinal have been dealt with."

"Good for you, Jeannie," said Wolverine. "As for Tessa, she ain't a fighter. Trick with her is to knock her down before she can worm her way into your head."

Cyclops nodded. "If both telepaths are present, Jean, forget Tesssa and concentrate on...Pryor." He had hesitated, just fractionally, before saying her name. She had always been 'Maddie' to him. He hoped the others hadn't noticed, although Jean certainly would have. "In that eventuality, Tessa becomes my responsibility." Wolverine was right: Tessa's threat could be ended with one optic blast, if only he could locate her and strike quickly enough.

"Looks like we got a plan then," said Wolverine. "I vote we strike now. Sooner we do it, the less time those suckers've got to prepare."

"Kurt, can you 'port back to the hotel and wake Hank?" asked Cyclops.

"Jawohl, mein fearless leader," said Nightcrawler, with a mock salute. The others crowded around him, preventing the few other diners in the café from seeing as he vanished into thin air. Cyclops couldn't help but wonder, however, what any onlooker might make of the sound and the brimstone smell of his teleportation effect.

The X-Men finished their breakfasts in silence, each lost in his or her own thoughts of the battle to come. Cyclops was playing through various possibilities in his mind, ensuring as far as possible that he was prepared for any eventuality, that he wouldn't lose control.

Then Nightcrawler returned, hurrying through the glass door from the street, still in his Errol Flynn disguise, having apparently teleported back to a discreet spot nearby rather than risking materializing where he might be seen. And Cyclops could tell, from the expression on his illusory face, that something was wrong. Something for which he hadn't prepared.

"He's gone!" Nightcrawler blurted out in a low voice, as soon as he was near enough to the table for the others to hear. "Hank's gone!"

"What do you mean?" asked Cyclops, urgently.

"He wasn't in the hotel room. And he hasn't been there for the last thirty minutes at least. The beds have been made up, so I checked with the cleaners. They haven't seen hide nor hair of him, no pun intended."

"Thirty minutes?" repeated Phoenix.

"More than long enough for him to have joined us here," said Rogue, "and I can't imagine where else he would have gone."

"Ain't it obvious?" grunted Wolverine. "The Hellfire Club are picking us off one by one. Looks like we got us two hostages to rescue now."

The costumed mercenaries were taking no chances. Four of them held on to the Beast, as four more covered him with their guns. They had wrestled him to the floor, but they lifted him to his knees as Trevor Fitzroy entered the Hellfire Club's ballroom, the boots of his bulky bio-armor thudding heavily into the thick carpet. More agents followed at his heels, along with a white-haired woman who could only have been the Red Rook, Scribe.

"Well, well, well, what do we have here?" said Fitzroy, in a mocking tone. "One of our enemies, delivering himself into my hands. To what do we owe this pleasure?"

"You expressed it eloquently enough yourself, Fitzroy," said the Beast. "I came here of my own volition, and allowed your rent-a-mob extras to believe they had overpowered me, because I wished to speak to you. It isn't necessary to engage in heavy-handed tactics."

"I'll be the judge of that, I think. What kind of a trap are you planning to spring here?"

"No trap," the Beast assured him. "I merely want to get a message to your Black King."

"A plea for the return of your associate, no doubt. I don't think so, X-Man. You've got nothing to say to the Lords Cardinal that we want to hear."

"I think we should let Mr. Shaw make that decision for himself," came a new voice.

The Beast recognized the woman known only as Tessa, as she swept into the room. She was young and slight of form, but Hank knew her power resided in her mind, not her body. Her black hair was piled up on top of her head, and she looked the very model of efficiency in a stylish black trouser suit.

"Shaw left me in charge while he was gone," said Fitzroy, pointedly.

"And he sent me to investigate the situation here," countered Tessa. Fitzroy was a member of the Inner Circle, and therefore technically Tessa's superior. Hank wouldn't have guessed it, though, from the young woman's demeanor. She had always been loyal to Sebastian Shaw—almost uniquely so—for as long as the X-Men had known them both. But, increasingly it seemed, she had little time for his associates. The Beast saw the barely disguised contempt in which she held Fitzroy, who was probably a few years her junior. He wondered if he might be able to use that rift against them both in the future.

"The situation," growled Fitzroy, "is that I've fought off the X-Men, as Shaw wanted, and now I've captured one of them. I think I can deal with him myself."

"He's telling the truth, Mr. Fitzroy," said Tessa, scornfully. "I can see it in his mind. He didn't come here to fight. His teammates don't even know where he is."

"So, we kill him before they find out!"

"They won't. I've constructed a psi-shield around his mind. Even Phoenix won't be able to detect his thoughts now. Not from a distance. He's on his own." As Fitzroy fumed in silence, Tessa stalked across the room and crouched down in front of the Beast, bringing her eyes level with his. "Now, little man, you said you had a message for my employer?"

The Beast returned her stare levelly. "I know what Shaw's plans are," he said. He was bluffing: he couldn't be sure that his deductions were correct.

"Do you indeed? And the X-Men intend to stop him, I suppose?"

"Maybe. But, as you have already inferred, I came here without their knowledge, and for an entirely different purpose."

Tessa grinned unexpectedly. "I know. You're here because you have come to think as I do: that Sebastian Shaw is mutantkind's best hope."

The Beast blanched at this unequivocal statement. "I wouldn't go that far."

"Oh, come now, Doctor McCoy. Does it shock you so much to hear your unspoken thoughts vocalized for the first time?"

She had a point, Hank couldn't deny it. Like Selene, Tessa had exposed what he was thinking, what he had hardly dared to admit to himself. Ever since his return to Muir Island, ever since he had found both Moira and her files missing, an idea had been building in his mind. A crazy idea; perhaps, in some ways, an unworthy one. But, as each piece of the jigsaw puzzle of Moira's disappearance had slotted into place, as the schemes of the Hellfire Club had been gradually revealed, it had become more and more natural. More insistent.

A few days ago, he would never have dreamed of coming here like this, of dealing with the X-Men's enemies. But then, a few days ago, William Montgomery had still been alive.

And so, Hank McCoy had walked into the clutches of the Hellfire Club, afraid of being proved wrong, and so ashamed of his own decision that he hadn't been able to face his friends with the truth. He was taking a huge gamble, but every fiber of his being screamed at him that he had to do this. And yet, he still couldn't bring himself to say the words, because saying them would expose his guilt, and make the decision too real.

"Come on," coaxed Tessa, "why don't you say it? Put Trevor here out of his misery."

"You're right," said Hank, reluctantly, casting his eyes down towards the floor. "I think Shaw might be our best hope. Our best hope for a cure to the Legacy Virus. And I'm committed to finding that cure, whatever it takes, whatever I might have to do."

"Say it," Tessa whispered in his ear. "Tell us why you came here."

"I want you to inform Shaw..." He hesitated then, and took a deep breath, steeling himself, before he let out the treacherous words at last. "...that I might be prepared to offer him my services."

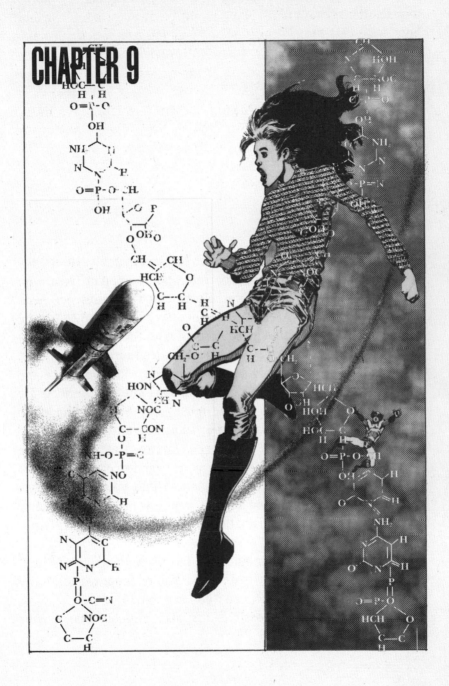

CHAPTER 9

STILL SAY it's a trap," said Trevor Fitzroy, irritably. He led the way down the deep-carpeted corridor, not looking at Tessa, who lagged two steps behind him. He resented her presence here. Had she not turned up—had Shaw not sent her to spy on him, despite his assurances that he could deal with the X-Men himself— then one of his enemies would have been dead already. As it was, this glorified secretary had had Scribe and Mountjoy take the Beast downstairs to a holding cell, while his fate was decided. He had gone without a fight, but he must have been feeling quite pleased with himself. He was getting what he wanted.

Tessa's office was next to Shaw's. Fitzroy tried to open the door, but it was locked. He sulked, as he was forced to step back and let her come forward with the key. "I told you, Mr. Fitzroy," she said, with an infuriating hint of condescension in her voice, "I've scanned his mind. The Beast's offer is sincere. He truly believes what he is saying."

"Then that psionic witch, Phoenix, has done something to him. She's disguised his thoughts somehow. You're supposed to be the bloody telepath around here, can't you see that?"

Tessa nodded. "It is possible. It's also possible that Doctor

McCoy has simply chosen to see things our way. He wants to cure the Legacy Virus as badly as we do."

They walked into the office, and Tessa took a seat behind her desk. Fitzroy remained on his feet, pacing up and down. He had sent his bio-armor back to its other-dimensional pocket of reality, where it awaited his mental command to protect him again. In the meantime, he was clad in a black and white, high-collared body-suit. "He wants us to believe him. He wants us to take him to the facility—and, mark my words, his teammates will follow."

"Perhaps," acknowledged Tessa, thoughtfully.

"Even if he is telling the truth, it won't stop the X-Men from looking for him."

"I'm still concealing his thought patterns."

"Oh, sure, that'll throw them off the track, won't it?" scoffed Fitzroy. "I mean, it's not like they'll ever think of coming here, is it?"

"That's why we need to make a decision quickly. We must remove the Beast from this building, one way or the other."

"Then we kill him. It's not worth the risk of keeping him alive."

"It might be."

"We don't need him!"

Tessa shook her head. "That, I'm afraid, is where you are wrong. If he is sincere about helping with our project, then his defection couldn't have come at a more opportune time. He could prove very useful to us."

"How? Shaw's already got the MacTaggert woman!"

"She wouldn't cooperate. We need a replacement, and McCoy would be ideal."

Fitzroy ceased his pacing, and pulled at his lower lip, stubbornly. This was news to him, and it changed everything. Clearly, Tessa thought their captive could make the difference between success and failure for the project. If she thought so, then doubtless Shaw did too. And, much as he hated to acknowledge the fact, Fitzroy dared not go against Shaw.

He remembered Wolverine's taunts, and knew that much of what he had said was painfully true. When Fitzroy had first come to this time, he had been running from a life in which he was nobody; from a father who took sadistic delight in humiliating him and making him look small. Here, he had thought, his advanced technology and his knowledge of things to come could give him an edge. He could gain power, respect and wealth.

Instead, he had been soundly beaten, several times over. He had even been left for dead by the gang of mutant terrorists known as X-Force.

Fitzroy played the long game now. He worked for people like Selene and Shaw because they could give him a taste of what he desired. But it was a temporary measure. When he had traveled back in time, this brash young mutant had promised himself that he would never be subservient to anyone again. He longed for the day when he would control the Hellfire Club, or an organization like it, himself. Until then, he had to rein in his impatience, curb his frustration. He couldn't afford to get on the wrong side of his current benefactors. Not while he still had a use for them.

"Unfortunately," said Tessa, "the communications blackout is still in force. We cannot contact Sebastian to request instructions. However, I believe he would want us to take the Beast to him. Don't you agree?" She looked at Fitzroy with an arched eyebrow, as if challenging him to argue. He didn't know why she had invited him to discuss the matter at all. She was just going through the motions of Hellfire Club protocol. She had already made up her mind, and she would get her own way.

"You really think he'll help us find a cure?" he asked, delaying the inevitable.

"Yes," said Tessa, "I think he will. There's a chance, at least— and I thought you, Mr. Fitzroy, of all people, would want to take every chance you could get."

"What's that supposed to mean?"

"Your greatest asset in the twenty-first century is your fore-knowledge—but the Legacy Virus isn't a part of your past, is it? It was created by a mutant from beyond your era: somebody who, like you, traveled back in time and made a difference. This isn't quite the world you read about in your history books. It must be very discomforting for you, to watch this plague spread without knowing when or how it will end."

Fitzroy grunted a reluctant agreement to that, smarting at the unspoken implication. Shaw had appointed him to his Inner Circle specifically because he knew of events that had not yet happened. The more those events were distorted, the less recognizable this era was to him, and the more dispensable he would become.

He bit his lip, dropped himself into a seat and said, resignedly: "So, we do what the X-Man wants, I suppose. We take him to Shaw."

"I think so," said Tessa. "In the meantime, I have been authorized to suspend all operations here in Hong Kong. The Lords Cardinal will regroup at the island facility, and remain there until the project is concluded."

"What? Why?"

"Because the X-Men will almost certainly attack this headquarters again, and we can only lose personnel and equipment by attempting to defend it. Better to let them find an empty building, and search it to their hearts' content. They will find nothing."

"Sounds to me like we're giving in to them," grumbled Fitzroy.

"While they waste precious time, we can be long gone from here."

"Right. The sooner we leave, then, the better. I absorbed enough energy from Wolverine last night. I reckon I can open a portal directly to the island."

"No, that won't be necessary. I came here in the helicopter. We need to take it back."

"But the X-Men—"

"The X-Men don't know we have their teammate. Yes, they might well find a way to follow us. But, if and when that happens—" Tessa smiled tightly. "We'll deal with it."

* * *

They're leaving the building. Three...no, four...five...a whole string of black limousines, coming out of an underground garage.

Phoenix was still five blocks away when Nightcrawler's message came in. The other X-Men had heard it too, thanks to the telepathic link that Jean had set up between them. She broke into a run, as did Cyclops, Wolverine and Iceman beside her.

I've got them, Rogue's voice sounded in their minds. *They're all identical, and they have black-tinted windows. I can't see if Hank's inside any of them. Jean...?*

Still no sign of him, Phoenix sent back. As soon as she had been told of the Beast's disappearance, she had performed a telepathic sweep of the area, searching for her old friend. Somehow, his thought patterns had been masked from her. However, there had been one obvious place to search.

Nightcrawler had teleported directly to the Hellfire Club building. Phoenix could sense him now, his adhesive feet clinging through his soft boots to the side of an overlooking skyscraper. Rogue and Storm had followed, flying under their own power.

I'm almost in sight of the building, Storm reported. *Yes, I can see them.*

They're all out now, sent Nightcrawler. *A dozen cars, in all. They're splitting up, each heading in a different direction.*

This is a deliberate attempt to confuse us, Storm considered.

Get on them, people, ordered Cyclops. *Hank might be in one of those vehicles. We can't let any of them escape.*

The four ground-based X-Men had been halted by a particularly busy road junction. Before Phoenix could suggest levitating the quartet over the traffic—an act that would have meant blowing their cover, as they were still wearing their street clothes—Wolverine had stuck out his hand and flagged down a cab. It threaded its way across two lanes and stopped beside them, at which point Logan wrenched open the door and removed the driver by force. Cyclops protested, but his Canadian teammate was already in the driving seat. "Anyone joining me?" he asked gruffly. The driver was on his back on the sidewalk, giving vent to a stream of expletives. Scott gave him an embarrassed smile, dropped some money into his hands and muttered an apology, as he followed Phoenix and Iceman into the back seat.

"We don't have time to be polite," said Wolverine. He reinforced his point by stepping on the gas, causing several vehicles to brake as he ran a red light. The cab skidded around a corner, pursued by a cacophony of angry horns.

Phoenix closed her eyes, and saw what Nightcrawler was seeing. He had waited for one of the black limousines to stop at a crossroads, and had teleported onto the top of it. Whoever was inside had evidently heard his arrival, as a volley of machine-gun fire chattered through the roof at his feet. He leapt forwards, spread-eagled himself upside-down across the windscreen, grinned and shouted "Boo!" at the unseen driver. Then he flipped backwards, landing on his feet even as the car swerved off the road and collided with a brick wall. Steam rose from beneath its bonnet, and the doors were thrown open. As four uniformed Hellfire Club agents emerged, Nightcrawler dropped into a crouch. He squinted to see past them, to ensure that there was nobody else inside their vehicle. "Sorry," he said cheerfully, "wrong car!" And he teleported away.

Rogue, meanwhile, had employed similar but more direct tactics. By simply landing in front of another limousine, she had forced it to stop. This car too contained only costumed mercenaries, so she returned to the air, shrugging off their bullets as she chose another target.

Phoenix switched her focus to Storm. The wind-rider was still soaring above the streets, keeping track of all the fleeing cars at once. Phoenix saw them through her eyes. The time of day was working to the X-Men's advantage: Hong Kong's morning rush hour was just starting, and the Hellfire Club's drivers were battling against growing traffic.

Phoenix drew Wolverine's attention to a cluster of three black cars, which hadn't yet been able to get away from each other. "Already on it, darlin'!" he responded. He took another corner, wide, and then threw the steering wheel hard right. With a squeal of tires and an odor of burnt rubber, the cab stopped almost within its own length, and turned sideways, effectively blocking the road. Almost immediately, a black limousine rammed into its back end, in an attempt to knock it out of its way. The cab conceded a quarter-turn, but it wasn't enough to clear a space for the larger vehicle. The limousine backed up, stopped, surged forwards again and mounted the sidewalk, scattering a knot of pedestrians.

By this time, the four X-Men had spilled out of the battered taxicab, and Cyclops lifted his glasses and took out the rogue vehicle's nearside tires with two well-placed optic blasts. Phoenix knew he was sparing a thought for the onlookers, who were beginning to panic. He wished this situation could have been handled more discreetly.

Further up the road, two more black limousines were trapped by the gridlock they had created. Iceman and Wolverine made towards them, the former 'icing up' and creating a slide for himself, the latter bounding, animal-like, across the roofs of the intervening cars. As he did so, he pulled off his shirt and flung it to one side, revealing the top half of his costume underneath.

Phoenix checked in with Storm again. She had swooped down to deal with a limousine that had almost escaped onto an open road. A precisely controlled bolt of lightning burnt out its engine, with a pyrotechnic display that was impressive but safe. Nightcrawler, meanwhile, had emptied another car in his own inimitable way. Phoenix searched Storm's memories for her most recent sighting of the next nearest vehicle, and directed Kurt towards it.

A particularly reckless driver had failed to brake at the sight of Rogue in his path. Phoenix felt her bracing herself for the impact, and watched from afar as the front half of the limousine hit her and came off worse. Metal crumpled, glass shattered, and now Rogue could see into the car. The Beast wasn't present. Nor, the X-Men now knew, was he in any of the three cars stopped by Phoenix's party.

Four Hellfire Club agents had attacked Cyclops, but they hadn't been a threat to him. He had taken out three of them, and Jean seized the fourth telekinetically, making him drop his gun and freezing him to the spot. She was about to enter his mind, to see what he knew about the whereabouts of her teammate, when Wolverine's voice popped into her head: *No need for that, Red. I already handled it; used the traditional method.* She turned, to see that Wolverine had pinned an agent to the side of his car, and was holding a claw to his throat. *McCoy was at the club all right. Took off with Tessa and Fitzroy, but none of these mooks know where they were headed. Got some useful information, though—and a hunch to try out. Rogue?*

I'm here, sugar, came the response through the psi-link.

Give me a lift, would you darling?

On my way!

A thought flashed through Cyclops's mind, so briefly that nobody but Phoenix could have known about it. He was suppressing a mild irritation at Wolverine, for going his own way rather than following orders. But he also knew that Wolverine's 'own way' was often very effective. Jean distracted him by relaying the news, from Storm, that there were only four cars left to search. Ororo was taking one, Nightcrawler another. Phoenix sent Iceman towards the third: with his ice slides, he could make good time. She levitated herself and Cyclops, and they passed over the heads of the confused and frightened crowd below, in the hope of intercepting the fourth. From this vantage point, she could see that several police cars were trying to fight their way through the snarled traffic towards them.

Rogue landed beside Wolverine, and he jumped onto her back, wrapping his arms and legs around her. She took to the air again, her Canadian teammate guiding her path. Phoenix listened in on his thoughts again, just long enough to know that he was directing her towards a small private airfield, a short way to the north.

Stepping through one of Trevor Fitzroy's portals was like being immersed in a split-second nightmare. The Beast felt cold and prickly, and he had an overwhelming sense of foreboding—and then it was gone, like a dream exposed to the daylight, and he wasn't sure he could even remember or describe the sensation any more. He wondered what manner of terrible realms the young mutant had to pass through, in order to bend real space as he did.

Hank ran across tarmac, with Tessa in front of him and Fitzroy behind, watching his every move. They reached a black helicopter and climbed into the front seat, Fitzroy taking the controls and Hank sandwiched between the two members of the Hellfire Club. Within seconds, the blades were rotating and the chopper was rising into the air. Less than two minutes later, they had swung out over the North Pacific Ocean. Hank looked down at the vast field of shimmering blue beneath him, and realized that there was no going back now.

"Worried yet?" asked Fitzroy, with a sly grin. "It's gonna be harder than you thought for your pals in the X-Men to follow you, isn't it?"

Hank didn't answer, but Tessa spoke up in a quiet voice, which betrayed no trace of alarm. "I wouldn't be so sure about that, Mr. Fitzroy. I'm reading the mental signatures of two people, about a mile behind us and closing. They're flying."

Fitzroy's expression was a mixture of surprise and anger; Hank would have found it quite comical, had it not been for the butter-flies in his stomach. A part of him felt that he ought to have been relieved, but his overall reaction was one of disappointment and disbelief. They couldn't have found him. Not yet. Not until he had a few more answers. He wasn't ready.

"I knew it," snapped Fitzroy. "I told you this was a trap."

"This has nothing to do with me, I can assure you," Hank rumbled. "I can only assume that my colleagues discovered our method of decampment on their own initiative."

"One of the mercenaries must have talked," said Tessa.

"They're trained to keep silent," argued Fitzroy, "and they know nothing about the island."

"But they do know the location of the airfield," said Tessa, reasonably.

"And some of my friends can be remarkably persuasive," Hank muttered.

Tessa was punching instructions into a black, futuristic console, which was plugged into the helicopter's instrument panel. A tiny LCD screen lit up, but at first it showed nothing more than a flat expanse of light blue. As Tessa continued to tap away, Hank realized that he was looking at the output of a rear-mounted video camera, which soon found its targets. Two figures jerked into view on the screen, in low resolution: Rogue was flying through the clear sky, her face set into a determined expression, Wolverine on her back.

"Pursuit confirmed," said Tessa. "Mr. Fitzroy, I think we need your particular skills."

"You mean—?"

"They can't follow us through one of your portals."

Fitzroy hesitated for less than a second. Then he grinned, took his hands off the controls, and furrowed his brow in concentration. The air in front of them split open, forming another circular gateway, much bigger than the one that had taken them to the airfield. Hank steeled himself as the helicopter plunged into it. He closed his eyes for a moment, and when he opened them again he could almost have believed that nothing had happened. The sky was still in front of him, the ocean still beneath. The view seemed completely unchanged.

Then Fitzroy brought the helicopter around, and Hank saw two familiar figures: Rogue and Wolverine, just as the miniature viewscreen had shown them, but seen from behind now and much, much closer.

"Fitzroy, what do you think you're doing?" Tessa didn't raise her voice, but she couldn't conceal her alarm. "You were supposed to take us straight to the facility."

"I had a better idea. This way, we get two X-Men out of our hair for good."

The Beast realized what he had in mind. "No!" he cried, lunging towards him, trying to knock his hands from the controls, but he was too late. The helicopter bucked, as two sleek missiles shot out from somewhere beneath the cockpit. They streaked into Hank's vision, trailing white smoke. Rogue was still reacting to the helicopter's unexpected appearance; by the time she started to take evasive action, the missiles were almost upon her.

"This wasn't part of the deal, Fitzroy!" Hank shouted. "If either of them are hurt—"

"You'll do what?" mocked Fitzroy. "You've already reneged on the deal, McCoy. But guess what? You still get to see the Black King, and to help him with the project. I think you'll find that we can be just as 'persuasive' as your friends."

Hank clenched his fists impotently, and held his breath. His heart sank as Rogue threw herself out of the missiles' path, only for them to turn and find her again. They were heat-seekers. She managed to lose one of them, by taking a turn so tight that it couldn't follow. But she had no chance against the other.

It was all over in seconds. Hank didn't see the impact, because the white smoke had billowed up around the helicopter, but he saw the flash and heard the bang of a tremendous explosion, and he felt the cockpit rocking so fiercely that Fitzroy had to fight just to keep them in the air.

As they finally emerged into clear skies again, Hank looked around desperately for a trace of his two teammates. There was nothing.

Wolverine twisted his body in midair, and hit the Pacific Ocean headfirst, breath held, his arms outstretched ahead of him like a champion diver. Even so, the impact from such a height was like smacking into concrete. Had it not been for his adamantium-laced skeleton, he would have been smashed unconscious. As it was, the shock to his system was enough to daze him, and to force air out of his mouth in a frenzy of bubbles.

The metal in his bones dragged him towards the seabed, but, in a way, this was a blessing, because otherwise he would have had no idea which way was up. The water was icily cold, and, despite the insulation provided by his costume—and the jeans that he still wore over it—his healing factor had its work cut out for it just staving off hypothermia and preventing his body from shutting itself down.

He struck out with strong, tireless arms, but his lungs had begun to ache and it seemed like an eternity before he finally broke the surface. He took two great, rasping breaths, pedaled frantically to keep himself afloat, and picked up the sound of the Hellfire Club's departing helicopter with his ultra-sensitive ears. The vehicle was a diminishing speck on the horizon. He would worry about it later. Right now, satisfied that he wasn't about to die yet, he turned his thoughts to the plight of his teammate.

As the missiles had streaked towards them, as Rogue had realized she couldn't avoid them both, she had hurled her passenger away from her, as far and as fast as she could. Wolverine had had no choice in the matter. Hurtling towards the ocean, he had been forced to concentrate on his own survival. He had winced inwardly at the almost deafening sound of an explosion above and behind him. A blast of hot air had buffeted him, throwing him yet further away from Rogue. She had saved his life, but at what cost to herself?

Wolverine had an excellent sense of space. Even in free-fall, he had thought to check the position of the sun, and to run some quick calculations in his head. He knew roughly how far he had been thrown, and in which direction. Without pausing for rest, he launched himself into a powerful front crawl, until he was directly below the spot where he and Rogue had parted company. He took a few more strokes, to account for the fact that she would have been flying away from him for a second before the impact, then he brought up his legs, lowered his head and dropped beneath the waves again.

But he could see nothing—and, as he dropped still further, and the water around him became darker and dirtier, and his lungs began to hurt again, he realized that he was probably wasting his time. He had glanced back, trying to see Rogue in the air, to fix her position, an instant after the big bang—but he had been dazzled by the flare, and then it had been too late. He knew where to begin his search, but he could only guess where the Southern X-Man might have been flung by the missile's detonation.

She was tough, he reminded himself. She had the near-invulnerability of his old friend Carol Danvers, from back when she was Ms. Marvel. And Carol's powers had come from the Kree, and were nothing to sneeze at. But even if she had survived the missile attack, she would be in no state to fend for herself in these frigid waters.

Again and again, Wolverine returned to the surface for fresh oxygen. Each time, he hoped against hope to see the shape of his friend against the waves. He wanted to know that she had made it up here by herself, that she wasn't unconscious and sinking slowly into the depths. Each time, he was bitterly disappointed.

He continued searching for minutes after common-sense told him that, if Rogue was still down there somewhere, then she couldn't be alive. He returned to the surface again, exhausted, and in no condition to consider undertaking the long swim back to the shore.

He trod water, waited for the rest of the X-Men to rescue him and swore that, if Rogue really was dead, then he would make the Hellfire Club pay.

"Nightcrawler? Nightcrawler! Kurt, are you all right?"

Nightcrawler took a deep breath, and something caught in his throat. He doubled up, his stomach aching, and coughed water out of his lungs. Wheezing, he opened his eyes, and blinked away dark blotches to find himself looking up at the roof of the Blackbird's main cabin. He was sprawled across the floor, and Rogue was bending over him, concern in her eyes. Iceman was behind her, and Phoenix and Cyclops were up in the cockpit. Nightcrawler could hear the engines, and feel that the plane was in flight.

"I'm fine," he panted. "Just need to catch my breath, that's all." He hauled himself into a sitting position, leaning back against the base of a seat, and Rogue reached out a gloved hand to help him. His costume, he realized, was wet. Soaked through. Somebody had wrapped a thick towel around his shoulders. He could taste salt on his tongue.

"Easy there," said Rogue, and a guilty expression crossed her face. "You've taken enough knocks already on my account." She didn't look too healthy herself. Her face was pale, her hair was plastered down on her head and her voice was more subdued than normal.

"Not at all, Fräulein," Kurt assured her, chivalrously. He closed his eyes and breathed deeply, composing himself as the pain in his guts receded. "All for one, and all that."

"You should get into some dry clothes, at least. You'll catch your death." Rogue had already changed into a spare costume, which must have been stored aboard the Blackbird. It was an old one: yellow with green highlights, over which she wore a bomber jacket with circled 'X' logos in red on each shoulder.

Memories were crashing back into Nightcrawler's mind. Through the telepathic link, he had been aware of Rogue and Wolverine's discovery at the airfield. The rest of the X-Men, eager to follow, had headed for their own vehicle. A frightened and overzealous police officer had fired two shots at Storm as she had passed overhead.

They had reached the Blackbird, at last, at another airfield. Wolverine had called in a favor from an old friend who worked there, and the plane had been hidden beneath an old tarpaulin, no questions asked. The heroes had piled into it, stripping down to their costumes, Cyclops taking the controls. Phoenix had dropped the link between her teammates by now, but she had still followed Rogue and Wolverine's progress herself. No sooner had the plane taken off when her face had turned ashen, and she had cried out: "They've been attacked!"

Nightcrawler had watched anxiously as the telepath had cocked her head to one side, as if listening. At last, she had announced: "Logan's OK, but Rogue's been clipped by a missile. She's down and out. Nightcrawler—"

"I'm on it. Where is she?"

She had beamed a location directly into his mind. Not coordinates exactly, but an intuitive understanding of where Rogue was, relative to his current position. A trail of thought. And a warning, that his target was already underwater.

Nightcrawler had taken a deep breath, and teleported. The next thing he had been aware of was the shocking cold. He had thought himself prepared for it, but it had almost stolen the air from his lungs. He had forced his eyes to open, and had seen a dark shape in front of him, sinking. Rogue.

He had swum after her, trying to ignore the fact that he couldn't feel his extremities. For an awful few seconds, she had been sinking faster than he could catch her up. The current had threatened to tear him away from her, and he had felt so tired, as if he were about to black out himself. But, with a Herculean effort, he had managed to take hold of her.

The front of Rogue's sweater, and her costume beneath it, had been shredded and singed by the missile strike. Nightcrawler had clung tightly on to her, but had been extra-careful not to touch her bare skin with his. He didn't want a repeat of yesterday's experience. He had drifted with her, trying to visualize the inside of the Blackbird, but his brain had been too numbed by the cold to concentrate. He had teleported, at last, the strain of taking another person with him doubled by the desperate conditions, and by the sharp twinge in his side that had reminded him of his injuries. He had exhausted his remaining oxygen in a cry of pain and defiance. And, he remembered now, he had collapsed as soon as he and Rogue had arrived back on the airplane.

"I'm not the one who got blasted out of the sky," he reminded his teammate. "How are you feeling?"

Rogue smiled, weakly. "Bruised and battered, if you want to know the truth. But I'll be OK. I might not be Wolverine, but this old body of mine's no slouch in the healing department."

"Where *is* Logan? How is he? Do you need me to—"

"The half-pint's fine. Holding out well, according to Jean. Ororo's gone to fetch him."

As if on cue, the main hatchway door was pulled open from the outside, and Storm carried a bedraggled Wolverine over the threshold, unconcerned by the fierce wind outside. His face cracked into a wide grin when he saw Rogue. "Good to see you, darling."

"Now that everybody's present and correct," Cyclops called over his shoulder, "we need to give some thought to what we're going to do next."

"I'm afraid I lost the chopper," said Rogue, ruefully.

"Jean, can you try locating Hank telepathically again?"

Phoenix shook her head. "I've been trying, Scott. If he was in that helicopter, then his thoughts have been shielded somehow. By Tessa, I'll bet."

"He was there," growled Wolverine. "I caught a glimpse of him, just before that scum Fitzroy pulled the trigger."

"I've been following the bearing they were on when Rogue last saw them," said Cyclops. "It looks like they were heading towards the Philippine Islands."

Wolverine shook his head. "They changed direction. Probably thought I was too busy drinking in seawater to notice. Roughly a hundred and thirty degrees from where Storm here picked me up."

Cyclops smiled tightly, as he turned the plane around. "Now we're getting somewhere."

"A vehicle like that can't have too long a range," surmised Storm.

"Certainly not enough to cross the Pacific Ocean," said Phoenix. "Either Fitzroy's planning to double back on himself again, or–"

"Or," concluded Wolverine, "the Hellfire Club are holed up on an island out there somewhere." He slapped his right fist into his left palm and muttered, under his breath: "In which case, it's only a matter of time..."

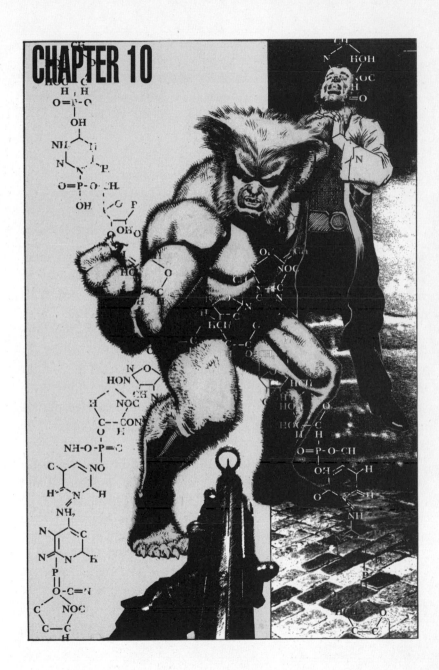

CHAPTER 10

BELOW HIM, the Beast could see a small island. It was covered, for the most part, by a lush, green forest, which gave way to rocky beaches only at the island's edges. He swallowed as he realized that Fitzroy was bringing the helicopter in to land.

He had spent the journey in a state of nervous anticipation. The fact that he was shut into a confined space with two of the X-Men's deadliest enemies hadn't helped. He was worried they might have harmed Rogue and Wolverine, although he kept telling himself that both had survived far worse than an unexpected plunge into the Pacific Ocean. Even so, he couldn't help but wonder if he was doing the right thing.

"Getting nervous are we, old chap?" taunted Fitzroy, casting a sideways glance at his passenger. Hank didn't answer. "Can't blame you if you are. You think Shaw needs your help? What if he doesn't? You're a long way from anyone who can save you."

"Just take us down, Fitzroy," the Beast growled, baring his fangs. "My business is with the organ-grinder, not with his monkey."

"I hope he *does* turn you down," snarled Fitzroy. "Perhaps he'll throw you to me."

He guided the helicopter down to the forest and into a small clearing, which could barely contain it. Its blades were almost close enough to the trees to shred the leaves in their uppermost branches. The landing site, Hank realized, benefited from the greatest possible natural cover. It would be difficult for anyone to find them here.

He looked at Tessa. She didn't return his gaze. She seemed relaxed enough, but she had to be concentrating to maintain her blockade around his mind. She hadn't spoken since his teammates had disappeared beneath the waves. Briefly, he considered attacking her, taking her by surprise, distracting her for just a second. That was all Phoenix would need to locate his thought patterns, to get a rough fix on his location. But then, if his meeting with Shaw went as he expected—and Fitzroy's snide comments aside, he had no reason to believe it wouldn't—then the last thing he would want was for the X-Men to interfere.

And, he thought belatedly, how could he surprise a telepath anyway? Tessa was inside his head, no doubt monitoring his thoughts. She probably knew about his plan, and about his decision not to implement it, already. He resisted the urge to flash her a guilty smile.

They stepped out of the helicopter, Tessa going first. Fitzroy placed a hand on the Beast's shoulder and gave him a helping push out of the cabin, as if he were a captive. Hank didn't rise to the bait. Let him play his power games.

At the edge of the clearing was an entranceway. It was constructed from thin beams of metal, and resembled nothing more than a phone booth put together with Meccano. However, Hank could see it housed the top of a stairway. Tessa made her way towards it, and he followed her, with Fitzroy behind him.

Then, suddenly, he was alerted by crashing sounds in the undergrowth, and Hellfire Club agents in their distinctive blue and red costumes burst into the clearing from all sides.

The Beast tensed and dropped into a crouch, but the agents just brought up their machine-guns to cover the newly arrived trio, and made no further move towards them. Tessa seemed to take the ambush in her stride, but Hank could sense Fitzroy twitching resentfully beside him. For a second, he thought he might actually attack his allies.

From the direction of the entranceway, came the sound of somebody clearing his throat deliberately. Hank turned to find Sebastian Shaw standing at the top of the stairs, flanked by two more uniformed guards.

"Welcome to my island," he said. He smiled, but the smile didn't reach his eyes.

"What the hell do you think you're playing at, Shaw?" snapped Fitzroy.

"You'll have to excuse the reception committee." Shaw's words were polite enough, but the tone of his voice was hard, betraying a hint of anger. "When your perimeter scanning systems inform you that two of your colleagues are bringing one of your sworn enemies to your base of operations... well, you can understand why one has to be careful."

"The X-Man is our prisoner!" contested Fitzroy. "Don't you see? We've managed to capture one of these 'sworn enemies' of yours."

"Actually," Hank spoke up, apologetically, "I would dispute the veracity of that statement."

"Doctor McCoy has volunteered his services for the project, sir," said Tessa.

"Oh?" Shaw looked surprised.

"In fact," Hank corrected her, "I merely intimated that I might be prepared to enter into a temporary alliance with you for the sake of our common purpose. Firstly, of course, I would need to know more about your operations. Secondly, my cooperation would be contingent upon your assurance that Moira MacTaggert is, and will remain, safe and unharmed."

Shaw nodded. "I see no problem with those conditions." He looked sharply at Fitzroy. "What precautions did you take to ensure the X-Men didn't follow you?"

"We shot two of them out of the sky," boasted Fitzroy. Shaw was treating him like a child, and the young mutant clearly resented him for it. "They didn't come back after that!"

"They will," said Shaw, "sooner or later. Tessa, put up the vibro-screen and man the defenses. Doctor McCoy, I won't deny I could use your help. But if I ever have cause to suspect that you plan to betray me..." He left the threat unfinished.

"I have deduced correctly, have I not?" said Hank, evenly. "You brought Moira here to assist you in your quest for a cure for the Legacy Virus?"

"Correct," said Shaw.

"For which you would require her willing participation."

"Unfortunately, Doctor MacTaggert chose not to accept my proposition."

"As she has before. So..." Hank took a deep breath, and tried not to betray his trepidation as he prepared to ask the most important question. The one that had brought him here. The one that mattered. "What made you think you could change her mind now?"

Shaw's smile grew broader as he stepped to one side and, with a sweep of his arm, indicated the entranceway behind him. "Allow me to show you."

Shaw led the way down the stairs, his two personal guards at his shoulder, followed by the Beast, then Tessa and Fitzroy. The face-less agents came behind them, booted feet clanging on metal steps as they filed back into the base. They reached a long hallway from which several corridors branched, along with more stairs leading further downwards. The walls were dull, metallic and gray. Hank suspected that they also gave off photons, as he could see no other light source.

"You should know," said Tessa, leaning close to his ear as if the information were confidential, "that this facility is proofed against psionic intrusion. Your telepathic friend won't be able to find you." Then she turned on her heel and marched smartly away, her duties here discharged.

The agents dispersed around Hank, many of them clattering

down to the next level, some disappearing down the various corridors. Fitzroy, he noted, stood guard at the stairs to the entrance, glowering at him as if daring the X-Man to try to get past him. Hank stood, taking in his surroundings, as Sebastian Shaw and his guards waited patiently.

"This is all very impressive," he remarked. "Your own island headquarters."

"A legacy, you might say. This facility was constructed many millennia ago by an alien race known as the Kree." Hank nodded. He had encountered the Kree before. "They used it as a spaceport and a scientific base during their early explorations of Earth. It was rediscovered by the Fantastic Four, some years ago."

"Ah yes, I recall the case." Hank's brow furrowed as he dredged up old memories of Avengers files. Reed Richards and his family had stumbled upon the abandoned Kree island by accident, and had found themselves drawn into a battle with a mechanical Sentry left behind by the ancient space-faring civilization. It had been the first of many recorded encounters between humankind and the Kree, and it had set the tone for most of those to come. Having only narrowly defeated their foe, the Fantastic Four had had to flee before the Sentry could destroy the island, and the Kree's secrets with it. "Clearly," he said out loud, "that initial encounter was less destructive than Professor Richards believed."

"The island was submerged, and there was extensive damage to this facility."

"And yet here it is now, raised from the seabed, good as new." Hank shot his host a penetrating glare. "And, if I'm not very much mistaken, several thousand miles from its original location. Who do you know, I wonder, who has the power to accomplish that?"

"I have my contacts," said Shaw, darkly. "But that isn't important." He led the way along the hallway and down one of the connecting corridors. Hank fell into step by his side. Shaw's two guards also accompanied them, their blank masks concealing their emotions as always. Hank was pleased to note that they left Fitzroy behind, at least. "The important thing," said Shaw, "is the technology I now possess. Alien technology, Doctor McCoy. Not to mention the records still contained within the core memory of the base's computer."

The Beast's eyes widened. "From a time when the Kree, by all accounts, were conducting genetic modifications willy-nilly upon our forefathers!" He hardly dared to let himself hope. Throughout the galaxy, the Kree were known not only as fierce and proud warriors but also as master geneticists. Even thousands of years ago, they had doubtless understood more about human mutation than Henry McCoy did now.

"It took months for my technicians to reconstruct the corrupted data," said Shaw. "Longer still for it to be deciphered."

"But now, you must have access to information that could revolutionize genetic science!"

Shaw smiled. "I see you are beginning to understand."

He pushed open a set of double doors, and ushered his guest into a large room. It shared the dull gray color scheme of the rest of the base, but the walls were lined with monitors, control banks and displays of various kinds. The bare floor was punctuated by four metal lab benches which were cluttered with discarded notes and medical equipment.

From various parts of the room four white-coated people looked up at the new arrivals. Hank recognized three of them from photographs he had seen at the mansion. Shaw reeled off the names of each in turn, starting with Doctor Scott. The gray-haired black man glowered at Hank and Shaw over the top of a pair of frameless spectacles. Professor Travers, similarly, made no attempt to disguise his hostility towards them. An elderly gentleman, his features were mostly concealed by a bushy, white beard. Perched on a stool, a microscope in front of her, Doctor Takamoto was a young, attractive Japanese woman with shoulder-length dark hair. She looked away quickly, as if afraid to let Hank read her expression.

"And, of course," Shaw concluded, "you already know Doctor Campbell."

"Hank, what are you doing here?" Rory Campbell was a tall, well-built man in his early thirties. A white streak ran through his swept-up brown hair, and beneath his coat he wore a bodysuit, which was also predominantly brown but blue around the shoulders, the colors separated by a slanting red stripe. If he was pleased to see Hank, then he didn't show it. He wore a habitually grim expression, and his green eyes were haunted by the future.

Campbell had once been afforded a glimpse of his own fate. He knew he would end his days as a savage, one-legged, mutant-hunting slave. He had vowed to fight against that destiny, but part of it had come to pass already. He hobbled across the laboratory on a crutch, having lost his left leg some time ago in an accident on Muir Island. He had refused to have a prosthetic limb fitted. Hank guessed he saw the inconvenience as a reminder to himself not to be careless again. And, of course, as a reminder that the future was getting closer.

"Doctor McCoy is considering joining our team," said Shaw.

Campbell tilted his head in mild surprise, but otherwise took the news in his stride. "You'd be a welcome addition," he said. "We've made some good progress here, but I can't deny we could be doing better. It would be useful to have a fresh pair of eyes looking over our work so far. And we have a few specific problems that you might be able to help us with. I was hoping to have Moira join us, but –"

"Doctor MacTaggert was quite stubborn, as I have explained," interrupted Shaw.

"You mean she had bothersome principles," said Hank. "I want to see her before I'll agree to anything. Where is she?"

"In living quarters downstairs," said Shaw, "where she is perfectly comfortable."

Campbell drew Hank to one side. "Before you talk to Moira, why don't you take a look up here for yourself? See what you might be getting yourself into." He punched a few short commands into a keypad, which was set into the nearest wall, and a monitor lit up with a string of numbers and letters. The characters raced across the screen so quickly that it took Hank a second to realize what he was seeing. When he did, his eyebrows shot up in surprise.

"I knew the Kree were experts," he breathed, "but...but they've mapped parts of our genetic structure that we hardly knew existed..." He wished he had his notepad with him. But even if he had, there wouldn't have been time to scribble down more than a tiny fraction of this information. He looked at Campbell. "They even seem to have postulated the eventual emergence of the mutant gene."

"The Kree conducted various studies into possible evolutions of the human race," explained Campbell. "Have you ever heard of the Inhumans?"

"Of course. An offshoot of humanity, created by the Kree thousands of years ago and yet similar in many respects to the species that is only now beginning to evolve naturally."

"This computer is a treasure trove of information," said Campbell. "Not only that, but it can run detailed analyses and accurate projections of staggering complexity, so fast that our only problem is keeping up with it. With somebody like you on board..."

"So, Doctor McCoy," said Shaw, who was waiting by the doors, "I think you've seen enough to agree that I am offering you an unparalleled opportunity to achieve your goal."

"Perhaps," said Hank guardedly, his mind still racing with the possibilities.

"Which is surely what you hoped to find when you first volunteered to come here."

"I can't deny that."

"Then perhaps you would like me to take you to see Doctor MacTaggert now."

"If looks could kill," muttered Hank, as he and Shaw retraced their steps to the entrance hall, the two Hellfire Club agents trailing a short distance behind them. "Campbell aside, your specialists don't appear to think much of you—or of me, by association. The usual mutant phobia? Or have you done something in particular to arouse their ire?"

"My fault, I confess," said Shaw. "They didn't exactly volunteer for this project."

"Oh yes," said Hank, with distaste, "I'm well aware that Moira wasn't your only recent kidnap victim. But it's more than that, isn't it? Why are those people working for you at all?"

"Do you find it so strange that *homo sapiens* would help to combat a disease associated primarily with *homo superior*?" It was a rhetorical question, apparently, as Shaw didn't give Hank time to answer. With a hollow laugh, he continued: "You're right, of course. You know as well as I do that scientists prepared to tackle the Legacy Virus have been thin on the ground, and funding even more so."

"That's beginning to change."

"Only now that that Legacy has spread to their kind!" spat Shaw. "Even so, too little, too late. I approached Scott, Takamoto and Travers with a reasonable offer. Good terms and conditions. They refused me. Even after I had brought them here, they needed...further persuasion."

Hank narrowed his eyes. "What did you do?"

"I gave them a personal stake in our project."

"You infected them with the virus, didn't you?"

Shaw's only answer was a smug smile, but it was enough for Hank to know that his accusation was true. He seized the lapels of the Black King's jacket and lifted him bodily, slamming him back into the metal wall of the corridor and screaming into his face: "You bastard, *you've given them the virus!*" The guards reacted instantly, bringing up their guns and training them upon the X-Man's head. By now, however, the Beast had Shaw pinned to the wall by his neck. He breathed heavily, bringing his anger back under control. His sudden outburst had surprised even him. But he had begun to see a solution to his problems, to the problems of the world. And then Shaw had reminded him of just how far he would have to compromise his ethics to achieve it. He had flaunted

Hank's helplessness, showed him that people were still dying around him, whatever he did.

To make matters worse, his enemy was unruffled. "May I remind you," he said smoothly, "of my mutant ability to absorb kinetic energy."

"It won't do you much good," said the Beast, tightening the hand that he held around Shaw's throat, just a little, "if I apply enough pressure to your larynx to crush it."

"Perhaps not," Shaw conceded, in a husky but perfectly even voice. "However, your assault upon my person has already improved my strength and stamina. I can guarantee that you wouldn't have time to do me serious harm before my agents could fire a considerable number of bullets into your brain."

The Beast glared into Shaw's inscrutable eyes for a long moment, then lowered him back to the floor and stepped away from him. The guards relaxed, and Shaw brushed out the creases in his maroon velvet jacket and picked off a blue hair. "Oh dear," he said, without regret, "am I to take it that I've lowered your opinion of me?"

"I doubt I could think any less of you than I already did!" the Beast growled.

Shaw smiled, as if he had been complimented rather than insulted. "But you're prepared to deal with me, nevertheless; to sell your soul to the devil in exchange for your heart's desire."

"That remains to be seen," said Hank.

But he knew, deep down, that it was true.

Moira MacTaggert didn't know what to expect when she heard footsteps outside her room.

It seemed like only a few minutes since Shaw had left her here. She had expected him to cast her into a dingy prison cell some-where. He had certainly been angry enough when she had refused his offer to join him, although he had tried to hide it behind his usual mask of confidence. But then he had escorted her down here, to these quarters: a small room, to be sure, but carpeted and wall-papered and with a comfortable bed.

She had slept since then, sinking into the soft mattress and allowing exhaustion to overtake her. This time, there had been no dreams.

Now, as sturdy bolts were pulled back on the other side of the door, she scrambled to her feet. She had no idea how long she had slept. There were no windows in this underground complex, and her body clock was shot. Perhaps Shaw felt he had given her long enough to reconsider her decision. Perhaps he was here to put his proposal to her again. Perhaps, this time, he would not take no for an answer.

The door opened, and Moira felt a surge of relief at the sight of her blue-furred friend and colleague, Hank McCoy. Then she realized that he was standing between Sebastian Shaw and two Hellfire Club agents. "Och, Hank!" she blurted out. "Don't tell me they got you too. Don't tell me they thought *you'd* throw in your lot with that madman!"

She expected the Beast to respond with a ready quip. Instead, he turned to Shaw, a dejected look on his face, and asked: "Can you give us a few minutes alone?" To Moira's puzzlement, Shaw nodded and motioned to his guards. They stepped aside, allowing Hank to enter the room. A guard closed the door behind him, but didn't bolt it again.

Moira's visitor greeted her with an embarrassed smile. "What's going on, Hank?" she asked, frowning, already suspecting what he had to tell her but not wanting to believe it. "Are the other X-Men here too?"

He shook his head. "I came here alone, and of my own volition."

"Lucky you!"

He raised an eyebrow. "Shaw led me to believe you hadn't been hurt. If he was being less than truthful—"

She waved aside his concern. "I'm still in one piece. He hasn't treated me too badly, all things considered. But Hank..." Her voice trailed off. She didn't want to say the words. But, as she looked into the Beast's face, she knew they were true, and that there was no escaping them. "Hank—you've agreed to help him, haven't you?"

He nodded, shamefacedly, avoiding her gaze. "I'm about to. I hoped you'd understand."

"Understand? Hank, we're talking about Sebastian Shaw!"

"I'm perfectly aware of that."

"Then perhaps you've forgotten who he is. This is a mutant who builds Sentinels—robots specifically designed to hunt and kill other mutants—and sells them to the government. A man who once allied himself with the X-Men's greatest enemy, Magneto. And how can you just overlook what he did to Jean?"

"I'm not overlooking anything," said Hank, although he flinched visibly at the memories that Moira had stirred up. Moira herself could feel her temper flaring, as she thought about how Shaw and his Inner Circle had unleashed the monster called Dark Phoenix upon the universe. "But if he can help us to achieve something worthwhile—"

"Then you're prepared to give him what he wants!"

"What he wants, Moira, is what we all want: a cure for the Legacy Virus."

She shook her head. "No, Hank, what Shaw wants is power. That's all he's ever wanted, and he doesn't care who he steps on in the process of acquiring it. If he can find a cure, then what do you think he'll do with it? Just hand it over to anyone who needs it?"

"I accept that his motives may not be entirely altruistic, but—"

"But nothing! Shaw as good as told me he'd have control over who'd receive his cure and who wouldn't. And he'd use that power, Hank, you know he would. Sebastian Shaw would decide who gets to live and who dies. Is that what you want?"

"If the alternative," said Hank, in a quiet voice, "is that every-body dies, then wouldn't it be preferable?"

"I don't believe I'm hearing this." Moira was almost lost for words. "After all the times we discussed this...after Campbell walked out on me...I thought you were on my side."

She must have touched a nerve, because Hank looked directly

at her for the first time, his eyes pleading with her. "I *am* on your side, Moira, and I appreciate what you're saying. I disapproved of Campbell's defection as strongly as you did, and for the same reasons—but things have changed. Shaw is on the verge of a breakthrough, whereas our research has floundered. It is no longer germane to ask who will be the first to reach our mutual goal. The question is, can it be reached at all?"

"It can," insisted Moira, "and we'll reach it in our own way. It's just a matter of time."

"But we could have a cure *now*. Think, Moira!" Hank reached out and took her hands in his. His clawed fingers were surprisingly gentle. "We'd be saving lives. We'd be saving *your* life. I can make it a condition of my assisting Shaw that you be among the first group of patients to be treated. Isn't that reason enough, on its own, to do this?"

"No! It's too high a price to pay. We'd just be exchanging one problem for another."

"A problem that seems insolvable for one that we can handle. It's a fair exchange."

"Oh, and you're so sure you can 'handle' Shaw?"

"We've beaten him before. If he gets his hands on a cure and misuses it, then we'll fight him again. We can take the cure from him."

"So you say now. But what if you can't?"

"Then at the very least I'll have learned something. I'll have had an opportunity to work with Kree technology, to study their records. And, just as importantly, we'll know that a cure *is* possible, that our problem isn't insolvable after all. Even without access to the machinery in this base we'll have taken an important step closer to finding an answer for ourselves."

"You'll just have given Sebastian Shaw a head start."

"Yes."

"And what do you think he'll do with that head start, Hank? Imagine an army of mutants, all doing his bidding because he's the only person who can keep them alive. And I'm not just talking about the people who are suffering from the Legacy Virus already.

How many more might he infect, if he knows it will give him complete control over them?"

"Or have you considered that he might just market the cure?" asked Hank. "That alone could earn him billions of dollars, and it would be perfectly legal."

"It's not enough for a man like him!"

"What I'm saying, Moira, is that this is only speculation. You're allying yourself with the Luddites; arguing that scientific advances shouldn't be made for fear that somebody, some day, might abuse them."

"That's not fair, Hank, and you know it!"

"I'm merely proposing that we deal with the immediate problem."

"And to hell with the consequences?"

"No. But we'll cross the next bridge if and when we come to it."

"There are no 'ifs' about it. For your information, Shaw has already kidnapped and infected three people. He's forcing them to work for him."

Hank bowed his head. "I know—and, granted, it does provide some cause for concern." He looked up again, and Moira could see that he had made up his mind. "But it's also one of the reasons I must do this. Those people upstairs are dying, and they have a cure for their ailment almost within their reach. How can I refuse to help them? How can I let them down, as I let William Montgomery—and too many before him—down?"

Moira breathed in deeply, and released her frustration in a long, heartfelt sigh. She sat down on the bed, and cradled her head in her hands. It was beginning to ache, so she closed her eyes and massaged her temples with her fingers.

After a few seconds, she heard the Beast padding across the room to join her, and felt the depression of the mattress as he seated himself by her side.

"I had hoped you would help me," he said, softly.

She shook her head, wearily. "I'm sorry. I can't."

"I share your reservations, but I truly believe this is the lesser of two evils."

"I know you do. But I can't agree."

"Will you wish me luck, at least?"

"I hope things turn out the way you want them to."

Hank smiled weakly, and they looked at each other with sad eyes. Then he stood again, walked over to the door and rapped sharply on it. Shaw came into the room, and glanced over at Moira. Hank responded with a mournful shake of his head.

They left without another word—and this time Moira heard the bolts sliding, making her a prisoner again. She lay back on the bed, a hundred thoughts chasing each other in her weary mind. Hank had seemed so sincere, so determined, and she respected his judgement. She had never imagined they could argue about something like this. What if she had been wrong? She thought she had taken a moral stand, acted on her principles. But what if she had just let her famous stubborn streak blind her? What if Hank had made the only practical choice?

Thanks to him, at least Shaw would leave her alone now, and—who knew?—his plans might come to fruition after all. The world would be rid of the scourge of the Legacy Virus and Moira wouldn't be dying any more and the X-Men would take the cure out of Shaw's hands and all she had to do was wait and everything would soon be all right.

Hope had long been a stranger to Moira MacTaggert, and she felt almost guilty about entertaining it now. But it was an intoxicating emotion, and she could quite see how it had entranced her erstwhile lab partner, creeping up on him when he had thought it gone.

The lure of a happy ending, no matter how improbable, was strong. But the more she thought about such an ending, the more unlikely it seemed.

Perhaps that made her a pessimist. But Moira couldn't bring herself to believe that anything but ill could come of Hank McCoy's decision today.

Tessa seated herself in her small, circular cubicle, and flexed her fingers as she prepared to go to work. She was surrounded by freestanding terminals, which gave her access to the colossal computer that serviced the alien base. The inscriptions on their keypads and display units were in the Kree language, but this didn't bother her. Tessa's mind had often been compared to a computer itself. She had deduced the purpose of every interface, learned how to operate each one and committed the information to her precise memory in hours. Sebastian Shaw had had experts analyze the computer for months, and Tessa herself had helped his scientists to access its basic functions—but nobody on this world knew it as well as she did.

She ran a series of basic checks on the island's defense systems, almost without having to think about it. Idly, she reflected on the Beast's arrival and wondered what effect it would have upon her employer's plans. Sebastian would have to let him talk to Moira MacTaggert, of course. The Scots woman would try to dissuade him from his proposed course of action. She had a chance of succeeding. But then Tessa had seen inside Hank McCoy's mind, and—despite his doubts—it was her considered opinion that he would not be swayed.

Tessa calculated that Sebastian might achieve his goals this time. If he did, it would be as much by luck as by judgement. As always, he had taken too many risks, and made some very bad decisions. She had cautioned him against involving Doctor Mac-Taggert in his schemes, predicting that she wouldn't cooperate with him. He had ignored her counsel.

It wasn't that he didn't listen to Tessa. He employed her as his personal assistant precisely because he admired her logic and valued her advice. But there was a definite limit to which he would let anybody change his mind once it had been made up. Tessa had realized this quickly, and had learned to stay in her place, to nudge her employer gently in the right direction without ever pushing him too hard.

She had long since given up trying to advise Sebastian about his alliances. It was almost as if he deliberately surrounded himself with people he couldn't trust, as if it were a game to him. And then he would test them. He had two personalities: he could be charismatic—even seductive—one minute, a coldhearted monomaniac the next. He drew people to him, and then challenged them to betray him. Tessa just did her job, kept out of the way of such monsters as Selene and Madelyne Pryor, and helped to pick up the pieces when Sebastian's power games inevitably exploded in his face.

Right now, she had an important role to play, and she intended to do her duty in the most efficient manner possible. Like Sebastian, Tessa had no doubt that the X-Men would locate this facility in time. She had to keep them from interfering with the project. With the technology at her disposal, she was confident she could do so.

She activated the vibro-screen that surrounded the island: its first line of defense. Then, with a practiced sweep of her hand, she brought a series of monitors to life in the curved wall around her. Each screen showed a different part of the forest above, each picture shot at an upward angle from ground level.

The computer reported that all other systems were active and standing by, and Tessa sat back in her seat and steepled her fingers. She was ready.

As if on cue, a red light began to wink on one of the alien terminals. The proximity alarm. This was how Sebastian had known about her own arrival, along with Fitzroy and the Beast. Tessa checked the readouts and smiled to herself, anticipating the challenge. An airplane was approaching the island, and the computer detected the energy signatures of seven mutants on board, none of whom were known to it. It could only mean one thing.

The X-Men were here.

CHAPTER 11

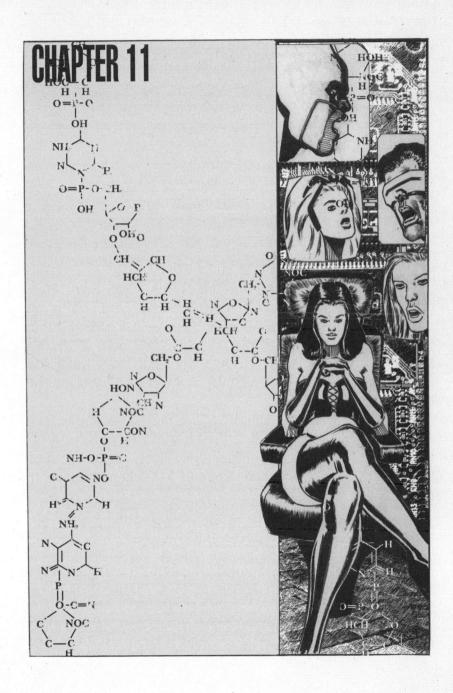

SOMETHING'S GOTTEN hold of the Blackbird!"

Cyclops had known something was wrong, even before Rogue's urgent cry had confirmed it. He had been looking out of a window, down at the small, uncharted, wooded island beneath them. Rogue had been guiding the plane in closer, as per his instructions. Cyclops had strained to make out as many features as he could, searching in particular for any signs of habitation. He hadn't found any.

At first, the gentle vibrations had been indistinguishable from normal air turbulence. But then, they had intensified a hundredfold. The X-Men had braced themselves as they were tossed from side to side, and the Blackbird's engines had begun to scream in protest.

Heedless of his own safety, Cyclops pulled off his seatbelt and jumped to his feet. The cabin bucked beneath him as he struggled to make his way forwards. It felt as if a giant fist had taken hold of the plane and was shaking it at will. Finally, he reached the pilot's seat and supported himself against its back. "What's happening, Rogue?" he asked tersely.

"We've flown into some sort of interference." Rogue didn't turn around. Her eyes were fixed on the dials before her, her knuckles white on the joystick and her expression grim. "I can't pull us out of it. It's taking all I've got to keep this crate in the air!"

"We're losing altitude and airspeed," Phoenix confirmed from beside her. Cyclops could see that for himself. The artificial horizon indicator was gyrating wildly, unable to keep up with the plane's repeated changes in altitude.

"This isn't a natural phenomenon," Storm informed them from behind. "I can summon winds to help keep us level, but I cannot calm the vibrations themselves."

"I'm gonna have to bring us down before we tear ourselves apart," said Rogue through gritted teeth. "Sorry, Cyke, looks like we're about to lose another 'Bird."

"That's the least of my worries right now, Rogue."

"I suggest y'all bail out," said Rogue. "Leave me to it. I might be able to keep the plane in one piece, but I can't guarantee a soft landing!"

"No," Nightcrawler spoke up. "I'll take the controls. If the worst comes to the worst, I can 'port myself out of here before we hit the ground."

"Agreed," said Cyclops. "Besides, we need all the fliers we can get to help us evacuate. Ororo, I want you to concentrate on keeping this plane as steady as you can. Jean, take the controls until Kurt gets into the pilot's seat. Rogue, take Wolverine and get out of here!"

The X-Men moved into action, obeying their leader's commands. Even if they disagreed with him, they were trained well enough to know that there was no time to argue. As Cyclops stepped aside to allow first Rogue and then Nightcrawler to pass him, the Blackbird gave a particularly violent jolt, and he tumbled against the hull. He rubbed his bruised shoulder ruefully, and clung to a chair for dear life as Rogue wrenched open the hatchway and a fierce gale gusted through the cabin. Wolverine wrapped his arms around her shoulders, and his legs around her hips, and she carried him out into the sky. Storm followed them, gliding gracefully on the wind.

"Jean!" yelled Cyclops, over the roaring sound of evacuating air, the increasingly sick whining of the engines and the screeching of the plane's tormented chassis.

"I'm ready!" she yelled back, as Nightcrawler took the controls from her.

Cyclops trusted her, enough to place his life in her hands. He made his way unsteadily to the hatch, and let the wind take him. His stomach lurched as he dropped away from the Blackbird, and saw the ground—far nearer than he had expected—rushing up towards him. He spread his arms and legs wide, and free-fell towards it, almost grateful for his visor because it kept the wind from stinging his eyes.

He could almost have reached out and touched the tops of the trees when, finally, he felt his rate of descent slowing. He smiled to himself, and angled his body so that he dropped into the forest feet first. He landed in the undergrowth, with no more force than if he had just stepped off the bottom rung of a ladder. He looked up in time to see Phoenix and Iceman gliding to a similarly gentle halt beside him. With Rogue carrying the heaviest X-Man, Jean's telekinesis had been more than up to the task of lowering the others.

"I think it's safe to say that we've found the right island," said Phoenix.

"Unless there's more than one super-villain base in these parts," said Iceman, dryly. "I didn't see any buildings as we came down, though."

"An underground installation, most likely," said Cyclops. "Can you sense Hank or Moira yet. Jean?"

"Not a trace. I've swept the island telepathically, but the only people I can detect are our own. If the Hellfire Club are under our feet, then they must have very good psi-bafflers."

The trio looked up in unison as the Blackbird screamed over their heads, trailing a plume of smoke. Cyclops resisted the urge to duck. The plane was low now, almost scraping the trees. He tried not to worry about Nightcrawler. He knew how to look after himself. And the X-Men were more than used to being shot out of the sky. It was beginning to seem like a monthly occurrence.

"I doubt we've seen the last of this island's defenses yet," he considered. "It's dangerous for us to be separated."

"I agree," said Phoenix. "We should get back to the others as quickly as possible."

"Gee," mugged Iceman, shielding his eyes as he looked up into the sky at the Blackbird's lingering smoke trail. "Do you think we'll be able to find them?"

Cyclops chose not to answer that. He set off through the forest at a run, and his teammates fell into step beside him.

Rogue hovered in midair, her fingers crossed as she watched the Blackbird diving towards the trees, Storm flying beside it. She was aware of Wolverine's breath, warm against her ear. "The imp's never gonna make it!" his rough voice growled in her ear. "He'd better have the sense to get out of there while he can."

The trees were clawing at the plane's hull now, gouging lines in the paint-work. One of the engines was on fire. With Storm's help, Nightcrawler had succeeded in lifting the nose so that the craft was almost level. Without a clear spot to land in, though, he was still in trouble. He had waited until the last possible minute before lowering the landing wheels, but Rogue could see that they were already taking a beating.

The Blackbird ran out of momentum at last, and belly-flopped into the forest, crashing through a nest of branches and sending up a cloud of smoke and dust, which obscured Rogue's view of the landing site for a full minute. She landed as near to it as she dared, and Wolverine immediately leapt to the ground and scuttled forwards.

The Blackbird lay lopsidedly on its broken undercarriage, at the end of a surprisingly short set of skid marks, in a clearing it had made for itself among the trees. It would need some work to get it into the air again—but, considering what it had just been through, it was a miracle that it wasn't a write-off. Storm had summoned a localized rain shower to extinguish the flames that still burnt in the engine housing, and to put out the small, scattered fires that had started in the wake of the plane's tumultuous landing. Steam rose from the battered metal as cold water pelted down upon it.

Anxiously, Rogue looked for the erstwhile pilot, but could see no sign of him. In front of her, Wolverine crouched and sniffed the air, but she doubted if he could pick up anything useful over the acrid smell of burning.

Someone was knocking on the inside of the Blackbird's dented hatch. Before she could react, the door flew open, to hang limply from one hinge. Framed in the aperture, Nightcrawler looked unsteady on his feet, and he held his shoulder as if wounded. Rogue's heart leapt in horror at the realization that he had stayed in the plane. But he sprang into the air, somersaulted to the ground and took an elaborate bow. "Please, please, no applause—just throw flowers!"

"You almost got yourself killed!" growled Wolverine, but he couldn't mask the affection and relief in his voice.

"Hey, where's the fun in fighting to protect a world that hates and fears you if you can't make a stupidly heroic gesture once in a while? And, whatever our fearless leader might say, I doubt if the X-Men's budget can stretch to another new Blackbird just yet."

He took a step towards them, and his legs buckled beneath him as his eyelids closed and his head lolled back on his shoulders. Wolverine must have seen it coming: he moved with lightning speed and was by his teammate's side in time to catch him.

"Is he all right?" asked Rogue.

"He'll live. He's just taken one too many knocks lately." Rogue was uncomfortably aware that she was largely responsible for that. If Kurt was badly injured, she would never be able to forgive herself.

Storm joined them, having dissipated her rain clouds. "Have you noticed the flowers around here?" she asked. "I don't believe I've ever seen anything quite like them."

She indicated the small flowers that grew between the roots of one of the nearby trees. Their star-shaped petals were a startling lime green in color, and they sprouted in cup formations around violet buds. To Rogue's eyes, the clashing colors made the flowers look quite ugly. She had never seen their type before, but then she didn't share Storm's interest in botany. Looking around, she saw more of the same flowers, growing in isolated clusters.

"Don't recognize the scent," said Wolverine, "but they aren't artificial."

"We have a mystery, then."

"Which I suggest we investigate later," said Rogue. "Somehow, I think we might have lost the element of surprise when we brought this here plane down."

"She's right," said Wolverine. "We need to find the others."

"She's right. We need to find the others."

"Too late," said Tessa to herself, with a confident smile.

Wolverine's grim expression was framed on one of the screens in front of her. Elsewhere on the single wall of the circular room, she could see worm's eye view images of the other six intruders. The sight of an unconscious Nightcrawler was especially gratifying to her. The vibro-screen had surpassed expectations. It had felled one of the X-Men and split them into two groups. Tessa intended to take full advantage of that latter fact.

Cyclops, Phoenix and Iceman were jogging through the forest towards their colleagues. They would reach them within minutes—unless somebody stopped them.

Wolverine had been right about the green flowers. They weren't artificial—not entirely—but he hadn't imagined that they might be alien in origin. The Kree were specialists in the fields of both mechanics and genetics. The flora of this island had been enhanced by a combination of DNA modification and cybernetic implants. The fact that it could act as a network of ground-level spy cameras was the least of its uses.

Tessa entered a series of commands into the Kree computer, her fingers moving quickly and confidently across the alien controls.

She smiled at the knowledge that somewhere above her head—but below her enemies' feet—mechanical devices were now releasing a controlled combination of pheromones, which in turn would awaken a biological imperative in the local plant-life.

An imperative to attack.

At first, Cyclops thought he had merely stumbled in the under-growth. But then something strong and slender wound itself around his left ankle, and he realized that the undergrowth itself was trying to trip him. "Jean, Bobby, face front!" he rapped. "We've got a situation."

"So I see," said Phoenix.

It was easy enough for Cyclops to tear his foot free—but, wher-ever else he placed it, he could see the ground churning, as roots and tendrils crept towards their target.

"Not another living island," moaned Iceman. "Please, not another living island!"

And then the trees themselves reached out, their branches like arms, and Cyclops barely had time to shout a warning before he was entangled. Thorns pricked at him, and snagged on his insu-lated uniform. He struggled, and felt the satisfying snap of a dozen twigs. But for every one that broke, more came grasping for him, scratching at the exposed skin of his face. He operated his visor, and branches crackled and withered in the destructive path of his eye-beam. In between blasts, he glanced over at his teammates. Phoenix was using her telekinesis. He could see it was an effort for her to locate and take hold of so many targets at once, but she was succeeding in pushing the branches away from her. Iceman too was keeping them at bay. He had surrounded himself with a field of intense cold, which rendered the living wood brittle and allowed him to snap anything that ventured too close to him.

In fact, it was Cyclops himself who was the least equipped of the three to deal with this threat. Effective as his optic blasts were, he could only shoot at what he could see. And, almost as if the vegetation could sense this, it launched a concerted attack upon him from behind. Before Cyclops could turn, his arms were bound to his side, and a creeper had wrapped itself around his throat and was squeezing tight. He gasped for breath as he clawed at it. By the time he had ripped it loose, more tendrils had seized his feet and pulled them from beneath him. He toppled sideways, landing awkwardly and still breathing heavily. He tried to stand, but he was already held fast. He found himself staring into the violet center of a flower with lime green petals. And, suddenly, the petals opened outwards and the flower puffed a sweet-smelling gas right into his face.

He was caught by surprise, unable to stop himself from breathing in until it was too late. He opened his visor again and pulverized the flower, but the smell of the gas was already overpowering, and he could feel himself beginning to black out. He could sense Jean's concern through their permanent telepathic link, but there was nothing she could do. She was weakening too. And Cyclops could feel himself being pulled into the soft earth, and he almost welcomed its embrace as he sank into a dreamless sleep.

Wolverine cut a swathe through the living forest like an angry whirlwind, running too fast for the trees and shrubs to fully react to his presence before he had passed, lashing out with his claws at any branch or creeper that was still able to get close to him. The vegetation around the Blackbird's landing site had been too damaged to pose a threat. But a telepathic distress cry from Phoenix had alerted him to the perils elsewhere.

He hadn't stopped to think. She was nearby, and she was in trouble.

If Wolverine was at all disappointed to find that Phoenix had summoned him on her husband's behalf, rather than her own, he didn't show it. He didn't let himself think it. He took in the situation at a glance. Cyclops had already sunk halfway into the ground. He was asleep, and Wolverine's keen sense of smell told him why. The green-and-red flowers were pumping an anaesthetic gas into the atmosphere. It had affected Phoenix and Iceman too:

they were groggy, but at least they were still standing, and still fighting. And Storm was already on the scene, having flown ahead. She had summoned a fresh breeze that was dispersing the gas before it could do more harm.

Wolverine leapt towards Cyclops, but a tangle of vines reared up before him, and he lost precious seconds as he hacked his way through it. By the time he reached the spot where the X-Men's leader had been, only his yellow-gloved hand was still visible, protruding forlornly from the ground. And, even as Wolverine reached for it, it sank beneath the surface.

He dug with his claws, carefully at first but more frantically as he realized that Cyclops was already deeply buried. Phoenix lent him a telekinetic assist, having extricated herself from her own predicament. But the more dirt they shifted aside, the more poured in to replace it, and their hole remained stubbornly shallow. Wolverine took a step back, recognizing the hopelessness of the situation—and, within seconds, the hole had been filled. There was no way of telling that it had ever existed.

A heavy silence fell. Storm landed quietly beside her teammates, and the X-Men stared at the ground and considered their loss. The plants were no longer a threat, although some broken branches and shredded vines still thrashed helplessly as if in death-throes.

"I can't feel Scott in my mind any more," said Phoenix, in a distant, hollow voice.

"Doesn't mean a thing," said Wolverine. "In case you ain't worked it out yet, whatever's down there is shielded from your telepathy."

"You're right," said Phoenix, with a determined nod.

"We assume that Cyclops is unharmed until we see evidence to the contrary," said Storm. As the X-Men's deputy leader, it was up to her to take command now.

"Fair enough," said Wolverine, "but I think there's more bad news on the way."

The others looked up, only now seeing what Wolverine had

scented seconds earlier. Rogue had stayed behind with the Black-bird, to look after the unconscious Nightcrawler. She flew towards them now, and the elf was not with her.

"The earth just swallowed him up," she explained, apologeti-cally. "I tried to keep hold of him, but it was too strong. If I hadn't let go, he would have been torn down the middle."

"We're getting creamed," grumbled Wolverine. "Two people down, and we ain't even seen the enemy yet."

"Then it is past time we took this fight to them," announced Storm. "Clearly, it is too dangerous to travel through the forest on foot. We will take to the air, and search for sites where their heli-copter could have landed."

From below, Tessa was still watching.

The X-Men had destroyed or disabled several of the flower cameras, but there were many more. The computer told her that Cyclops and Nightcrawler had been brought to the base. She had transmitted an order to a team of Hellfire Club agents, to collect the anaesthetized heroes from their arrival bays and to take them to the holding cells until she was ready to deal with them. She concentrated on tracking the flight path of the remaining five, allowing herself a smile at the thought of what lay in store for them.

The Kree's security systems had been effective so far. But their greatest defense—their most powerful weapon—had yet to be employed.

When the Kree had abandoned this island base in the distant past, they had left a custom-built guardian behind: a mechanical life form, fitted with the strongest armor and the most devastating weaponry that their advanced civilization had developed. It had gone now—but the base still housed its repair facilities, and its schematics were still held in the computer's databanks. Sebastian Shaw had hired some of the world's foremost robotics experts. They hadn't been able to duplicate the life form exactly—some of the materials hadn't been available, and they hadn't entirely grasped the complexities of its artificial brain; their version was less independent, more robotic—but they had come up with something almost as formidable.

The X-Men were approaching the entrance to the base.

It was time, decided Tessa, to bring the Sentry into play.

"This must be the place," said Phoenix. They were standing in a tiny clearing, towards the forest's edge. She could tell that it was manmade, quite recently. The stumps of felled trees were still new. The ground was strewn with rocks, but a space had been cleared. A makeshift landing pad, she reasoned. The helicopter itself had probably been taken underground by some means. Like Kurt and her husband.

"It is," said Wolverine. "It's thick with the stench of Hellfire Club goon. I've got McCoy's scent too. A few hours old." He crouched down and snuffled his way across the clearing, like a sniffer dog. Phoenix wasn't surprised when the trail led him to the area's most notable landmark: a freestanding spire of rock, about four feet tall, surrounded by smaller stones at its base. "It ends here," said Wolverine. "Looks like we've got our way in."

He sniffed at the spire, and then—seemingly satisfied that there was no danger—took hold of it and pulled. And pushed. And twisted. Nothing happened.

"I guess they've locked the secret door behind them," said Iceman.

"I'll take a look," offered Storm. Wolverine stepped back, deferring to her experience. As a poor child living on the streets of Cairo, before her mutant gene had manifested itself, Ororo Munroe had been forced to steal to survive. Amongst the skills she had had to learn during that time was an expertise in defeating all kinds of locks.

It took Storm mere seconds to uncover a small hatch set into the spire. She pried it open to reveal a recess filled with circuitry and wiring. "It is activated by an ultrasonic signal," she reported. "However, I believe I can disengage it." She reached for the set of picks that she kept in her belt, and lowered one carefully towards the electronic lock.

The other X-Men withdrew, so as not to distract her from her delicate task. Phoenix cast an eye around the clearing, and reassured herself that no further threat was about to make itself evident. She had every confidence in Storm's abilities.

But then something unexpected happened.

Black bolts of electricity exploded from the spire. Storm cried out in surprise and pain, her body arcing backwards as it was flung away. More bolts flew out, apparently at random. Phoenix leapt for cover behind a tree, and a bolt just missed her. It crackled into the ground, and left behind a sizzling pool of mud.

Rogue was hit. She winced and fell to her knees, but her tough skin spared her serious harm. Iceman wasn't so lucky. With its shell of ice, his body was a natural conductor. He screamed as he was hurled back against a tree. He slid to the ground, but Phoenix was relieved to see that he was still conscious, albeit shaken.

The stones at the base of the spire were moving. It took Phoenix a moment to realize that something was pushing them up from below. As the metal-framed structure revealed itself, she saw that it was an entranceway. She could see steps leading down behind it.

And something was coming up those steps. Something big.

Phoenix took stock of the situation. Storm was down; she had taken the brunt of the electrical attack. Iceman needed time to recover. Rogue was back on her feet. And Wolverine was already rushing headlong to meet the enemy.

It was humanoid, mechanical, and about fifteen feet tall. It had to bend almost double to get through the entranceway, and that was when Wolverine hit it. His senses must have confirmed that it wasn't a living being, for he sliced savagely at its chest with his claws. Outside of one of his berserker rages—and he had those more or less under control these days—he wouldn't normally have attacked an unknown foe with such ferocity. A human being would certainly have been killed. But this adversary was barely scratched.

Out in the open now, it drew itself up to its full height. It was a bulky, imposing figure. Its armor was tinted red around its head and torso, light blue around its limbs. Twin nodules protruded from each side of its head, resembling malformed ears, and a crude approximation of human features had been carved out of the blue metal of its face. The robot's mouth was set into a thin, angry line, and its eyes were covered with black plates, which gave the ludicrous impression that it was wearing sunglasses. Nevertheless, combined with its unchanging expression, they served to emphasize its dispassionate, uncaring nature. Phoenix shuddered involuntarily. She hated robots. You couldn't read their body language, couldn't predict them, couldn't reason with them. It was worse for her: with most people, even if she wasn't actively reading their minds, she received a background buzz of psychic chatter, some confirmation that they were alive and thinking. With a robot, she felt nothing. Just a cold, empty void. And against a robotic adversary, her telepathic abilities were useless.

She remembered where she had seen this particular model before. She was well aware of the Kree, of course—not least because of the X-Men's connections to their sworn enemies, the Shi'ar. And Jean had always lived by the axiom that it paid to be prepared. She had learned all she could about the Kree's incursions into the affairs of Earth. If certain government officials only knew how willing some Avengers were to open their restricted files to a band of mutant outlaws, they would have had conniptions.

It's a Kree Sentry, she telesent to the others. *It has built-in weaponry. It's fast and it's strong, and it's pretty near invulnerable.*

'*Pretty near*,' Wolverine sent back, *that's what I like to hear, Red!*

He attacked the Sentry again, aiming for its arms and legs this time. They must have had less protection than the chest, as his claws left silver scratches. Still, it was hardly significant damage. And the Sentry was preparing to fight back. It raised its huge arms, bunched its fists and brought them down together. Wolverine leapt out of the path of a blow that made the earth shake, blasted dust into the air and almost knocked Phoenix over. She held onto a tree to steady herself, and struck back. Her enemy might have had no mind for her to attack, but she still had her telekinesis. She tried to reach inside its casing, to find wires and components to pull apart. A gentle force repulsed her, and she felt as if she were trying to run through a mattress. The casing was shielded from mental attacks.

Rogue took to the air and swooped past the Sentry, delivering a powerful punch to its face. Knowing how strong she was, Phoenix was dismayed to see that the automaton was unfazed. Indeed, it reacted quickly enough to take a vicious swipe at its flying opponent, almost hitting her. With her mind, Phoenix lifted the heaviest rock she could find, and hurled it at the Sentry's head. It crumbled into fragments, but this too had no visible effect.

Nevertheless, Wolverine took advantage of the twin distractions. He ducked and dived between the Sentry's legs, never staying in the same place for more than a fraction of a second, getting blows in when and where he could. Phoenix held her breath as the Sentry lifted a giant foot and drove it down, and Wolverine only just rolled out of its way. For an instant, he was down and helpless, but Rogue saw the situation and flew right at the Sentry's hooded eyes, making herself a more enticing target. "What's wrong, sugar?" she taunted, as she struck another resounding blow. "Can't find someone your own size to pick on?" The Sentry didn't respond, even though Phoenix was sure that it should have had a voice.

It swung at Rogue again, but Phoenix helped her out with a concentrated barrage of small rocks. She aimed for the plates over the robot's eyes, hoping at best to knock out its optical sensors and at least to obstruct its vision temporarily. Emboldened by this, Rogue turned and launched herself on another attack run. But, as if it could sense her rather than just see her, the Sentry struck out with its fist and knocked her right out of the air. Rogue plummeted into the surrounding trees, and Phoenix couldn't see where she had landed although she could sense from her thoughts that she was more stunned than hurt.

There was a method, she realized, to Wolverine's apparently random strikes. He was aiming the majority of his blows at the same spot, at the top of the Sentry's right leg. And it was working. He was beginning to cut into the metal.

Iceman was on his feet, although he still looked unsteady. He brought his hands together to point at the Sentry, and unleashed a stream of ice that coalesced into a solid lump around its head. It would have been an effective strategy against a human target. But the Sentry didn't need to breathe, and the ice didn't bother it at all. It focussed its attention upon Wolverine, and its chest-plate opened outwards to reveal the huge, round muzzle of what could only have been a weapon. Wolverine hadn't seen it—it was some way above his head—but Phoenix's telepathic warning alerted him in time. With no more than a quick glance upwards, he ducked and sprang aside as the muzzle pivoted down towards him. But it had a wider field than he had anticipated. The air itself seemed to explode, and Wolverine was caught by the edge of the ferocious blast and knocked sideways. Only then did the Sentry reach up with both hands and, with an almost casual squeeze, shatter the ice in which its head was encased.

In the meantime, Iceman had aimed a jet of snow into the muzzle of its weapon, effectively blocking it. He poured layer after layer of ice on top of it, before the Sentry had time to close its chest-plate. Then he gave a startled cry as the robot thundered towards him, with a speed that belied its size. He tried to jump out of its way, but he must still have been dazed from the black electricity, and he wasn't fast enough. The Sentry floored him with a single swipe from its great fist, and Phoenix knew he was out for the count.

It turned towards her, then: the only X-Man left standing. She ran first one way and then the other, but it bore down upon her unerringly.

Then Rogue shot out of the trees, like a bullet from a gun, and hit the Sentry from behind just as Wolverine charged it from the side. Both heroes had obviously gotten their second winds. They grappled with the robot, long hours of training allowing them to coordinate their attacks without having to exchange words. Phoenix felt a thrill of elation as they threw it off-balance and it toppled backwards, falling with an almighty thud that made the ground tremble again and dislodged leaves from the branches above her head.

But the danger wasn't over yet. The Sentry activated its weapon again. A deep groan emanated from its inner workings, and Phoenix allowed herself to hope that Iceman's blockage would do its job; that the weapon would backfire.

Instead, icy shards erupted from the Sentry's chest. They couldn't penetrate Rogue's hide, but they cut thin lines across the exposed parts of Wolverine's face and arms. It was nothing his mutant healing factor couldn't handle, but he was momentarily beaten back. Rogue aimed blow after blow at the Sentry's head, but it shrugged off the onslaught. It was already climbing back to its feet, and its right hand shot out, enormous fingers circling Rogue's midriff. She struggled to break free, but to no avail. The Sentry squeezed her, tighter and tighter, until Phoenix felt her mind surrendering at last.

By this time, the automaton was fully upright again, and Wolverine had renewed his assault, aiming for the same spot as before, on its right leg. His claws struck blue sparks from the metal, and finally penetrated the casing: just a small hole, but it was enough. It was the opportunity that Phoenix had been waiting for: a gap in the psi-resistant armor.

She entered the gap with her mind, and sent a tendril of psychic force snaking up the Sentry's leg and into its abdomen. She pressed on upwards, feeling her way around its inner workings, but its brain-box was a long way up, and the further she ventured inside the shielded casing, the more extreme was the effort required.

In the meantime, with a casual flick of its wrist, the Sentry had tossed the unconscious Rogue aside. Unaware of Phoenix's actions, it had logically shifted the whole of its attention to Wolverine, its most persistent foe. This time, he was ready when it used its chest weapon—he somersaulted out of its way, but he was back before the echoes of the blast had died down—but even he couldn't stay out of the reach of those powerful fists for much longer.

Phoenix had reached the Sentry's chest cavity. She might have been able to deactivate its weapon, but that would have alerted it to her telekinetic presence. It was best, she thought, to trust Wolverine to keep it occupied, for just a minute more. She struck out for the throat, but her head was beginning to ache now. Sweat dripped into her eyes, and she sagged to her knees and pressed her hands to her temples, trying to block out the pain even though it was inside her. If her concentration wavered now, all would be lost.

If she could just...push...a little bit...further...

But then, the moment that Phoenix had been dreading arrived at last. The Sentry caught Wolverine a glancing blow, and he fell. He lay, stunned, on his back, still conscious but in no position to defend himself. The Sentry stood astride him, and the muzzle of its weapon pivoted downwards again. Phoenix was sure he couldn't survive a blast from that range.

She had to act now.

She gritted her teeth, and drove the psychic tendril up into the Sentry's brain, despite the shrieking protestations of her own. Blinded, gasping for air, she fumbled for something, anything, to pull apart, to twist, to rend, to damage in any way she could. Something gave, but she didn't know what. She felt as if she were passing jolt after jolt of electrical current through her brain. She let go, screaming, and sprawled face-first into the mud, no longer able to control her muscles, to even raise her head.

She passed out, not knowing if she had done any good.

At first, Tessa didn't know what was happening. The Sentry put its hands to its head, in an almost human gesture of anguish. Then, with no more warning than that, it collapsed. Even Wolverine was hard-pressed to get out of its way before he was crushed beneath its weight.

The X-Men had destroyed the Hellfire Club's greatest weapon, and Tessa wasn't even sure how they had done it. She felt a pang of consternation, but she reassured herself that there was no cause for alarm. The robot had defeated Storm, Iceman and Rogue—and Phoenix, she now saw, was also down. That left just one. And, of course, she had taken precautions against even such an unlikely event as this. Tessa never left anything to chance.

She watched on her monitors as six Hellfire Club agents rushed out of the base. They dropped to their knees, brought their machine guns up to their shoulders and strafed the clearing at chest height. Wolverine, naturally, was already back on his feet, avoiding the bullets with superhuman speed and dexterity, and taking the fight to his attackers. The first agent fell, with triple claw marks across his chest. Tessa wasn't concerned. The outcome of the battle was a foregone conclusion. She had staged it only to provide a short delay.

She abandoned her post at the Kree computer and walked confidently, unhurriedly, down the stark, gray corridors that led to the base's main entranceway. By the time she had climbed the steps to the surface, her agents were all down—she had expected no less—and Wolverine was crouched by Phoenix's side, trying to coax her awake. His costume was torn, and rivulets of blood stained his face from wounds that had already healed. He smelt Tessa coming and looked up at her with a scowl on his face and murder in his eyes.

She reached into his mind as he came at her, claws extended. He had been trained well. His psychic blocks were better than any she had ever encountered in a non-telepath. But he was tired and hurt, and it was a simple matter for Tessa to turn his brain off.

She allowed herself a smile of quiet satisfaction as the last X-Man fell at her feet.

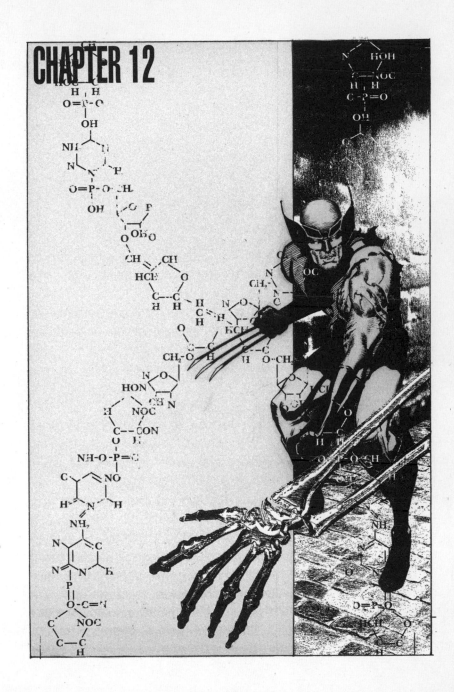

CHAPTER 12

CYCLOPS WOKE, his limbs feeling heavy and his head feeling light, and the first thing he realized was that he couldn't sense Jean's presence in his mind any more.

He denied himself a small pang of fear, and concentrated on getting to his feet, on forcing his tired eyes to open so he could see where he was and take appropriate action.

He felt embarrassed at having been felled so easily. He was worried about the other X-Men.

He felt alone without her.

The room in which he found himself was red. Very red indeed. At first, he assumed his vision was still blurry, that he wasn't focussing past his visor. Cyclops was used to seeing the world through a scarlet haze. But no, it was different this time.

He took a few steps forward, reached out and touched a wall that felt like multi-faceted glass. Red, multi-faceted glass. He turned around, hoping to find something, anything, to suggest that what he feared wasn't true. But the redness surrounded him.

He cut loose with his eye-beams, but he wasn't surprised when the walls simply swallowed them, as darkness swallows light. The walls themselves were translucent, but opaque enough to deny him a glimpse of what might lie beyond them. He stared at a thousand images of his own worried expression, reflected to infinity and all washed in red. He wondered how much a prison like this would cost, and then remembered who he was dealing with: the owner of Shaw Industries, Black King of the Hellfire Club and one of the richest men in the world. One of the few men who could afford to manufacture a giant ruby quartz crystal.

Ruby quartz: the substance from which his visors—and his glasses, when he wasn't in costume—were made. The only substance that could keep his destructive power in check.

Nevertheless, Cyclops opened his visor again and pivoted slowly on the spot, in a full circle, testing every square inch of the walls, floor and ceiling. The crystal glowed a brighter red wherever it was hit, but showed no signs of breaking. He had to accept that his powers were useless to him in here. But that didn't mean he was beaten.

He couldn't see any kind of opening. But logically, there had to be one. He spent the next several minutes running his hands patiently over every surface—even the ceiling, which he could just about reach if he stood on his tiptoes. He was searching for a hidden mechanism, or even just a seam in the crystal to show that a door existed. He found nothing.

Which left only one option: brute force.

He removed his boot and struck with the heel, as hard as he could, again and again at the unyielding red wall. Intellectually, he knew it was hopeless. It would have taken somebody of Rogue's strength to smash through ruby quartz, and even she would have found it difficult. But if he could just find one flaw, one stress point in the crystal. . . .

To his elation, he felt something give way. A thin crack spread across the red surface, and he set to work with renewed strength, concentrating his blows upon the same point, smiling as ruby shards flaked away to collect at his feet. The more he worked, the faster his progress became. Within minutes, layers of crystal were shattering like glass with each swing of his boot, and even before his flailing fists. Shaw must have cut costs, used imperfect materials.

At last, Cyclops punched his way through to air, whereupon it was the work of just seconds to widen the hole, to propel himself through the disintegrating red barrier, one arm in front of his face to protect his exposed skin. He couldn't see where he was going—and he was hardly likely to take any prospective foes by surprise. So, he had to be ready for anything.

But he was not prepared at all for what greeted him on the far side of the wall.

He had broken through to another cell exactly like the first. Another giant ruby quartz crystal. Another room with no doors.

And as Cyclops stared, aghast, at his own myriad reflections, he thought he could hear Sebastian Shaw's rich, mocking laughter echoing from the red walls.

Storm woke to the dark, and a stifling atmosphere which stirred an old fear.

She was lying on her back on a hard wooden surface, her arms folded across her chest, her skin dry and hot and prickling, her own breath loud in her ears. She stirred and felt more wood, hemming her in on each side. She reached up, but there was wood there too. It was only an inch or two above her upturned face but, in the absolute darkness, she couldn't see it.

Goddess, don't let this be!

A wooden box.

No. Something worse.

She reached past her head, but felt more wood. She stretched out her legs and kicked at yet another wooden surface. It surrounded her, confined her, and took her back to the worst hours of her life.

She fought down a rising tide of panic. She had confronted and beaten this phobia before. She could do so again. But had she ever really vanquished it, or had she just learned to cope? Had she only sent the fear to lurk in the shadowy corners of her subconscious mind?

She pushed frantically against the box's upper surface—the lid of the coffin, she knew with a cold, sick certainty—hoping against hope that her worries were unfounded. But the lid didn't budge. Something weighed it down.

They had buried her alive. Encased her in wood and left her to rot in the earth.

She screamed and thrashed, and brought her full strength to bear on the walls of her cramped prison. The release of emotions was cathartic, but ineffective. She forced herself to calm down, before she exhausted her scant reserves of air. She closed her eyes—although open or closed, it made little difference—and breathed, slowly and deeply, concentrating on the gentle rhythm and trying to forget where she was. She pictured herself in the African rainforest, and tried to imagine she was still there, enjoying her years-long respite from a life of hardship. Before Professor Xavier had brought her back to painful reality.

Instead, her thoughts drifted back to an even earlier time.

She was five years old, lying in the rubble of her house in Cairo, pinned by fallen beams and choking on thick dust. Her mother lay beside her, battered, bloody and deathly pale. Ororo Munroe screamed her throat raw, and cried until there were no tears left. Then, at last, she allowed the pain and the dizziness to reclaim her, and drifted into a restless sleep.

She never saw her mother again. Nor her father, whose last words to her had been that he would protect her, protect them all, as the fighter plane had careened towards them.

He had lied.

The fear had crept up on Storm again. Her heart raced, and she was on the verge of hyperventilation. She gritted her teeth and scolded herself inwardly. She was not five years old now. She would not let this scar from her childhood, this irrational claustrophobia, defeat her. The rescue parties had overlooked her then, salvaging her parents' corpses but leaving young Ororo sleeping. She had had to dig her own way to freedom, even though it had taken long, hard, suffocating hours. She could do it again.

She reached out with her very soul, working blindly, trying to shape weather patterns that she could neither see nor feel. Perhaps she wasn't too deeply buried. Perhaps she could turn the soil above her head to mud, wash some of it away, give herself a chance to break free. But as more time went by, the air in her coffin grew staler, and Storm couldn't even hear the rain and the thunder and the lightning that she thought she was bringing down.

She kept on trying. What else could she do? Perhaps, at least, a freak rainstorm might alert somebody to her plight. It might bring help.

From down here in the darkness, though, there was no way of telling.

"Incredible!" breathed the Beast. "Amazing, stupendous, sensational!" His borrowed white lab coat billowed out behind him as he leapt across the laboratory, ricocheting off the wall and coming to rest beside a laser printer, which was spewing out paper like tickertape. He glanced over the freshly inked numbers, even though he had just seen them on a computer screen. Then, with a whoop of delight, he performed a standing backflip, bounced off a desk and landed back where he had started, at Rory Campbell's side.

"I take it you're impressed," said Campbell, with a raised eyebrow.

" 'Impressed' would be a major understatement of my condition of exuberance," Hank assured him, sorting frantically through a stack of papers on the bench in front of him, scribbling notes on some with a red ballpoint pen, which he produced from behind his ear. "I had no idea the Kree had carried out so much research into the human genome. Why, the work they've done with the Inhumans alone—the records they've kept here on the long-term effects of their genetic experimentation—it's as if I've spent the last few months fumbling my way around a forest in the dark, and somebody has just handed me the map."

"A partial map, at best," said Campbell.

Hank refused to be daunted. "To substitute another metaphor, then, it's as if I've found a dozen missing pieces of a jigsaw. Not enough to complete it, perhaps, but at last I can see what the picture ought to be." To himself, he muttered: "As soon as I get a few spare weeks, I have a lot of reading to catch up on." Aloud, he said: "In the meantime, you and your people have done some very useful number crunching with this remarkable computer."

"You think we might be heading in the right direction?"

"Oh, I do, Doctor Campbell, I most certainly do. The Legacy Virus was specifically designed to attack the mutant gene, to catalyze a reaction that eventually causes total cellular collapse. If we can change the nature of the gene, and consequently of that reaction...." He let out a whistle at the sheer possibilities. "Moira and I pursued a similar line of research some time ago, but came up against what we thought were insurmountable obstacles. If only we had known then what you know now...."

He bounded across the room again, startling Doctor Scott as he dropped a sheaf of papers into his arms. "Very impressive, my friend, very impressive. I've made a few corrections to your calculations and marked some areas you might wish to pursue further." He moved on, making similar observations to Takamoto, encouraging Travers to re-run some tests and pretending not to notice that all three of the scientists regarded him with open resentment.

"You know, I'm actually beginning to see a solution to all this," he said, pacing the room fretfully. "Ideally, of course, we should have some Inhumans here to examine first-hand."

"I'm sure Shaw could arrange it," put in Campbell.

"No, no, no," said the Beast hurriedly. "I think we've all seen quite enough of our kind benefactor's recruitment methods." His words were meant at least partly for the others, but he had his back to them and couldn't tell if he had made an impression or not.

"The computer's database has all the information we need," said Campbell.

"Indeed it has. I would have liked to have run some empirical tests, that's all. Still, no matter. We have been given the opportunity to take some bold steps forward. We should take it. You've already carried out trials on the alpha and beta vaccines?"

Campbell nodded. "Mr. Shaw donated a few pints of mutant blood."

"His own?"

"Fitzroy's. The results were informative, but not very encouraging."

"With the alterations I've suggested—and with a modicum of fortune—we might be able to change that. I'll need to see those figures."

"I'll get them for you," said Campbell.

"I do hope I'm not interrupting." The Beast recognized the voice before he turned to face its owner. Sebastian Shaw stood in the doorway, wearing his usual old-fashioned attire and his usual smug expression. Hank hadn't heard him enter.

"As a matter of fact," he said shortly, "you've distracted me from a very delicate stage of my calculations." It was partially true: he had a thousand figures and as many possibilities running through his head. The real problem, however, was that the mere sight of Shaw had dampened his ebullient mood.

For the past few hours, he had immersed himself in work, forgetting all else. The Legacy Virus was the most knotty problem he had ever had to face, and to see those knots unraveling at last had been a wondrous experience. After too long, he had begun to rediscover the joys of scientific achievement. Now, all he could think of was the circumstances under which those gains had come about, the compromises he had made.

"I don't suppose there have been any sightings of my teammates?" he asked.

"None," said Shaw.

Hank nodded. "They'll be here, sooner or later."

"I don't doubt it. I know how persistent your friends can be."

"And I'd like to talk to them when they arrive."

"Yes, I think you should." Hank was surprised at Shaw's willing agreement to his demand. He raised an eyebrow, and the Black King elaborated: "The X-Men have a tendency to—how shall I put this?—break things. It would be a shame if they were to end this project before you had a chance to explain its importance to them."

"I shall certainly endeavor to do so," Hank rumbled.

Shaw hesitated for a moment, then, as if unsure whether to say more. However, he turned and left without a further word, and the Beast watched him go with a despondent sigh.

He wasn't looking forward to meeting the rest of the X-Men. He feared that they would react as Moira had, when they learned what he was doing—and he couldn't face explaining himself again. Not yet. He didn't want another argument that he wasn't sure he could win.

Perhaps if they could stay away for a little longer, just until he had something more tangible to give them, some proof that he had made the right decision...

Campbell reappeared at his elbow and, without a word, handed him a manila folder crammed with paper: the file he had requested. Hank opened it and looked at the top sheet, hardly taking in the words and numbers upon it, unable to recall his enthusiasm of just a moment earlier.

He turned slowly, examining his surroundings as if for the first time; as if only now realizing the possible consequences of the deal he had made.

Doctor Takamoto looked quickly down at her work before his gaze could meet hers—but not quickly enough to conceal the naked hatred in her eyes.

Wolverine's cell was a large, white room, and somebody had left the door open.

There was only one problem. He wasn't the room's only occupant.

Standing between him and the door—through which he could see only a gray corridor wall—was a silver, skeletal figure. In fact, Wolverine realized, it was a perfect human skeleton, of a short man, fashioned from metal. *Not another flaming robot,* he thought.

As if sensing his interest, the figure dropped into a combat-ready crouch. Wolverine wasn't sure how it could move at all without joints or muscles, but it could. He circled it warily, and it shifted its position to follow him around the room, always staring at him with the blank eye sockets of its leering skull, always blocking his path to the door.

All right, bub, thought Wolverine, *if that's how you want it!*

He extended his claws, only to hear the familiar *snikt* sound repeated a half-second later. A feral smile spread across his face as he saw what had happened. Three claws, identical to his own, had extended from the backs of each of the figure's hands.

Cute, Shaw. Very cute!

So, not just a human skeleton, then. A replica of his own skeleton. And sheathed with the same near-invulnerable material?

There was one way to find out.

The skeleton made no attempt to evade Wolverine as he rushed it. It simply braced itself for the impact, then lashed out with incredible speed and matched him blow for blow. It was strong—far stronger than its spindly frame suggested—and it had all his moves. It was like fighting a taciturn, scrawnier version of himself. His claws clanged against the skeleton's bones without damaging them, confirming his theory that, like his own, they were laced with adamantium. But, unlike his opponent, Wolverine had flesh to cut, blood to spill.

He winced as he took a deep gash to his side. He fell back and, to his surprise, the skeleton let him go. Clearly, it was programmed to leave him alone so long as he didn't attack it, and so long as he wasn't trying to get to the door. *Your first mistake, Shaw!* he thought. The skeleton had shredded what little had been left of his costume above the waist, but his body was healing. He could feel the pain in his side receding, and new skin was already growing over some of his more shallow cuts. He flung the remnants of his mask aside and flexed his fingers. Seconds later, not only restored to full health but with the experience of his first defeat to inform him, he hurled himself at his opponent again.

With the same result.

For a second time, Wolverine withdrew, wiping blood from his face with the back of his hand, his heart burning with a rage that he knew he couldn't afford to surrender to.

When his healing factor had done its work again, he tried a different approach.

He ran at the skeleton a third time, and it dropped into its usual defensive stance. But, instead of attacking it, Wolverine leapt over it, performing a handspring off its shoulders.

For an instant, the open door beckoned to him.

But, before he had even landed, the skeleton pivoted and knocked his legs from under him with a sweep of its arm. Wolverine landed heavily, and the skeleton stood astride him. It lashed out with its claws, and he knew he had given it the opportunity to drive them through his heart. But it simply cut his skin, and, once again, allowed him to scramble away from it, beaten.

On his fourth attack, Wolverine grabbed the skeleton's wrists and concentrated on keeping its claws away from him. He grappled with it, forcing it around until he had his back to the door. Then he pushed it away from him and turned to flee, but the skeleton had anticipated this move too, and it leapt on him from behind and wrestled him down.

On his fifth attack, he used his claws again and simply tried in vain to outfight his opponent, because he had to let off some steam.

And, somewhere between the sixth and seventh attacks, he succumbed to the voice in his head. The voice that told him that the skeleton was too good at predicting his moves, at countering them. And that the way to beat it was to become more unpredictable.

His eighth attack was the most brutal and sustained yet. A red mist descended over Wolverine's eyes, and he punched and slashed at his android foe with no regard for the injuries he was taking in turn. He had no intention of disengaging again, but the skeleton made the decision for him. It lifted him bodily, and hurled him away. He got to his feet, let out an animal roar and immediately rushed back into the fray.

He had lost count of the number of attacks he had made when the skeleton finally punched him too hard, and he slipped into unconsciousness.

An indeterminate time later, he woke to find his injuries all but healed, his heart rate slowed and the crazy fog lifted from his mind. The skeleton had returned to its guard position, the door still temptingly open behind it. Wolverine regarded it through hooded eyes, and it glared back at him sightlessly.

He began the process all over again.

The corridor was lit only dimly, by a blue-tinted source, which Nightcrawler couldn't see. He could barely make out his own three-fingered hand in front of his face, but this was quite normal. His body was melting into the shadows, as it always did.

He spread his arms and found that, as expected, he could touch the dull, gray metal walls on each side of him simultaneously. That wasn't good. Nor was the fact that the ceiling was low, only a foot or so above his head. He felt hemmed in.

In front of him, the corridor turned to the left. Behind him, it passed the openings of three side passages—two the left and, between them, one to the right—before it stopped short at a T-junction. In all, six possible directions to take.

He turned around and scuttled along the right hand wall, because it was as easy as walking on the floor and it might just allow him to avoid a trap or take a foe by surprise.

He paused as he drew level with the first opening. He found himself looking down another long passageway, with more junctions at irregular intervals along it.

A maze, then.

Despite the possible perils of the situation, Nightcrawler found himself grinning. He enjoyed this sort of challenge.

He took the right turn, and the first right after it. He came to a crossroads, at which he headed right again. This took him up a blind alley. He checked the wall at the end of it, just in case it was an illusion or it concealed a secret door. There was nothing.

He tried taking every first left turn instead, but soon became convinced that he was walking in circles. He considered pulling a thread off his costume, to mark his path. Perhaps later, he thought, if things became desperate.

He felt a surge of triumph as he sighted something in the distance: a narrow flight of metal steps, twisted around a pole. He teleported towards it in his eagerness. It led both up and down. He climbed up first, and was dismayed to find himself in a corridor identical to the one he had come from. Climbing down, he found the same. He returned to the highest level, guessing that his objective was more likely to be above than below. When he found another, identical ladder a few minutes later, he climbed that too. And another. And another.

Nightcrawler lost track of the time he had spent wandering the dark corridors. He tried to keep walking in broadly the same direction, and to move up through the levels of the labyrinth whenever he was able. But he never reached its outside edge, nor its roof. Finally, to confirm his suspicions, he dropped a white handkerchief onto the metal floor in the center of a corridor. He found it again, half an hour later, three floors and almost two miles away.

He had only one option. He had realized this some time ago, but he had wanted to be absolutely sure before he committed himself to taking such a risk.

Somehow, this labyrinth was confounding his senses, clouding his thoughts, sending him around in circles without him knowing it. It wasn't a fair challenge. But he could teleport out of here. The problem was, it would have to be a blind 'port. He had no destination to visualize, no idea if he was ten yards inside the labyrinth or ten miles. And, under those circumstances, he could easily find himself trying to occupy the same space as an unexpected wall or a piece of furniture. Nightcrawler swallowed at the very thought. He had no choice but to do this—he knew that—but he also knew he might be about to commit suicide.

He closed his eyes, breathed in deeply, and focussed on a virtual spot one mile straight up from his present position. At least, this way, he could be sure of clearing this maze with its danger-ously narrow corridors and low ceilings. Of course, it also meant he was more likely to find himself in a fatal plunge towards the roof of whichever building he was in.

Nightcrawler let out a therapeutic yell as he made the 'port.

When he opened his eyes again, he was standing with his nose pressed against a cold metal wall, and he recoiled from it with a startled gasp...

...to find, to his despair, that he was still inside the labyrinth.

Rogue was floating.

At first, she thought she was underwater. Her lungs balked at the act of respiration, and she suffered a minor coughing fit.

Somehow, though, she could breathe.

The liquid around her was green-tinged, cold and, apparently, super-oxygenated.

It was also full of people.

They stretched for as far as she could see—which wasn't too far, through the murk—in all directions, in rows and columns, all float-ing upright as she did, all unconscious, arms limp by their sides. Their heads tilted forwards at identical angles, their chins resting on their chests. Their faces were composed into identical expres-sions of contentment.

They *were* identical. Dozens of identical men with the same short, sandy hair, the same bland features, the same slight dimple in each of their chins. Rogue wondered if they were all clones.

The identical men were all naked. She realized, with a start, that she was too.

Automatically, she folded in her arms and legs, looking around warily in case any of the men came towards her. If she touched one—even brushed against him—with her bare skin, her mutant ability of absorption would kick in.

She needn't have worried. The men weren't moving. They remained in their perfect rows and columns, not even drifting. But this gave Rogue a problem: how to get past them?

There was space between them, but not a great deal. She could swim through it, but only if she kept tight control over every movement of her body. Could she do it? She was used to fighting with strength, not precision. And the consequences of failure terrified her. All those people, all those personalities, those ideas and emotions. She shuddered at the thought of them invading her mind, destroying her sense of self.

Best, perhaps, not to take the chance; to stay where she was.

Or was that what her captors wanted her to think?

Whatever these things around her were, they weren't real people. They were artificial life forms, grown in a laboratory. What if they were empty vessels, with no thoughts of their own? What if it was safe for her to touch them after all? What if the only thing keeping her here, floating in this tank or whatever it was, was her own paranoia?

It wasn't the most convincing argument, but it was enough to persuade Rogue that she had to take a risk.

She kicked out tentatively, and sent herself drifting upwards. It didn't feel like swimming, more like maneuvering in zero gravity. Fortunately, she had been trained to do just that. She floated between two of the clone men, her arms above her head, heels pressed together. She even pulled in her stomach, taking up as little space as she could. She resisted the urge to close her eyes, to prevent herself from seeing if this all went wrong. Never before in her life had she felt so exposed, so much in danger.

She took a deep, calming breath as she came face to face with one of the clone men, her nose inches from his. Her first impulse was to flinch, but there was an identical man only the same distance behind her. The first man's eyes remained closed, his expression unchanging. Tiny bubbles emerged from his mouth as he breathed out gently.

Rogue had stopped moving. She gave another tiny kick, as soft as she could manage, and resumed her slow rise. She didn't even dare to look up; she just hoped that, soon, she would bump into a roof. One with a hatch in it, preferably.

And then, to her horror, she realized she was drifting off-course. Almost touching one of the clone men, she back-pedaled frantically.

A little too frantically.

She felt the awful press of skin against her skin—a bare foot against her back—and she screamed as a thousand unwanted thoughts flooded into her mind. She recoiled instinctively, only to collide with another clone. She gritted her teeth and closed her eyes, and tried not to let the images of other lives, the opinions of other people, affect her; just let them sluice through her mind without *changing* her. Her body spiraling out of control, she touched another man, and another, and suddenly a dozen more voices were shouting to be heard, protesting at what she was doing to them and at the same time assailing her with their mundane lives, and she couldn't stand it any more.

With a yell of pain, Rogue lashed out. She didn't care how hard she hit the men, she just had to get them away from her. She created a space for herself, but at the expense of adding a few new voices to the cacophony in her head. She hardly knew who she was any more. She curled into a ball and tried to find an essential, inviolate part of herself upon which she could focus, to tune out all else. She didn't want to listen, to think, to feel. All notions of escape were pushed out of her mind as she drifted in the greenish liquid and sobbed quietly to herself.

"I think we've done it," whispered Rory Campbell. "We've actually done it."

The five scientists stared up in awe at the wall-mounted main screen of the Kree computer. Travers, Scott and Takamoto crowded around the Beast in their eagerness to see, their hostility towards him temporarily forgotten in the sheer excitement of discovery.

"Let's wait and see how the simulation plays itself out," Hank cautioned, although he could feel the same excitement building within himself.

The screen displayed a graphical representation of a human

blood cell. It was stained around the edges, as if somebody had injected black ink into the cytoplasm. And the ink spot was wriggling, reaching out towards the center of the cell, trying to grow. But it wasn't succeeding. Its questing tendrils were blocked by a similarly amorphous white blob, its equal and opposite. And, as the two forces met in combat, they were canceling each other out, until only the healthy cell remained.

"It's unbelievable!" said Campbell. "All the time and effort we put into finding a cure, and you come along and finish the job in a matter of hours. Doctor McCoy, you are a genius!"

The Beast waved aside the compliment, graciously. "You would have reached this same conclusion sooner or later. Your team had already laid the groundwork. I was simply able to utilize my experience to build upon it all the faster." His experience, he thought, refreshed by Moira MacTaggert's purloined notes of their research together. He felt a twinge of guilt. "I should also remind you that this is only a computer projection. We have months of trials ahead of us before we can even think about testing our formula on a living subject." He looked up at the screen again. Both the black and white stains were appreciably smaller. "Nevertheless," he said, "I think I can safely state that congratulations are due."

The last remnants of black and white merged, and blinked out in a final whimper of mutual destruction. Professor Travers drew a sharp breath, Rory Campbell laughed giddily, and Doctors Takamoto and Scott began to applaud. Hank felt like throwing his arms around all four of them, but restrained himself. Even in their present mood, that might not have gone down too well.

"My fellow scientists," he announced, "I believe we have found our cure."

Iceman was standing on a circular white platform, only inches above the ground, in a circular white room. The wall was about thirty feet away, and it rose towards a white dome about ten feet above his head. There were several doors, evenly spaced around the wall. He could see nothing amiss, nothing to stop him from just walking away. So, every fiber of his being told him that this had to be a trap.

He 'iced up' with a thought, surrounding himself with his customary protective shell. When the trap was sprung, he would be ready. At least, as ready as he could be.

"I hate this!" he said, to fill the unnerving silence. "I hate it when the bad guys have watched too many episodes of *Batman*. I hate it when they build these elaborate prisons. I mean, why go to all this trouble just to make our lives miserable?" No answer came, but for the echo of his own voice from the blank walls.

The platform itself was suspicious. "No prizes for guessing that, whatever's gonna happen, it'll happen the second I step off this thing," he considered. He reached out with a tentative foot, but snatched it back. "On second thought, let's show a tiny bit of caution."

Iceman rarely gave much consideration to the mechanics of his powers. He just used them. He didn't think about how he was condensing moisture from the air—nor about how, in that same instant, he was draining every iota of heat from a small, localized area. As far as he was concerned, he was just doing something that came naturally: he was making ice cubes. And, once they were made, he sent them skittering and bouncing along the white floor.

"And, to my immense surprise, nothing happens. Perhaps I got this place wrong after all?" He thought for a moment, then shook his head. "Nah, I don't think so!"

Still, there was only one thing to do, much as he disliked it.

He extended his leg again and, this time, he let his foot touch the floor.

Immediately, the room was filled with fire.

With a strangulated cry, Iceman leapt back, almost falling. The fire burnt fiercely, giving off waves of heat that began to melt his armor, but it didn't touch the platform.

Then, in the space of a second, it died down and went out altogether.

He looked around, wide-eyed, but he couldn't see where the

flames had come from. From beneath the floor, he guessed, although he could see no gaps in the smooth surface. Nor were there any scorch marks, nor lingering traces of smoke. Iceman entertained the possibility that the fire had been an illusion. But he had felt its heat against his face, and he saw now that there was nothing left of his ice cubes. They had melted.

"OK," he muttered to himself, "if the floor is pressure-sensitive...."

He created an ice slide: a cantilever structure, anchored to the platform. The far end of it was within reach of a door handle. But, as soon as he took his first cautious step along it, the fire erupted again, its flames touching the ceiling. This time, as it beat him back, he lost control of his armor altogether, and he was just plain, helpless Bobby Drake, cowering from his natural enemy, sweat running down his brow.

The fire was extinguished again, and Bobby felt a shiver of fear running through him. The slide had gone. Not just melted but evaporated, leaving only a misshapen lump of ice on the platform itself. What would happen to him, he wondered, if he was caught in that furnace? If he tried to make it all the way to a door? He could reach one in seconds, using his powers to replenish a slide beneath him as fast as it could be melted. But what if he wasn't strong enough? What if he couldn't keep his protective shell up all the way?

No, he decided, sitting down on the platform, knees up against his chest and arms around his knees. It was too much of a risk. He didn't have that kind of control over his powers. He wasn't good enough. He couldn't make it out of here alone.

It was up to the others to find him.

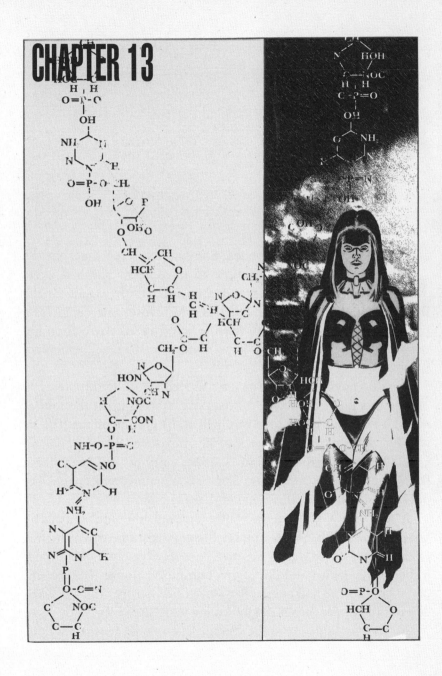

CHAPTER 13

JEAN GREY'S head throbbed. She had expected that, but the pain was worse than it ought to have been. She had over-extended herself, overtaxed her powers, but it wasn't for the first time, and it had never felt this bad before. She could taste blood on her lips, and she realized it had trickled down from her nose. She feared she might have done herself some permanent damage.

But that possibility was the least immediate of her problems.

She was lying on a hard rock surface, staring up at the roof of a rough-hewn cavern, which was held up by granite pillars. The air was hot and dry, and the back of her throat felt like parchment. Carefully, she eased herself to her feet, carrying her head like a fragile egg on her shoulders. She took a handkerchief from her pocket and dabbed at the blood on her face.

It took her a moment to realize that she shouldn't have *had* pockets. She had been wearing her Phoenix costume when she was felled, but now she was in her own conservative civilian clothing: a smart, gray jacket and skirt, over a turquoise blouse. She remembered how Selene had altered her attire in New York, and she wondered if the Black Queen was in league with Shaw after all.

As her eyes adjusted to the gloom, Jean saw there was only one way out of the cave. The flickering light of flames glowed in the jagged opening, and she crept towards it, poking a cautious head around the corner of the slime-encrusted rock.

She gasped at the sight of an enormous pit of fire, from some medieval vision of Hell itself. It was crisscrossed by crumbling stone walkways, which in turn were guarded by malformed gargoyle statues. The infernal vista stretched for as far as Jean could see. She heard a papery rustle of batwings, and a sinister shadow slid across the roof. Somewhere, somebody was screaming, and somebody—or something—responded with a demonic cackle.

"Where am I?" she whispered, in awe and horror.

She jumped, as the answer leapt into her head from nowhere. *Where do you think?*

The voice was Jean Grey's own. Or rather, it wasn't.

I thought you'd be familiar enough with this place, cow. Look into your subconscious, your repressed memories. You've been here before. We both have. We've both returned from death.

I never died! she insisted, ramming the words home with telepathic force.

Time to remedy that, then.

Jean could see her now, standing on a walkway in the mid-distance, hot smoke and glowing ashes roiling in the air behind her. It was like staring into a funhouse mirror, at a woman who should have been her twin, but who looked very different. Madelyne Pryor: the erstwhile Goblin Queen, the current Black Rook of Sebastian Shaw's Inner Circle, and the living embodiment of everything Jean Grey had ever feared she could become. She was a nightmare in a black leather bodice, her garb reminiscent of Selene's, the Hellfire Club's trident symbol embossed upon a clasp at her throat, and a smile of pure evil darkening her face.

Madelyne was walking slowly, confidently, towards Jean. Jean stayed put and let her foe approach her, but she was nervous. As she had noted before, Madelyne's powers were equal to her own. In this unfamiliar realm, she might even have the advantage.

You had your crack at life, you witch, said Madelyne Pryor's voice, full of hate, in Jean Grey's mind. *You screwed it up. You don't get another chance. You don't get to take* my *life!*

I didn't take anything from you!

"You took *everything* from me!" spat Madelyne, near enough for her voice to carry now. "This should be my time, not yours. It will be my time again."

"So, you want to kill me," said Jean. She struggled to keep her own voice from trembling. She wasn't afraid of dying in combat, not really. But she was chilled by the thought of what might happen after her death (of *what happened last time*, screamed a part of her mind, which she tried to tune out). She couldn't stand the idea of Madelyne walking back into her life and taking it over, taking her place with Scott. Logically, she knew it couldn't happen. She knew Scott better than to think he could ever go back to his first wife, no matter how much he might be hurting. She had to keep telling herself that.

"It won't make a difference," she insisted, out loud. "You think that, with me out of the way, you can just waltz in and replace me again? It won't happen, lady. Not this time."

Madelyne was nose to nose with Jean now, and the X-Man braced herself for an attack, trying to clear her mind. "I'm putting things right," snarled the Black Rook, "putting things back the way they should be. Me up there, and you down here."

And suddenly, the world itself twisted around Jean, and the rock wall behind her reached out to push her onto a walkway, which bucked and rotated beneath her. She tried to steady herself, but a gargoyle flew at her, its grotesque face leering at her and its stone wings beating in front of her eyes, and she couldn't hold on.

It all happened in an instant. She had no time to react, to fight back. Jean Grey couldn't even draw breath to scream, as she was plunged into the fire.

"Mr. Shaw? Sebastian?"

Tessa leaned forward in her seat and waved a hand in front of her employer's eyes. He was sitting behind his desk, elbows resting upon its metallic top, fingers pressed together in front of his mouth, and his thoughts had evidently drifted far from this basic underground office. Tessa was used to seeing him in a contemplative mood, but rarely this distracted.

He focussed back upon her, shifted his position and smiled slightly, as if trying to show her that everything was all right, that he was still in control.

"There isn't a problem is there, sir?" she asked. "Nothing I should know about? I thought everything was going according to plan now."

"Inasmuch as it can," he sighed, "with the X-Men here. They may be helpless for now, but they do have a rather irritating penchant for throwing spanners into my works. Perhaps Fitzroy was right. Perhaps it would be safer to kill them."

"You still need Doctor McCoy's cooperation," she reminded him.

"Do I? Perhaps it's time to accept that the risks of having the Beast around outweigh the benefits. Doctor Campbell and the others may be able to complete his work now."

"But what if they cannot?"

"You're right," conceded Shaw. "I can't take that chance. I want this cure, Tessa, and I won't allow my enemies to keep it from me. Not even for a day." He looked at her sharply. "If we could tell McCoy that his teammates were here..."

She shook her head. "No. Not until he's ready. We discussed this before, sir. The Beast isn't sure enough of his own motives. If he talks to his friends now, they will almost certainly dissuade him from helping us."

Sebastian seemed to accept this point, but Tessa could sense his impatience seething just below the surface. "We can do nothing, then, but wait," he concluded, "and hope that time proves to be on our side. Madelyne has assured me that she can keep our guests in line for as long as may be necessary."

A look of distaste crossed Tessa's face, before she could stop it. Sebastian saw it, and regarded her through hooded eyes. "You don't care much for our Black Rook, do you?"

The comment surprised her. He knew full well her feelings about both Pryor and Fitzroy—and Selene, for that matter—but he had never brought up the subject openly before. This project meant a lot to him, she realized, and his anxiety was prompting this unusually reflective mood of his. She decided to take full advantage of the opportunity. "No," she said. "She'll betray you, Sebastian. She'll turn on you, like they all do."

"Perhaps."

"She's using you. She's only interested in becoming the Black Queen in Selene's absence. Once she has that, she'll have no further use for you."

Sebastian didn't argue. He seemed to consider her words for a moment, then the metaphorical shutters came back down over his eyes, and Tessa knew he would pay no further heed to her advice. Perhaps, at least, he would think about what she had said. She got to her feet. "If there's nothing else, sir, I thought I might take a walk downstairs myself, make sure everything is as it should be."

Sebastian nodded. "Yes. A good idea, Tessa. Leave me to my thoughts."

She did so, wondering as she walked briskly through the Kree installation whether she had told him anything he hadn't already known. Sebastian might have let Madelyne Pryor into his bed, but his heart was far more carefully guarded.

The exasperating thing was that it didn't seem to bother him. It was as if he was happier knowing that Madelyne probably *was* plotting behind his back, because at least he could understand that. He could relate to her, deal with her, predict her actions, more easily than he could with an altruist like Moira MacTaggert. They were kindred spirits.

On the base's lowest level, Tessa passed two Hellfire Club guards and opened three doors one by one, checking inside three small, cubic rooms. Each one was devoid of furniture. In the first, Wolverine, Rogue and Storm were sprawled across the floor, all still unconscious. Wolverine's muscles were twitching, and he was muttering curses under his breath. Rogue was rolled into a ball, sobbing. The second room was occupied by Cyclops, Nightcrawler and Iceman. Their positions hadn't changed at all since she had last looked in on them.

In the third and final room, Phoenix lay on her side, also out cold. Beside her, sitting cross-legged on the hard, metal floor, was Madelyne Pryor.

The Black Rook's eyes were closed too, but she was smiling.

The flames licked around Jean, but didn't burn her skin.

She rose on a column of hot air, to face her tormentor. Behind her, one of the stone walkways exploded; her doing, more for effect than for any practical reason.

"The Phoenix rises from the flames," noted Madelyne. "How apposite!" And indeed, Jean was now wearing her Phoenix costume again.

"Did you think you could fool me?" she cried. "Did you think I wouldn't realize where we were, what this place is? The astral plane was my domain long before you came along!" She was angry, mostly with herself. She really hadn't put two and two together before now, which was almost unforgivable for someone of her experience. Her only excuse was that her head was still pounding, and she wasn't thinking straight. She had to pull herself together.

"Your domain no longer," hissed Madelyne. "You've been unconscious for a long while, Jeannie." She said the name with a snarl. "While your mind was hiding itself in its protective shell, I was making preparations. You aren't fighting on home turf any more." She gestured with one hand, and another walkway uprooted itself and crumbled into fragments, which flew toward her enemy's head. Phoenix concentrated, stealing their momentum until they hovered in midair. Then she reversed their direction, and sent the makeshift missiles toward their creator, but Madelyne disintegrated them without apparent effort.

Phoenix feared that her doppelganger had a point. Here, in the virtual realm, the power of the mind was all that counted—and she was still groggy, dazed from her battle with the Kree Sentry, whereas Madelyne was fresh and hungry and ready for this. Jean could already feel stone fists closing around her ankles, pulling her down, and she had to fight to remain aloft. If she fell into the fire again, if Madelyne gained the upper hand, then the flames might scorch her this time. They might even kill her.

"You're all alone, Jeannie," taunted Madelyne. "No Nathan Grey or Scott Summers to help you this time. No one to save you."

"My teammates. What have you done to them?"

"Imprisoned them," she said, with a boastful laugh. "I've trapped them in self-defeating mental prisons of their own creation. Their cells are the products of their own imaginations, their own fears. They don't believe they can ever break free, and so they won't. It would never have worked on you, though. You required my personal attention."

Phoenix had been pulled down almost into the flames again— but by giving her foe an opportunity to gloat about her own cleverness, she had gained time to compose herself. The certainty that she would never have fallen for such an obvious ploy herself, that she wasn't vain enough, also comforted her and gave her strength. Madelyne Pryor wasn't like her at all.

"You may have wormed your way into my mind," she swore, "but you'll never defeat me here!" She was taking control now. She could *feel* everything around her, every molecule in the cave walls, every flicker from the fires below. She could feel them, and manipulate them according to her own desires. She was all-powerful, invincible. It was a heady, exultant sensation, and she almost lost herself in it as she freed herself and reshaped Madelyne's own flames, directing them to raze her world of thoughts to the ground.

And then, the Black Rook hit her with a mental image: herself, as Madelyne Pryor was seeing her now. A fierce creature in human form, its face dark but its eyes alight with lust, as it hovered in the center of a shape sculpted from the flames themselves: a fiery phoenix, like the one upon her chest. The symbol of the force that had once consumed her. *No*, she told herself, almost desperately, *not me! And this image isn't real. This is Madelyne's doing.*

An image from your thoughts, an image from mine. Does it make any difference?

"Yes!" she screamed, and the twisted walls cracked open. Water cascaded into the cavern, putting out the flames, as Jean Grey—and her clothes were Jean Grey's again now—leapt at Madelyne Pryor, and knocked her over with the sheer force of her will.

The walls around them had dropped, the fire had been extinguished and they were clinging to a sturdy rock for dear life, lashing out at each other as and when they could, swept along in the deluge. "You hate me so much," snarled Madelyne. "You wish to deny me my very existence. But I'm a part of you, witch. I'm inside you. That's why you can't face me. And it's why you'll never beat me, never be rid of me!"

"You're wrong. You're twisted. I won't become like you. I *can't* become like you!"

"Like me? Or like the Phoenix? You've even taken its name for yourself. It's inside you, Jeannie. The taint is inside you. I know it, you know it."

They were pitched onto a muddy bank, and the river ran on by them. They grappled with each other in a primeval landscape, the earth dark and wet, jagged forks of lightning sundering the blood-red sky. And although their struggle was, in reality, mental not physical, Jean could feel her heart pounding, her muscles pumping, and adrenaline surging through her system.

"And the longer you deny it," spluttered Madelyne, choking on mud, "the more strength it will have when you're finally forced to set it free. Like I was. Like the Phoenix force was."

Jean slammed her into the ground, winding her, and wrapped her fingers around her throat. She wanted to shut her up, to stop the painful words. Madelyne Pryor wasn't her. The Phoenix force hadn't been her. Their crimes, their failings, their hungers had been their own. But the words continued inside her head: *Let it out, Jeannie. Give in to your dark side. Become me!* And she was no longer sure if they came from Madelyne or from herself.

But she was sure of one thing: that there was only one way to stop them.

Her grip on Madelyne Pryor's throat tightened.

Rory Campbell had left, to deliver a printed report of the scientists' encouraging findings to Shaw. The rest of the team had gathered in a small annex off the laboratory where they could relax, fix themselves drinks and talk. Hank hadn't been invited to join them, and he chose not to gatecrash their celebrations. He sat alone in the lab and listened to the distant mumbling of their voices, their tones more optimistic than he had heard them before. Travers was looking forward to seeing his grandchildren again. Scott just wanted to be reunited with his wife.

Takamoto dampened the mood by reminding them that, as Hank had already said, there was still a long way to go before they held a fully tested cure for the Legacy Virus in their hands. Scott pointed out that at least there was an end in sight now, a chance of surviving this and getting back home. But he sounded considerably less hopeful now.

Hank knew how he felt. After the excitement of a few minutes earlier, reality was beginning to sink in again. He sat on a tall, wooden stool, rubbed his tired eyes and began to really think— because he had run out of excuses not to—about what he was doing here. He remembered what he had said to Rogue, in the Blackbird, on the way back from Newhill to Muir Island: "I pride myself on being a man of words, a man of science—and yet I appear to be most at peace with myself when I can attack a problem with my fists!" His greatest fear had always been that the mutation which had turned his body into that of a beast would eventually do the same to his mind. Was that what was happening here, slowly but surely? Was that what he was doing? Giving up on the intellectual struggle, because he would rather be engaged in a physical one against Sebastian Shaw and his cohorts? What if the X-Men couldn't do anything and Shaw ended up as the sole possessor of the Legacy cure, as Moira had suggested? The possible ramifications hardly bore thinking about. But were they any worse than the ramifications of doing nothing, of allowing this disease to run rampant?

Even now, with a cure within his reach, Hank ached inside at the knowledge that there was still so much work to do, and that more people would die before it was done.

He looked up as Campbell walked back into the room, Shaw at his side. The Black King was grinning from ear to ear, and Hank wanted to punch the smile off his face. He grimaced and forced himself to overcome the primitive, brutish instinct.

Campbell ran through the computer projections with Shaw, and Hank peered over his shoulder, watching for the fifth time as the black and white blobs fought and neutralized each other. The sight still gave him a thrill of excitement, despite himself.

"Our serum," Campbell explained to his attentive employer, "works not by targeting the Legacy Virus itself, but rather the very gene it was designed to attack."

"The mutant gene," said Shaw.

"Exactly. We aim to give it the ability to fight back."

"How so?"

"Over a period of several days, the serum—aided by a course of radiation treatments from Kree machinery—will catalyze a fresh mutation in the gene, evolving it into a kind of super-cell, which in turn will sponge up the virus and overwrite its effects on the DNA sequences, before regressing to its original state. That's what these graphics represent."

"A complete cure, then," mused Shaw. "With no side-effects?"

"None at all."

"At least," Hank interjected, "that's the theory."

"But the computer," said Campbell, "predicts a 100% likelihood of success."

"The outlook is promising, I grant you," said Hank, "but no computer, not even an alien one, can fully predict all the effects of a serum like this one on the human body. We will have to conduct an extensive battery of tests."

Shaw shook his head. "We don't have time."

"We don't have a choice!"

Shaw turned back to Campbell with a thoughtful expression. "Are you telling me this serum of yours will only work on somebody with the mutant gene?"

"Initially, yes. Indeed, it has to be a mutant who has only recently contracted Legacy. His DNA still has to be relatively uncorrupted for the serum to stand a chance of working."

"However," said Hank, "once we have facilitated the development of this super-cell within our first patient, we can isolate it before it burns itself out, and reproduce it in a laboratory."

"That way," said Campbell, "we can short-circuit the process in future patients by injecting the super-cell directly into the bloodstream."

Hank took up the baton again. "By which means, we ought to be able to cure those in whom the disease is more advanced—along with baseline humans, of course."

Shaw nodded curtly. "I've heard enough, gentlemen. So, what we need now is a mutant test subject, correct?"

Hank narrowed his eyes. "I don't think you were listening closely enough, Shaw. We aren't ready to try out the serum on a living being. The possible consequences—"

"The certain consequences of delay," Shaw interrupted, "are that people will die. This isn't up for discussion, Doctor McCoy. I will not wait any longer than I have to."

"Perhaps we could find a volunteer," said Campbell, trying to keep the peace. "I mean, it's difficult to identify Legacy in its earliest stages, I know, but if we could find someone—"

Hank shook his head, still glaring at Shaw. "But it might be a long search. No, Doctor Campbell, I don't think that's what our impatient benefactor has in mind at all. I think he'd rather save time by creating a suitable guinea-pig for us. Isn't that right, Shaw?"

"You mean..." Campbell glanced at Shaw, nervously. "You mean by infecting a healthy mutant with Legacy?"

"What's wrong, Doctor Campbell?" asked Hank. "He's already infected three humans, without appearing to distress you unduly."

"I didn't know..." stammered Campbell, looking between Hank and Shaw, obviously wanting to refute the allegation but not sure if he should speak out in front of his employer. "I mean, I didn't know he was going to...to...I didn't approve..." Until now, Campbell had gone about his work in a resigned, businesslike fashion. Only now did Hank realize that he must share his own deep reservations, at least to an extent.

"It's your choice, gentlemen," said Shaw abruptly, heading for the door. "By chance, I happen to have seven suitable subjects for experimentation housed in this very base, should you require them. Alternatively, you have four hours to explain how else you intend to deliver a working cure to me within the next fortnight."

"Seven subjects?" Hank repeated, feeling a sudden sense of dread, which quickly turned into anger. He had been lied to again. "Shaw!"

Shaw paused in the doorway and looked directly back at Hank, a malevolent gleam in his eye. "But that's your deadline, gentlemen. Four hours, no longer. And then, we'll do it my way. We'll test your serum on a member of the X-Men."

Iceman was cramped and restless, and becoming more anxious by the minute. He paced up and down, and walked impatiently around the small circular platform—but he had precious little space, and he could only succeed in making himself dizzy.

He didn't know how long he had been here, but it felt like a long time.

What if the other X-Men weren't coming? What if they were all trapped in cells like this one? What if they were all waiting, like he was, for somebody else to rescue them?

What if it was up to him to do something after all?

He scowled, and resisted the unpleasant notion. "It can't be up to me," he muttered under his breath. "It can't be my responsibility." One of the others would escape. One of the stronger X-Men. Storm, perhaps, or Phoenix or Wolverine. But a little voice inside his head told him otherwise. He *was* one of the stronger ones, it told him; one of the strongest mutants alive, if only he could accept the fact. But he didn't want to hear it.

He looked at the doors around the circular room, so close but unreachable. He even formed another ice slide, towards what he judged to be the nearest exit by a fraction, but the very act of doing so made his heart beat faster with fear.

He could do it. He could get out of this room. It would be the work of seconds. The flames would hardly touch him. They couldn't get through his protective ice coating.

No, he couldn't. It was too far. He wouldn't be able to keep his armor up all the way. The heat would melt it, and his slide, and then his skin and bones. He wasn't strong enough.

He put one foot on the base of the slide, not far enough along to activate the flames. An idea occurred to him, and he walked to the opposite edge of the platform. He could run across it, and then along his frozen construct, picking up some precious extra momentum before he crossed the platform's edge. He could shave a vital half-second off his time.

He almost went for it, he really did. But something paralyzed his legs: the part of himself that knew he was weak, the part that knew—no matter how many times he was told otherwise—that his power was useless, childish, no more than a gimmick, good for snowball fights but not much else.

The moment passed, and Iceman returned to the center of the platform. He sat down again and looked at the slide, his path to freedom—and the door, so close to him.

But so far away.

Jean pulled away from Madelyne, breathing hard, appalled at herself, appalled at what she had thought of doing, however briefly. She could see the marks left by her fingers, vivid red against the white skin of her enemy's throat. This wasn't her, she told himself. That evil witch had got into her mind, perverted her thoughts. The battle had only been a distraction.

"Go on then," challenged Madelyne Pryor, "do it! Kill me! Because I swear to you, Jean Grey, that, as long as I live, I'll haunt you. I will fight for the life you stole from me!" But there was disappointment in her eyes, for she, like Jean, knew the moment had passed.

"I wanted to," she breathed. "More than anything, I wanted to do it. You did a good job on me, Madelyne. You made me fear my future, what I could become. You made me want to destroy you, as the symbol of that fear. And then you would have won, wouldn't you? Then I would have become you." She didn't reveal how hard it had been to pull herself back from that brink. But she had managed it, and she felt a new strength for having done so.

She looked at her twin, still lying in the mud, and she almost felt sorry for her, with her half-life and her longing to become something more than a shadow. And she realized she would never again be afraid of Madelyne Pryor. Not like she had been.

"I'm not you, Madelyne," she reiterated—and, for the first time, she believed the words herself. "And I've told you before, I won't become like you. You can't make me doubt myself. I know who I am." With a hint of pity, she added: "I hope you can say the same, one day."

It was too much for Madelyne. With a cry of rage and frustration that was more animal than human, she leapt to her feet and launched herself at Jean, who was ready for her.

The two women grappled, Jean employing all her mental strength to protect her from her foe, who was fighting more savagely than ever before. This time, however, no words were spoken, no taunts or insults hurled.

The time for talking was past.

Tessa had had an idea. She had worked out how to solve her employer's problems.

For once, she hadn't told Sebastian about it. It was important that he should be able to retain plausible deniability. He would have to assure the X-Men that he hadn't authorized what she was about to do—and to be telling the truth, because Phoenix would detect any lies. He needed to be able to persuade the Beast that nothing had changed, that the unfortunate actions of one disobedient subordinate shouldn't keep him from concluding his research here. He might even have to issue his assistant with a reprimand. But, secretly, he would be pleased with her work, unsanctioned or not, because, by taking the initiative, she would have given him what he wanted.

Sebastian's greatest worry was that the X-Men would interfere in his plans. But he couldn't do anything to harm them himself, because he needed the Beast's help.

So, Tessa would act in his stead.

She passed the guards again, and stood outside one of the cells, using her telepathic abilities to eavesdrop upon the thoughts of the three men within. They were still trapped inside their mental prisons. Nightcrawler had become disheartened, but he hadn't given up. He still wandered around his gloomy labyrinth, looking for a way out. Cyclops smashed his way out of his fourth ruby quartz cell, refusing to surrender, refusing to believe that there wouldn't be an end to this madness. By contrast, Iceman was resigned to his fate, accepting that he could never leave his room of fire without help.

Tessa had to admit, begrudgingly, that Pryor had done her job well. But, as Sebastian himself knew, the X-Men could never be underestimated. They had escaped from seemingly inescapable situations before. It would only take one of them to break the Black Rook's mind-grip—or for Pryor herself to lose the upper hand in her ongoing battle against Phoenix. It behooved the Hellfire Club to be prepared for such a possibility, to guard against it.

Tessa unbolted the cell door, and entered. She took a pair of silk gloves from her pocket, and slipped her fingers into them. Then she produced a clear plastic bag, which she opened to reveal two items that she had taken from the vault in Sebastian Shaw's office, while he had been absent. She removed them carefully.

One of the items was a large, stoppered vial, which contained a transparent liquid. It looked harmless enough, but Tessa held it gingerly away from her. The liquid was swarming with viral cultures, and she was determined not to let a drop of it touch her skin. She wouldn't even breathe in its fumes if she could help it.

The other item was a syringe.

It was a simple enough plan, really. Sebastian had already forced three human scientists to help him by infecting them with the Legacy Virus. She would do the same to his mutant prisoners. That way, even if they did escape, they would face a dilemma.

Tessa knew the X-Men. She knew, as Sebastian did, that they would be fully prepared to wreck this project on a point of principle; that, like Moira MacTaggert, they would rather ensure that no cure for the Legacy Virus existed than see one in the Black King's hands. But how many of them might find the choice more difficult, might even come to think as the Beast had, if they were dying themselves; if the Hellfire Club offered them their only chance of survival? It would, at least, be enough to plant seeds of dissent among their ranks.

She decided to start with the X-Men's leader. She lowered herself into a kneeling position on the metal floor beside Cyclops. She removed the stopper from the vial, concentrating to keep her hands from trembling as she did so. She siphoned a tiny measure of the clear liquid into the syringe. She didn't need much. She breathed a small sigh of relief as she sealed the dangerous vial again. Then she took Cyclops's left hand in hers, reached under his yellow glove and rolled back his dark blue sleeve. She rubbed his skin, until she could see the faint blue outline of a vein beneath it.

Then she lowered the needlepoint of the syringe towards Cyclops's arm.

"Oh no you don't, sister!"

Tessa whirled at the sound of the voice behind her. She barely had time to register the sight of Iceman, somehow impossibly awake and springing across the room, his arms outstretched, a clear shell crackling into existence around his body. She put up her hands by reflex, and the syringe dropped to the floor and rolled away, as she reached for his mind telepathically. Then something hard and cold slammed into her face.

Tessa's last thought, as she felt herself slumping forwards, black spots beginning to crowd her vision, was a simple prayer that she wouldn't land on top of the vial of Legacy Virus.

"You can't seriously be considering this," said Rory Campbell.

The Beast was sitting on his lab stool again, staring down at the object in his hands, and turning it over and over. He looked up at Campbell, with a melancholy expression. "Can't I? From where I'm sitting, it makes perfect logical sense. Sebastian Shaw has us over a metaphorical barrel. If I agree to his terms, then I will become responsible for infecting an innocent mutant, and probably a good friend, with Legacy. I can't let that happen. But what are my realistic alternatives?"

Campbell looked quickly around the room, as if fearing that somebody might be watching. Then he leaned closer to Hank, and lowered his voice. "The rest of your team can't be more than a few floors away. We could release them."

"I'd wager we would have to fight our way through several Lords Cardinal and sundry mercenary agents first. All the same, I am sorely tempted. The question is, could we prevent the resultant hostilities from escalating out of control?"

"If we could," said Campbell, "we'd have everything we wanted." Hank looked at him for a moment, wondering if this was some sort of a trick, a test engineered by Shaw. But he was doing Rory Campbell an injustice, he decided. Like Hank himself, Moira's former assistant wasn't working for the Hellfire Club by choice. He was working for them because he thought they could give the world its best chance of curing a seemingly incurable disease. He had just come to that conclusion a little more quickly, that was all. "We'd still have our cure," said Campbell, "but we—not Shaw—would have control over it."

Hank thought about that, but shook his head. "As much as the possibility of such an outcome appeals to me, I can't believe it's very likely. If it came to a battle between the X-Men and the Hell-fire Club, and if it appeared that our side was gaining the advantage..."

Campbell's face fell. "You're right. Shaw could destroy this island, the Kree computer and all our work with the touch of a button. And he'd do it too, rather than be defeated."

"Which brings us back to our original dilemma. Is it better for a cure not to exist at all then for one to exist in the hands of such a man?"

"And have you changed your answer?"

"No," said the Beast quietly.

"So," said Campbell hesitantly, glancing at the object in his colleague's hands: a medical syringe, filled with a clear liquid. "You're going to do it then?"

"I don't believe I have a choice."

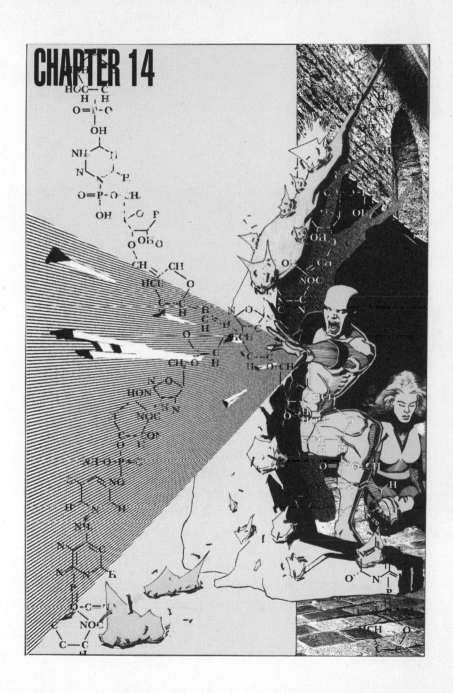

CHAPTER 14

ICEMAN WAS still shaking. He had rarely been so terrified in his life as when he had been steeling himself to race across that circular, white room, thinking about the consequences if he wasn't fast enough. In the end, though, once he had made up his mind, it had been over in seconds. There had been a blast of heat and a blazing light in his eyes, but he had tried to ignore both, concentrating until his head ached upon the act of creating fresh ice to keep up both the slide and his armor. He had hardly even seen where he was going.

His armor had fallen, and he had felt a tremendous heat upon his skin, but by that time he had already reached the door. And then he had awoken, in this metal-walled cell.

He smiled to himself as his fear began to wear off and was replaced by relief. He had done it. He had escaped from his prison—his mental prison, he now knew—when he had thought it impossible. And, it seemed, he was the first of the X-Men to have done so.

Cyclops and Nightcrawler were still lying on the floor, unconscious. So, rather more comfortably, was the mutant known as Tessa. It had taken Iceman a moment, upon awakening, to adjust to the fact that he wasn't where he had thought he was. But, quickly enough, he had realized what was happening: Shaw's assistant had been kneeling beside Cyclops, about to inject something into his arm. Iceman could see the syringe now, lying beside the telepath's outstretched hand. He couldn't identify the clear liquid inside it, but it was unlikely to be anything medicinal.

He remembered Wolverine's advice about Tessa: "Trick with her," he had said, "is to knock her down before she can worm her way into your head." He had done just that, pulling no punches, hitting her with a solid block of ice, shards of which still lay on the floor around her, and glistened in her black hair. She had sustained a shallow cut to her forehead.

Iceman hurried to Cyclops's side and tried to shake him awake. When this didn't work he mischievously dropped an ice cube down his leader's back. It provoked no reaction, not even a grunt, and a quick check told Iceman that Nightcrawler was in a similarly deep slumber. Presumably, they were both trapped in virtual prisons like his own.

He decided to find the other X-Men. Phoenix would be able to deal with this far better than he could—at least, as long as she wasn't in a comatose state too.

The door of the cell was standing open, so Iceman poked his head out into the corridor. He looked left: the passageway continued for a few yards, with more doors at each side, before reaching a dead end. He looked right: two of the Hellfire Club's mercenaries were staring at him. He ducked back into the room, narrowly avoiding a furious volley of machine-gun fire.

As the mercenaries' footsteps pounded towards him, he gave the floor inside the doorway a thin, icy coating. They ran into the room, and lost their footing. One fell on his back and riddled the ceiling with bullets. The other dropped his gun as he waved his arms frantically to keep himself upright. Iceman blocked the weapon of the former, filling its barrel with snow, in case a ricochet caught one of his friends. In the meantime, the second agent regained control of his limbs. He lunged toward the X-Man and punched his ice-encased jaw, hurting him but hurting himself

more. Iceman floored him with one blow, then dispatched his partner with similar efficiency, even as he was trying to stand.

Only then did he realize that the lights in the room—and in the
corridor outside—had dimmed, taking on a dull red hue. From
somewhere not too far away, he could hear the wail of a klaxon.
He gritted his teeth and cursed under his breath. The agents had
activated an alarm. Any second now, this area would be swarming
with more of their kind.

He raced back into the corridor, and to the nearest closed door.
It was sealed by a pair of sturdy bolts, which seemed to have been
screwed into its metal surface recently. Iceman pulled them back,
pushed the door open and found an empty room. The next room
was empty too. In the next, he found Wolverine, Rogue and Storm,
but no Phoenix.

He was heading further down the corridor, worried that he was
about to run out of time, when he heard a scream behind him. It
was a long, drawn-out scream of pain and frustration. And he recognized the screamer's voice.

"Jean!" he yelled, running as fast as he could toward the source
of the noise, terrified that something dreadful might have happened to her. He shot back two more bolts, and yanked open
another door. She was there all right, sitting in the middle of
another small, Spartan cell, blinking and wiping sweat from her
forehead. And there was somebody else too: another woman, in
black leather, apparently unconscious but staring blankly.

"Jean, are you all right?"

"Never better," said Phoenix, with a faint but genuine smile.
She looked down at the other woman, and Iceman started as he
recognized her. Madelyne Pryor, Scott Summers' former wife and
one-time member of the X-Men. Of course, he thought, she was a
clone of Jean, her voice was the same. It must have been her, not
his teammate, who had screamed. And that made him wonder
what Jean had done to her to hurt her so much. "She attacked me,"
said Phoenix, as if she had picked up the thought. "We fought on
the astral plane. I won."

"Look, Jeannie, we haven't got much time." Iceman reached out a hand to help her to her feet. It worried him how weak she seemed. He needed her.

"So I hear." The klaxon was still wailing.

"The others, they're trapped in their own minds somehow."

Phoenix nodded. "Madelyne told me what she'd done to them. Where are they?"

"I'll show you."

They ran back to the room that had once served as Bobby's cell. Phoenix saw Tessa, and Iceman quickly explained what had happened. He waited at the door so he could watch down the corridor for unwelcome arrivals, as Jean went to her husband's side. She laid a hand on Cyclops's masked forehead, and her green eyes flashed red, a telltale sign that she was employing her powers. But the red wasn't as deep as usual, and, just for a second, Iceman thought he saw green again. She was exhausted. Nevertheless, she looked up at him after a couple of seconds, with a quizzical expression.

"He's built his own prison in there—under Madelyne's direction, of course. I can lead him out of it easily enough—but if she did this to everyone, then how on earth did you get free?"

Iceman shrugged. "I don't know. I guess I had more willpower than the others."

It sounded unlikely, even to him—and he was a little embarrassed to see that Phoenix clearly didn't believe it either. She frowned, and he felt her gentle presence in his mind. Then her face cleared, and she smiled. "You underestimated yourself, as usual. You only created a prison you *thought* you couldn't get out of. Luckily for Scott, you learned better."

Bobby didn't know what to say to that. He stumbled over his words, and was almost grateful when the next wave of Hellfire Club agents ran into sight, interrupting him.

He stepped out to meet them, leaving Phoenix to her work. The agents were numerous, but the cramped confines of the corridor worked to Iceman's advantage. They had to approach him two at a time, and even if they aimed over each other's shoulders, no more than four of them could shoot at once. He created a shield of ice for himself and crouched behind it, letting the nearest men expend valuable ammunition. Bullets whizzed around him, but he rebuilt the shield faster than they could chip it away.

With his enemies almost upon him, Iceman changed tack. He lashed out with a hail of ice darts. They weren't sharp enough to penetrate the agents' padded uniforms; nevertheless, they fell back, bringing up hands to protect their eye-slits. Bobby took the opportunity to repeat his earlier trick, applying a light frost to the metal floor beneath them. In these close quarters, it only took one agent to slip and fall, whereupon he brought down another six with him. The ranks of Iceman's attackers collapsed in the middle.

He wondered how long it would take for Phoenix to wake the others. It occurred to him that he could buy some time by simply blocking the passageway with a glacier—but then, there didn't seem to be another way out of this section. The X-Men would have to break through the barrier themselves to escape, and the Hellfire Club could amass forces on the far side in the meantime. Anyway, it felt good to take the offensive. Much as he pretended not to care, a part of him burnt resentfully at what Jean had revealed.

He had been the only X-Man to overcome Madelyne's mind traps—and, secretly, he had felt quite proud of himself. Now he knew that he had only escaped because he had given himself the easiest task.

He set his jaw determinedly, and rained frozen stalactites upon the disoriented mercenaries.

"Scott!"

"Jean!" Cyclops turned, his face lighting up with hope at the sight of his wife behind him. He had been working on a fifth wall of ruby quartz crystal, beginning to feel that was no way out of here, but still driven on by his own stubborn insistence that, logically, there had to be. She had entered his scarlet-hued cell, the wall apparently peeling aside to allow her access. He strained to see through the gap behind her, but it seemed to open out onto a dark void. He frowned, and took an involuntary step away from her. "How did you get in here?"

"This place isn't what it seems."

"And what about you? Are you really my wife?"

"I can see why you're confused, Scott. Madelyne has you doubting yourself, trapped in your own nightmares. But reach out to me. Feel my thoughts."

Cyclops did so—and her warm, unmistakable presence rushed back into his mind, filling him with relief, joy and love. He ran towards her, and took her proffered hand.

"I can lead you out of here," said Jean. "Everything will be clearer then."

They ran into the void together.

Shaw sat behind his desk, his chin resting on his upturned knuckles. His eyes were closed, but he could still see the red glow of the emergency lighting through his eyelids. He was alone, as ultimately he always found himself, and his heart ached with the familiar sensation of impending defeat.

He didn't even have to know the details of what had happened. The alarm itself was enough. The X-Men had to be free, which meant that his Black Rook had almost certainly been taken already. He hadn't heard from Tessa since she had left to check up on his prisoners—and even at full strength, the Inner Circle would have been outnumbered anyway.

The X-Men didn't even have to win. The fight itself would probably be enough to destroy everything that Shaw had worked towards for months. Even if it wasn't, if there was still enough of the Kree facility left for McCoy, Campbell and the others to synthesize their cure later, then it would be Xavier's children who controlled it. Shaw drew in a deep breath, and let out a heavy sigh at the inevitability of it all.

There was only one thing left to do. He unlocked and pulled open the top drawer of his desk. Attached to the side of the drawer, inside, was a small, metal box. It opened like a Chinese puzzle box; Shaw applied pressure to various points on its surface in an exact sequence, until the lid sprang up.

Anybody who had ever seen an action movie, or read a comic book, could have guessed the purpose of the single red button that was thereby revealed.

He could set the timer running now. Hidden explosives would destroy the base, and return the island to the seabed from which his ally had raised it, in thirty minutes. That left him plenty of time to get away, taking Tessa and the other Lords Cardinal with him if possible.

With luck, at least some of the X-Men would be caught in the explosion. The important thing, however, was that they wouldn't be able to take the fruits of his work away with them.

One touch of the red button. That was all it would take.

Then he thought about Moira MacTaggert. He thought about her determination that it was better to have no cure for the Legacy Virus than to have one exist in the hands of an enemy. He hadn't been able to understand her attitude. Now he understood it only too well. Despite the situation, Shaw smiled to himself at the irony of his dilemma. He had more in common with the good doctor than he had thought.

The sounds of battle were approaching his small office. Shaw could hear the rhythmic chattering of his pawns' machine guns, and the all too recognizable energy discharges of Cyclops's optic blasts. It was time to make a decision, time to act.

Instead he sat alone in the gloom, deep in thought, listening as his dreams were torn apart around him.

His hand rested lightly on the red button, but he didn't press it yet.

Every muscle in Cyclops's body screamed that it was tired and sore. He made himself ignore the pain. He had been asleep for hours, but a part of his mind that he couldn't control remembered his imaginary toils, and insisted that he ought to be exhausted.

An icy trickle of water ran down his back, and he wondered where it had come from.

The Hellfire Club's agents were little threat individually, well trained though they were, but they seemed impossibly numerous. For each one that Cyclops brought down with a fist or a carefully gauged blast, two more appeared to replace him. However, the X-Men's numbers were increasing too, as Phoenix woke her team-mates one by one, and sent them to join the ongoing battle. Iceman, Cyclops and Nightcrawler had already succeeded in beating their foes back to the stairs, and their progress only became quicker as their ranks were swelled, first by the addition of Storm and then by Wolverine.

Finally, Rogue came flying along the corridor, Phoenix running at her heels. *Hank's here,* Jean told the others, linking them telepathically again. *Now that we're inside the Hellfire Club's base, their psi-shielding isn't as effective. I detected his thoughts a few minutes ago.*

Where is he? asked Cyclops.

Above us. I'm still working on the precise location. I think I can sense Moira, too.

Looks like we hit the jackpot, opined Wolverine.

OK, people, Cyclops commanded, *time is of the essence. We can't let Shaw get away with his hostages—and we don't know what else he might be preparing. We need to clear a way through his goons as efficiently as possible.*

He had already gained a few steps up the staircase, but Hellfire Club agents at the next level were leaning over the railings, sighting along their rifles. They had a good vantage point; Cyclops fought to ensure that they couldn't get a clear shot at him, through their allies. Then Storm took the matter into her hands. She flew straight up the stairwell, her cloak billowing behind her and confusing anyone who tried to get a bead on her. She manipulated the air itself, to snatch the snipers' weapons from their grips.

Soon after that, the mercenaries surrendered the staircase, falling back and taking up new defensive positions on the topmost level of the base. *I've got a fix on Moira,* reported Phoenix, as the X-Men climbed after them. *She's behind us—on the floor we've just passed. She's guarded, but only by two people. The Hellfire Club seem more intent on keeping us away from Hank. He's just above us now. And he's with the kidnapped geneticists.*

I'll go fetch Moira, offered Rogue. As she followed Jean's telepathic directions, the rest of the X-Men closed with their foes again. The agents were hopelessly outmatched. They couldn't even set up an effective ambush, thanks to Nightcrawler's ability to teleport behind them, not to mention Wolverine's willingness to simply run the gauntlet of their blazing machine guns, somehow reaching them unscathed. Still, for every second the heroes were delayed in their quest to reach their captured teammate, Cyclops grew more worried.

He found himself grappling hand-to-hand with a small group of agents. Three of them held him from behind, and one pulled back his head so that he was staring at the ceiling and couldn't aim his optic blasts. He kicked and struggled, determined to deprive them too of the chance to use their weapons against him. But tiredness crept up and threatened to overcome him, his head began to swim, and all the strength drained out of his limbs.

At first, he thought he was suffering a delayed reaction to his recent exertions. He concentrated on overcoming his physical shortcomings, on keeping control. Then he realized what was actually happening.

One of the agents had clamped a gloved hand onto his shoulder. Cyclops tried to dislodge it, but he was no longer strong enough. With a supreme effort, he twisted around and looked into the fervent eyes of his attacker. Despite the blank-faced mask, he knew without a doubt that he was being held by a disguised Trevor Fitzroy.

And that, courtesy of Fitzroy's energy-draining powers, he had mere seconds to live.

He tried to operate his visor, to blast the young Lord Cardinal away from him, but he couldn't even summon up the strength to close his fingers on the sensor. The world was growing dark, and it was all he could do to cry out to Jean, in his mind, as his legs turned to jelly and the floor rushed up to meet his face.

For a moment, he was lost in a forest of red-booted feet, hardly able to keep his eyes open, his entire body feeling like lead, waiting for Fitzroy to sap the last iota of his life force from him. Then something yellow hurtled over his head, he heard the dull impact of one body hitting another, and one pair of red boots was propelled away from him. Blearily, he pieced together what must have happened: Wolverine had received his psychic distress call and tackled Fitzroy, knocking him away before he could finish off his target. Cyclops mouthed a silent prayer of gratitude for the blessing of teamwork as he blacked out.

He fought his way back to consciousness, seconds or minutes later, to find that he was still on the floor and still surrounded. Now, however, he recognized the feet of his teammates. In the midst of the battle, they had gathered around him to prevent their enemies from taking advantage of his condition.

Wh-where's Fitzroy? he telesent to Jean. It was difficult even to form the words in his mind.

Wolverine dealt with him.

Is he...?

Unconscious. Logan hit him before he could summon his bio-armor.

Satisfied, Cyclops moved to his next most pressing concern: *I can't move, Jean. Can you help me?*

She sounded doubtful. *I can boost your mental resilience. I can help you to ignore your weakness. But it won't last long, Scott. I can't affect your physical condition. Once the boost wears off, you'll be dead on your feet.*

That's acceptable. Do it, Jean!

He felt the strength flowing back into his muscles, as Phoenix stooped down and lifted him. He tried not to think about the fact that his renewed vitality was only an illusion.

The ranks of the Hellfire Club's agents were thinning out, and he smiled grimly. "We're almost there, X-Men. Let's mop up the last of these people and rescue our friend!"

The laboratory, like the rest of the complex, was washed in a dull shade of red, and that infernal klaxon alarm wouldn't stop howling.

Hank McCoy was sitting on a lab stool, looking at the main screen of the Kree computer, trying in vain to memorize as much precious information as he could. His head was aching, his stomach was churning and he couldn't bring the figures into focus. And, as the sounds of battle reached his ears, he knew that he had run out of time.

He got to his feet, and the world lurched around him. He couldn't remember ever feeling more tired. He clutched at a lab bench for support. Rory Campbell stepped forward, hobbling on his crutch, and offered him a hand, but Hank waved it away. The other three geneticists sat quietly at the far side of the room, and watched him, tensely. Nobody spoke. They looked at their mutant colleague in a new light now. They were relying on him to do something, to save the project and their lives.

Hank had gone over what he had to say to the X-Men many, many times in his mind. He couldn't get the words right.

And then the sounds of battle drew nearer, and the combatants finally spilled into the laboratory, just as Hank had always known they would.

The Hellfire Club's agents came first, fighting a rearguard action. They spread across the room, taking up the most advantageous positions, scattering papers across the work surfaces and aiming machine guns at the doors. A second later, three more agents appeared in the doorway. It took Hank a moment to see that they were grappling with one of his teammates. Wolverine was almost invisible beneath their dark blue uniforms, but that soon changed. He hurled one of them away from him, tripped a second and grabbed the third, twisting him around so that, when the inevitable barrage of bullets came from inside the room, it was he who took the brunt of the attack. A line of red dots exploded across the agent's back, and Hank felt sickened. The first death. How many more would there be?

He leapt up onto a bench, and shouted to Campbell and the others to take shelter. He waved his arms, and yelled hoarsely: "There's no need for this violence! Do you hear me?"

Wolverine flew at another agent, kicking him in the head as he fired his gun. His shot went wild, and the Beast found himself dancing out of the way of his bullets, one of which ricocheted off a computer bank. Hank stifled a wail of dismay, as something fizzled and burned behind a control panel.

More people were pouring into the room: more Hellfire Club agents, more X-Men. Cyclops and Phoenix came last; Scott must have been injured, as he was leaning heavily against his wife's shoulder—but he still lashed out gamely with his optic blasts. If Hank had ever imagined he could calm things down, then he knew better now. But he still had to try.

Iceman was thrown back against the bench on which he stood. Hank hopped down to the floor beside him, thinking that maybe he could get through to his friends one by one. "Bobby, we've got to bring a halt to this. Neither side can win, but we might all lose far more than you can know."

His teammate threw him an uncertain look, but was distracted as a costumed mercenary came at him, using his empty machine-gun as a bludgeon. Iceman dodged, but took a crack to his shoulder. He retaliated with a barrage of ice darts. "I'll do what I can, Hank," he promised, "but I think it's these guys you need to be talking to." And, with that, he hurled himself back into the fray.

Hank looked around desperately, and saw Moira MacTaggert arriving with Rogue. She might not have had the X-Men's powers, nor the weapons of their adversaries, but she threw herself into the battle all the same, fighting hand-to-hand and managing to hold her own. Hank bounded towards her, handing off three Hellfire Club goons, and he pulled her to one side, to a position of relative safety. "Moira, you have to assist me. It's imperative that we do not damage the equipment in this room."

"Hank, we've already talked about this."

He seized her by the shoulders, and stared urgently into her eyes. "You don't understand." The words came out as an anguished cry. "We've done it, Moira. We've found our cure—but this skirmish is jeopardizing our hopes of ever being able to employ it."

Moira opened her mouth, but no words came out. She looked uncertain.

Hank pressed his advantage. "It doesn't have to fall to the Hellfire Club to control it. The X-Men have the upper hand now. Assuming that Shaw is as keen to preserve this discovery as I am, then surely we can reach an accommodation." He was aware of his own voice racing, its pitch becoming higher. "But only if we can stop this now!" And only, he thought, if Shaw hadn't already taken drastic measures. Too many ifs.

Moira's doubts were plain in her expression, but Hank could see that he had almost convinced her—to discuss the matter, at least. By now, though, the laboratory was in chaos, its floor almost invisible beneath a mass of undulating bodies. Even Campbell and the others had been dragged into the melee; Storm had taken it upon herself to protect them. Instinct told Hank to duck, just in time to avoid a spray of bullets. He heard a fragile piece of equipment breaking, and realized that the support of one friend wasn't nearly enough. She was as helpless to stop this as he was.

That was when his gaze alighted upon somebody else: a new arrival, who had reached the doorway and halted there. It was Sebastian Shaw. And for once, he wasn't smiling. He surveyed the chaos, lips set into a grim line. Then his eyes met Hank's, and a flash of understanding passed between the two men.

Moira saw it too. "Hank, you can't!" she whispered, but he was already making his way across the packed room. Shaw came to meet him, finding a path more easily. Whereas the Beast had to keep on his toes, ducking and dodging, twisting this way and that, forever alert for any attempt to attack him, Shaw strode almost casually, never losing sight of his target, and the crowd just seemed to part around him.

"We've got to stop this," said Hank, as they met, and the Black King just nodded.

Then his eyes widened and became bloodshot, and, as much as he tried to control it, Hank could see that he was in agony.

A second later, he saw the reason.

"Jeannie, no!" Phoenix had appeared behind Shaw, her eyes a dangerous red. Her foe's energy-absorbing powers couldn't defend him against a mental attack. As his eyeballs started to roll back into his head, Hank leapt at his friend, took hold of her and shook her, breaking her concentration. Shaw, still staggered, breathed heavily and put a hand to his forehead. Phoenix looked at the Beast, quizzically.

"There's no time to explain," Hank panted. "You've got to trust me on this one, Jean. Can you do that?"

"You don't have to ask," she said, but she was still confused.

"I've negotiated a truce." Despite her promise, it looked like Phoenix was about to say something. Hank forestalled the objection. "It's entirely in our interests, believe me. It is vital that we bring this unfortunate contretemps to as swift a conclusion as possible!"

"I can order my men to lay down their weapons," offered Shaw. He was still pale, but otherwise he seemed to have recovered from Phoenix's assault with incredible speed. "Under the circumstances, though, I'd have difficulty making myself heard."

Phoenix nodded. "OK."

She lowered her head and concentrated, and suddenly an impression formed in Hank's mind. He thought—no, *knew*—that Shaw was reaching out to him personally, making it clear that he didn't want this fight to continue. Jean must have reached into the Black King's thoughts, found that strong, genuine desire and communicated it to everybody, along with her own endorsement for the sake of the X-Men.

The tactic proved effective. Silence descended upon the laboratory, and everybody looked towards Shaw and Phoenix to see what they should do next. Rogue froze, with one hand pinning a

Hellfire Club agent to the wall, the other drawn back and clenched into a fist. Storm took advantage of the cessation of hostilities to usher a frightened Professor Travers into a slightly safer position, behind her.

"This isn't a trick," said Shaw, his voice calm and measured now, but carrying easily across the hushed room to his attentive servants. "The X-Men and I have reached an...agreement. As of now, they are to be considered my guests. Return to your normal duties." As the uniformed agents began to file, obediently and unquestioningly, out into the corridor, he glanced down at the floor, which was strewn with the unconscious bodies of the fallen. "Those of you who can," he added wryly. He still wasn't smiling.

Cyclops found his way to Phoenix's side, still hobbling slightly. "Jean?"

Phoenix glanced meaningfully towards Hank, and he knew this was the moment of truth. The room was emptying: only a small team of agents had stayed behind to revive their colleagues, or to carry them out where revival proved impossible. Shaw himself stepped into the shadows, watching quietly as the X-Men gathered expectantly around their blue-furred teammate. The rest of the scientists also drew closer, anxious for news of their fate.

Hank looked around the room, assessing the condition of the Kree computer banks. They had certainly been battered; one panel had been blown out altogether, and several screens were broken. He prayed that the damage was not too extensive.

He looked at each of the X-Men in turn, then his gaze lingered last and longest upon Moira. She hesitated for a second, before folding her arms tightly across her chest, and giving him a winsome smile and a nod of support. Grateful for that, at least, Hank took a deep breath, trying to drive back the pain in his head for long enough to give what seemed, at that moment, to be the most crucial speech of his life.

And then, the pain attacked him with a vengeance. The world shot out of focus, and Hank doubled up in a coughing fit so violent that he felt as if his heart and lungs were straining to escape from his body. He blacked out for an instant, and, when he came to, he was sitting on a stool, sweat matting his fur, concerned friends hovering around him, and Moira was dabbing at his forehead with a cold, wet cloth.

"Och, Hank," she groaned, "you didn't, did you? Please tell me you didn't."

Hank wanted to answer her, but his throat was too dry, and he couldn't speak.

"Is someone gonna tell us what's going on?" asked Wolverine, impatiently.

"He's infected himself, that's what," said Moira, with a hint of bitterness.

"Infected himself?" echoed Iceman. "With what?"

But some of the others were quicker on the uptake. "Oh Goddess, no..." breathed Storm, putting a hand to her mouth in horror.

"We needed a test subject," croaked Hank, each word burning in his throat. "It had to be a healthy mutant. I had no choice. But...Legacy..." He coughed again, and breathed deeply to compose himself before continuing. "Legacy is unpredictable. Some people can live with it for months, others for days or less. I...I find myself in the latter group, I'm afraid."

"But Moira said you were looking for a cure," protested Rogue. "She said you were..." She hesitated, but chose to complete the sentence. "She said you were working with Shaw."

"She was correct," said Hank. He cast his eyes downwards, sparing himself the sight of his friends' reactions. He pressed on quickly: "And we can debate the rights and wrongs of my decision at a more opportune time. For now, all that matters is that I have been given a chance to rid the world of the Legacy Virus at last. I can save potentially thousands of lives, including those of several good colleagues here present. You—and I mean all of you –" He looked pointedly at Shaw. "– must decide now whether you will allow me to take that chance. You might feel—" He transferred his attention to Moira. "—that you'd rather find the cure some other way. Most of you can afford to wait. If that is your decision, then so be it—but, whatever you decide, you will have to do so quickly.

"Forty minutes ago, I infected myself with the Legacy Virus. Ten minutes after that, I injected the serum that is the first stage of our untested Legacy cure into my system. So far, its effect upon the diseased cells has been negligible.

"Without further treatment, I can measure my life expectancy in hours."

CHAPTER 15

AS WITH much of the recovered Kree facility, the Hellfire Club had done little to brighten up the area that they had designated their conference room. They had restored it to full functionality, but nothing more. Ororo Munroe looked at the dull, gray, windowless walls and the single closed door, and was reminded that she was still underground. She felt confined, but she refused to be distracted by her illogical fears. Not now. Not while there were still important issues to be resolved.

As the X-Men's deputy leader, Storm was speaking for the team at this hastily convened meeting. She was backed up by Phoenix, who sat beside her at the circular conference table. Shortly after hostilities had ceased in the laboratory, Cyclops had collapsed, succumbing at last to a telepathically-delayed reaction to the power drain inflicted upon him by Fitzroy. He was sleeping now, with his teammates watching over him, in a neighboring bunkroom.

The Beast had wanted to be here as well, but Moira had forbidden it. His condition was too fragile. He too was resting, and she had promised to put his point of view across to this gathering, as well as her own. She was seated to Ororo's right, with Doctor Rory Campbell next to her. Moira had been civil enough to her former assistant, but Storm could tell from her body language that he made her uncomfortable. She didn't trust his motives.

Ororo had seen nothing of either Madelyne or Fitzroy. Presumably, the Black and White Rooks had made themselves scarce after their recent defeats. The Inner Circle was represented by its Black King, Shaw. He sat next to Campbell, directly across the table from his opposite number, whom he regarded coolly. He had regained his usual self-assured demeanor. Ororo would hardly have guessed from looking at him that the X-Men had just ruined his plans. To Shaw's right, between him and Jean, was his seemingly ever-present assistant, Tessa.

Moira opened the meeting by recounting what she knew of the Hellfire Club's actions so far, for the benefit of Ororo and Jean. Her voice carried an accusatory tone, especially as she described her own kidnapping and Shaw's inhuman treatment of his team of geneticists. But Shaw himself said nothing to dispute her version of events. He simply nodded quietly at appropriate junctures, and the ghost of a smile played about his lips. Ororo was saddened. Life seemed to mean so little to him. No more than just another commodity, to be used and abused. She had met too many people with similar attitudes, though, to be particularly surprised or angered. In contrast, Moira looked like she could flare up at any minute, incensed by Shaw's smugness. To Ororo's relief, she contained herself.

What did surprise her was the revelation of how Hank McCoy, far from being snatched by the Hellfire Club as the X-Men had assumed, had offered his services to them willingly. However, by the time Moira had explained his reasons, calmly and without any personal bias, Ororo thought she understood.

"We knew he had been affected by recent events," she reflected. "If only we had realized quite how badly."

"May I suggest," said Shaw, "that such recriminations are of no use to us now."

"Fine," said Moira, with heavy sarcasm. "So, we'll not talk about the innocent people you've kidnapped and infected then, shall we not?"

"The important thing, my dear," said Shaw, and Ororo saw a scowl flicker across Moira's face at the familiar term of address, "is to deal with the situation as it currently stands—and, specifically, with the fact that we are on the verge of finding a cure for the Legacy Virus."

"How close are you, exactly?" asked Jean.

Shaw turned to Campbell. "Theoretically," said the scientist, "we're already there. According to the projections we ran on the Kree computer, our treatment should work."

"In practice, though," Moira pointed out, "there's some way to go yet."

"The serum that Doctor McCoy has taken should react with his mutant gene."

"It should. But so far, it hasn't."

"However," countered Campbell, "this wasn't an unexpected development. We've already prepared a course of safe radiation treatment, using Kree machinery. It should be possible to jumpstart the reaction."

"And how long might that take?" asked Ororo.

"We should see some positive effect within an hour or so of the first dose. After that, it's difficult to say. Days, perhaps weeks, before Hank goes into remission. As soon as he does, though, we'll have a new, improved serum, which we can extract from his bloodstream."

Ororo glanced questioningly at Moira. The Scots woman shrugged. "Hank described the process to me. I can't say for sure that it'll work, but—well, it's feasible. I only wish he'd carried out proper tests before throwing himself in at the deep end like this." She shot a filthy look at Shaw. "No prizes for guessing who takes the blame for that."

"We don't appear to have much choice," said Ororo, with a sigh. "As Henry himself said, he doesn't have much time. If we wish to save his life, then we must allow this project to continue." She noticed Shaw's satisfied expression, and added sharply: "However, there will be certain conditions."

"For a start," said Moira, "I'll have nothing to do with this cure of yours without a guarantee that it will be freely available to anyone who wants it."

"I might remind you," said Shaw, "that the Hellfire Club, not to mention my own company, Shaw Industries, have invested a considerable amount of capital in this venture."

"Aye, and you've broken a considerable number of laws as well!"

"I think that's a matter for the courts to decide, don't you?"

"Oh, I get it!" snapped Moira. "I suppose, once you were finished with your unwilling slaves, you were planning to get one of your tame telepaths to mess with their memories, were you? Make sure they didn't testify?" She glared at Tessa, who had contributed nothing to the discussion so far. She seemed happy to sit at her employer's side, observing. "Well, you can forget that too, Shaw. You've done enough to those people already!"

The Black King shrugged, appearing unconcerned. Ororo wondered if it was a bluff, but it was certainly possible that he had the right contacts to ensure that any charges laid against him were thrown out, or at least dealt with in a way that didn't inconvenience him too much. Perhaps his company would receive a token fine. It annoyed her to think that, legally as well as physically, Shaw himself might be virtually untouchable.

"Nevertheless," he said, "I do expect some return from my outlay." He smiled tightly. "Otherwise, what possible motive do I have for allowing McCoy and his colleagues to continue their work at all? Need I remind you that this island, like everything upon and beneath it, is the property of the Hellfire Club? The X-Men are trespassers here."

"Trespassers who could bring this whole place down on top of you," grumbled Moira.

"Then do so," challenged Shaw.

"All right," said Ororo, "suppose we were to agree that if this cure does prove viable, then you can market it at a reasonable cost." She stressed the word 'reasonable'.

"That's all I ask."

"But we take a sample away with us too," said Moira, "just in case."

"I think that's fair," said Jean. She smiled at Shaw, sweetly. "We wouldn't want you to be tempted to go back on your word, now would we?"

"Acceptable," said Shaw, with a brusque nod.

"You will also allow Professor Travers, and Doctors Scott and Takamoto, to leave with us now if they wish," said Ororo, "or to contact their families, if they'd prefer to stay."

Shaw shrugged nonchalantly, as if it were of no importance to him.

"And the X-Men will maintain a presence at this facility, until the cure is ready."

"Ms. Munroe, you will already have the Beast on site—and Doctor MacTaggert as well, if she is prepared to swallow her precious principles and help us now." Shaw looked at Moira. "I'm sure that, even at this late stage, her expertise would prove invaluable."

"Henry McCoy is very ill," said Ororo, "and I intend to ensure that he's looked after. Three more X-Men will remain on this island at all times."

"Two," said Shaw.

"Only if you withdraw any personnel who aren't required to keep the base running."

"Agreed."

"And that includes the Lords Cardinal."

Shaw thought about it for a few seconds. "Agreed," he said again. "But I will remain here to supervise the proceedings myself—and, of course, I will need Tessa with me."

"Very well then," said Ororo. "Goddess help us all, but I think we have an agreement."

"I think we do," said Shaw. He got to his feet, and reached across the table, his smile turning into a broad grin. Ororo stood too, took his hand and shook it.

She tried not to show how much she was revolted by the very touch of his skin.

Wolverine put Storm's misgivings into words, when he heard what had been decided. "Seems to me we're just rolling over and letting Shaw and his flunkies get away with it," he complained from beneath the landing wheels of the crippled Blackbird. He and Rogue had ventured out into the forest, even though the evening had drawn in and a light rain had begun to fall. They were checking up on the plane, seeing what they could do about patching it up, at least enough to get them home.

"I know how you feel," said Ororo, "but there were other people to consider in all this."

"Those poor scientists," said Rogue, sympathetically.

Wolverine showed his oil-streaked face, which wore a disgruntled scowl. "Yeah, and I'd happily pop a claw or two through Shaw's heart just for what he's done to them, let alone to McCoy and Moira. Doesn't seem right that he's gonna profit from it."

"But we've put a dent in his plans," Rogue pointed out. "What else can we do? We can't very well leave Hank and Doctor Scott and the rest to die, can we?"

"Unfortunately," said Storm, "a deal with Shaw seemed the lesser of two evils."

"And at least, this way, we get a cure for the Legacy Virus," said Rogue. "We can save Moira too, and who-knows-how-many other people in the future."

"Let's hope so," said Wolverine. "I'm not complaining, 'Ro. You did the right thing." Darkly, he added: "But Shaw's day will come—and that's a promise!"

Shaw was trailed by Tessa all the way to his temporary office in the underground facility. He had almost forgotten she was there, until they reached the door and she quietly asked him if he required anything more of her. He told her to arrange the partial evacuation of the island, as agreed with Storm, and the reopening of the Hellfire Club's mainland headquarters. Then he turned his back, closed the door on her, and retreated into solitude behind his desk.

Alone now, Shaw dropped his confident, indifferent façade. His face darkened, his fists tightened, and he sat and brooded for several minutes. The X-Men, it seemed, were always able to thwart his ambitions. He should have seen this coming. Worse, he *had* seen it coming, but he had been too arrogant to do anything about it, to change his plans. He should have left the MacTaggert woman alone. But then if he had, the Beast would never have come to him, and he might not have come so close to finding his longed-for cure. No, he decided, he hadn't come out of this too badly, all things considered.

He repeated that affirmation to himself until he almost believed it. But still, his dark mood persisted. Shaw knew the reason why, although he had been trying to deny it. It irritated him to think that one person—any one person—should have this sort of power over him. He was angry with himself for feeling nervous; afraid, even. And, worst of all, for feeling inferior.

He bit down hard and tried to override his trepidation. He stabbed out with a determined finger, and booted up his laptop computer. He didn't allow himself to hesitate as he ran the communications program. He seethed with indignation as a pop-up window informed him that his business partner couldn't take his call right now, but would speak with him at his earliest convenience.

Shaw waited, rehearsing arguments in his head, becoming ever more impatient.

When the shadowy figure with the burning eyes appeared at last on his screen, he forgot all his carefully planned words. "I take it you have something to report, Shaw?" came the familiar inhuman strains of a digitally-altered voice.

Shaw took a deep, controlled breath, and resolved not to let himself be treated like a subordinate. He had entered into this business arrangement as an equal—and, even if his so-called ally wouldn't address him as such, then at least he would act the part.

"There's been a change of plan," he said.

"The X-Men," surmised his partner, with an unmistakable hint of contempt.

"Indeed," said Shaw, tightly. He recapped recent events, emphasizing the benefits of McCoy's cooperation. But his partner was not to be mollified.

"I told you what would happen if you involved Xavier's whelps in our plans," he snapped.

"They're prepared to let us finish our work," stated Shaw, flatly.

"Under their supervision! This cure is only half as much use to us if we don't exercise sole control over it. You know that, Shaw!"

The Black King's temperature was rising now, as he turned his fear into resentment, which in turn became anger. Fortunately, he was used to controlling his emotions. But he could see his own eyes flashing dangerously in his reflection in the screen.

"I took the necessary steps to ensure that a cure will exist at all," he said, tartly. "I salvaged success from a project that was going nowhere."

"If you call this 'success,' submitting to the wishes of our greatest enemies. I raised an island for you, Shaw. I helped to fund your miserable operation—only for you to overreach yourself again. Your incompetence has brought down everything we've worked for!"

Shaw's lips curled into a snarl. "This game isn't over yet…" He almost addressed his partner by name over the link, but that would only have riled him even more. "The X-Men might find I've still got a trick or two up my sleeve." *As might you, you imperious blowhard!* he added silently, to himself.

"You'd better, Shaw—for your own sake."

The shadowy face disappeared from Shaw's screen, and another window appeared to tell him that the link had been severed from the other side. He stared at the message in disbelief, and felt a rare, uncontrollable fury rising inside him. He threw himself to his feet, overturning his chair in the process. He swept his arm across the desk, scattering papers and knocking his laptop computer to the floor. He picked up a paperweight and hurled it viciously across the room. Then, running out of targets upon which to vent his wrath, he turned and punched the wall repeatedly. His mutant ability didn't protect him—because he was creating kinetic energy himself, and turning it outwards—and his knuckles became bruised. But the sharp pain helped him to focus, and his rage eventually subsided.

He was relieved, at least, that nobody had been around to witness his outburst. To other people—most other people—Sebastian Shaw was a cool, collected businessman, a controlled force to be reckoned with. He had no wish to alter that perception.

There were some sides of himself that he preferred to keep hidden.

The rain had passed now, and the sky was clear again. But water seeped into Hank McCoy's trunks and fur as he sat on the damp grass, leaning back against a tree-trunk and staring upwards. He was tired, and he wanted to close his eyes—but the night sky, untainted by the electric lighting of civilization, was a sight well worth a little effort to see.

Hank marveled at the uncountable thousands of stars that freckled the dark void, each one a blazing sun, perhaps supporting life on its orbiting planets. He was luckier than most: he had been out there, several times, and had witnessed wonders far beyond the imagination of most earthbound humans. But, from this perspective, he could see how vast the universe was, and he knew he had glimpsed only the tiniest fraction of what Creation had to offer.

There was still so much to see. So much to do.

Behind him, he heard footsteps, climbing the metal steps from the underground base. He sighed. His moment of quiet solitude had been all too brief.

The intruder walked through the clearing and straight towards him, even though he had thought himself concealed from the entranceway by the tree against which he rested. That told him who she was, even before he scented her gentle perfume on the fresh breeze.

"Hello, Jean," he said, without looking at her.

"I bet Moira wouldn't be too pleased with you if she knew you'd come out here alone," said Jean Grey Summers, but the good-humored tone of her voice belied the admonishing words. "Aren't you meant to be hooked up to all types of monitoring equipment downstairs?"

"I was weary of being poked and prodded and analyzed," said Hank. "This might be my last opportunity to view the night sky, and to breathe in fresh air. I thought I'd take it."

Phoenix sat beside him. "I thought your first dose of radiation treatment went well?"

"As well as could be expected, yes. There have been no unpleasant side-effects, which is something to be grateful for. The idea of a balding, blue Beast hardly bears thinking about."

"But your mutant gene—it is fighting back now, isn't it?"

Hank nodded. "The rate at which the Legacy Virus is corrupting my DNA strands has slowed considerably. However, the long-term prognosis is still somewhat uncertain."

"Well, Moira seems to think you might make a full recovery. So does Doctor Campbell. You ought to have more faith in yourself, Hank. I do."

"I am simply being pragmatic, Jeannie." With another heavy sigh, Hank wrenched his gaze away from the stars and turned to her. "Nobody can be sure precisely what this treatment will do to me. I have to face the possibility that I might still die." He held up a hand to forestall her next words. "And don't tell me not to think like that, because I'd rather be prepared."

"Fair enough," said Jean quietly. "So, how do you feel right now?"

"Exhausted. Fragile. Sick. Dizzy. My immune system is divert-ing all the resources it can marshal into an all-out war, win or lose. I feel burnt out, scoured clean inside. My body is failing me, and I feel helpless. I feel like William Montgomery must have felt, except that I'm the lucky one, because I still have some hope of being able to reverse my deterioration."

Jean didn't say anything. Hank closed his eyes. He longed for sleep, but he feared that if he were to doze off now he might never wake again. If this was his last day on Earth, then he wanted it to last a little longer. He wasn't ready to leave yet.

"According to Logan, the Blackbird's almost ready." Jean's attempt to change the subject was transparent. She thought it might help him to have something else to discuss, bless her. "We should be flying back to Westchester tomorrow."

Hank nodded. "Who's staying behind?"

"Ororo and Bobby. And Moira, of course. Scott and I would have stayed, but he's still so weak. It'll take him a couple of days to recover from what Fitzroy did to him."

"How *is* Scott?"

"Sleeping like a lamb. Don't worry about him, he'll be fine. Well, apart from a few battle scars—but we've all got them, I think."

"We certainly have," said Hank, morosely. He opened his eyes and looked up at the stars again. "How did we get here, Jeannie? It seems like only yesterday that we were enrolling at Professor Xavier's School for Gifted Youngsters, the eager new students. The world seemed a much simpler place, then."

"I know," sighed Jean.

"It's early afternoon on the East Coast of America. Sunday afternoon. Just over three days since I attended the funeral in Newhill. It's one of the quirks of memory, I suppose, that whereas our halcyon school days feel so recent, it seems like a lifetime since I heard that William Montgomery had died."

"But you've achieved so much since then!" insisted Jean.

"I just hope it's enough."

"You're prepared to sacrifice your life to cure the Legacy Virus! How can anybody expect any more of you than that?"

Hank shook his head. "No, Jean. I wish that was the case, but it's not. I'd die happily if I thought I could save others by so doing. But if I die now, it will be because the project has failed, because a cure is still beyond us after all. I will have achieved nothing."

"That's not true!"

"Which makes me wonder," he continued, ignoring the interruption, "have I been misguided all along? By throwing in my lot with the Hellfire Club and then infecting myself as I have, have I acted in a rational manner? Or have I allowed my impatience and feelings of guilt to override my better judgement? Have I thrown away my life, and my chances of discovering a real cure for Legacy, on a foolish whim? Have I, in effect, committed suicide?"

"You did what you thought to be the right thing," said Jean, "in a difficult situation. Nobody will judge you for that."

Selene sat back comfortably in her cushioned throne, as the image of Phoenix's concerned face faded into the milky white depths of her hovering crystal ball. Her conversation with the Beast had been recorded, some hours earlier, while Selene had slumbered through the daylight hours. Now, with a flick of her hand, she returned the scrying device to its dais and thought about what she had learned.

It had always been difficult to spy on Sebastian Shaw; he knew what precautions to take to foil her efforts. However, he had not yet learned that, for the Black Queen, nothing was impossible. As soon as she had met Doctor Henry McCoy, she had known he was searching for information that she too might appreciate. And she had known he would find it. It had been a simple matter for Selene to combine her dark arts and her mutant powers of the mind, and to cast a spell upon him surreptitiously.

She could see through the Beast's eyes now—and, from his unique point of view, she had witnessed much that had interested her.

"So, my 'dear friend'," she muttered to herself, "my Black King, Sebastian. You thought you could keep this project from me, did you? You couldn't bring yourself to trust me. Well, perhaps you had good cause..."

Selene had never worried overmuch about the Legacy Virus. She had thought of it as something she would deal with, in time, if she had to. But the possibilities of a cure...and of being the only person to possess that cure....

She smiled, as ideas began to form in her mind. But there was no sense, she knew, in acting hastily. She would monitor the situation on Shaw's Pacific island, bide her time, and strike only when the opportune moment presented itself.

In the meantime, she had plenty to occupy her thoughts. The sounds of torment from the catacombs below had been mystically amplified to echo through her sanctum. They called to her, and she answered them, drifting serenely out into the corridor and down into the depths.

The night was still young, after all.